the Full Picture

JESSICA CARMICHAEL

hibiscus press

Published in 2025 by hibiscus press
www.hibiscuspress.com

This is a work of fiction. Unless otherwise indicated, all the names, characters, businesses, places, events and incidents in this book are either the product of the author's imagination or used in a fictitious manner. Any resemblance to actual persons, living or dead, or actual events is purely coincidental.

Copyright © Jessica Carmichael 2025

All rights reserved.
No part of this book may be reproduced in any form or by any electronic or mechanical means, including information storage and retrieval systems, without the prior permission in writing from both the copyright owner and the above publisher of this book.

ISBN 978-1-0693354-0-1 (Paperback)
ISBN 978-1-0693354-2-5 (EPUB)
ISBN 978-1-0693354-1-8 (Audiobook)

Cover design by Fatima Baig
Title design by Sophia Chunn

This project is supported by the Edmonton Arts Council and the City of Edmonton.

*To Mommy Anna and Grandma Julie.
This story doesn't exist without you.*

one

I DON'T KNOW why I thought learning my mother's native language while flying 35,000 feet in the air would be easy. Sure, I passed French with flying colours in high school, but it wouldn't have been possible without a whole lotta Google Translate.

I slam shut the *Beginner's Guide to Twi* just as the plane dips, starting its descent to our destination. From my aisle seat, it's hard to make out the details of the city below, but I reach within myself, searching for a feeling that proves my body knows where I am. A sense of déjà vu that can confirm that I've been here before. Instead, I only feel the plane's wheels hitting the tarmac with a resounding thud.

"Ladies and gentlemen, KLM welcomes you to Accra, Ghana. The local time is nine forty-five, and the temperature is thirty-three degrees. I know many of you are returning home for the holidays and I sincerely hope you enjoy your stay! On behalf of KLM and the entire crew, I'd like to thank you for joining us on this trip."

As passengers flood the aisles, my palms begin to itch so I instinctively drag them against the length of my black leggings. The friction from the cotton rubbing against my skin is typically all it takes to stop my anxious tick, but today, it does nothing for me. Seeing your extended family for the first time since your mother's passing causes a level of anxiety far more significant than any grounding trick can relieve.

"My friend, are you going to move or just sit there," barks the older man squished into the seat beside me. It is our row's turn to exit and I've been holding them hostage from leaving.

"Sorry," I mumble sheepishly, scrambling to unbuckle my seat belt and shuffling into the aisle. Come on, Robyn, get it together! If Grandma Lily didn't want you to be here, she wouldn't have invited you.

After struggling to bring down my carry-on, I follow the passengers exiting the plane. As we enter the tunnel that leads us into the airport, sticky heat seeps through the crevices, and I have to move to the side to yank off my airplane sweater and stop my body from overheating. Once it's tied firmly around my waist, I merge back between the shuffling bodies as they descend the escalator, taking in the commotion beneath me. At the bottom of the escalator, airport personnel direct traffic flow, splitting us into various customs lines based on our nationalities. My line takes its time to wind around the maze of stanchions, but eventually, I reach the stone-faced customs officer in an army green uniform, who sits behind a plexiglass barrier.

"Please, what is the purpose of your trip?" He asks without looking up from thumbing through my passport.

"Um, I'm visiting my mom's family." At this, he turns his attention to me, and his intense gaze makes me feel obligated to blurt out more details than necessary. "It's my grandma's seventieth birthday on Christmas day and she's throwing a massive party to celebrate the beginning of a new decade. She demanded the presence of all her grandkids, so here I am." I nervously giggle as I regurgitate the e-vite my older cousin Ama sent on behalf of Grandma Lily earlier this year.

"I see." He blinks at me blankly and I swallow the lump forming in my throat. What is it about going through customs that makes you feel as if you're smuggling drugs when you know damn well you're not? I can assure you the hardest drug in my belongings is Pepto-Bismol, Mr. Customs Officer, sir.

"Robyn Carter? You are a Ghanaian?" He squints at the last name printed on the biodata sheet of my passport, then looks back up at me.

"Half," I say, forcing myself to smile. "My dad is from Barbados, and my mom is from Ghana." If I had a dollar for every time I've had this conversation, I could have flown here first class. Heck, I could have chartered a private plane straight from Canada.

"Interesting. And is it your first time in Ghana?" He peers at me curiously through the transparent divider and I wonder if a trip you can hardly remember – but have seen enough pictures to know you were there – counts.

"Um, yeah, it is," I lie, biting down on my bottom lip to prevent any more incessant rambles from tumbling out. Robyn, this man does not care that the last time you were in Ghana was to bury your mom when you were seven years old. It means nothing to him that you've barely kept in touch with her family these last ten years. And there's no need to tell him that even though you're nervous, you've secretly longed for this reunion because it means you'll finally learn about the woman your dad can't bring himself to talk about.

The officer nods and the corners of his mouth turn upward in an empathetic smile that makes me wonder if I've somehow shared my musings aloud. But instead of responding to the thoughts that occupy my mind, he stamps my passport before handing it back to me.

"Akwaaba. Welcome to Ghana."

* * *

I've been trying my best not to exaggerate these days, since my best friend and roommate Chelsea Ankrah claims it's one of my worst traits, but my first hour in Ghana has been an absolute nightmare. Only one out of my two suitcases has made it to Accra. The luggage containing my toiletries, underwear and pyjamas never left the Amsterdam airport where I spent my six-hour layover. How exactly does one suitcase make a flight and the other miss it? I couldn't tell you, but it better be here tomorrow like they promised. This is the last thing I need right now; I think, as I chew on my bottom lip. It's bad enough that I've flown across the world to meet family that I barely know. How am I going to make a good first impression when I have to rotate through the limited outfits in my sole suitcase? Okay, fine, I know they'd probably accept me if I rocked up wearing a burlap sack, but it still doesn't change the fact that I want, no I *need*, to make a good impression. It's imperative that they take one look at me and know that I've got my shit together. Even if that's not entirely the truth.

Sighing, I try not to think about next month's phone bill surge as I turn on data roaming. My phone is refusing to connect to the airport's free Wi-Fi and I need to find out if Ama is already here to pick me up. It takes a moment to get on to the local carrier, but a dozen messages come rushing in when it finally does. Seven texts from Chelsea telling me which restaurants she wants to try when she gets here, three 'ETA?' texts from Dad and one voice note from Ama. I quickly like Chelsea's messages, let Dad know I've landed safely and then switch to WhatsApp to play Ama's recording.

"Robyn! Welcome to Ghana, love! A bit of bad news, yeah.

Something urgent has come up and I can't leave work. You know how these startups are. But no worries, Grandma Lily has arranged for our neighbour Osei to pick you up. We don't stay too far from the airport so he should be there by now, holding up a sign with your name. I'm so sorry I couldn't be there to greet you. I really wanted to be the somewhat familiar face you saw when you walked through those doors. I know how crazy it can feel being back here for the first time after so long. It also doesn't help that so many people will bombard you. Like my goodness, no, I don't need a taxi! Anyways love, Osei is a great kid, so I know you're in good hands. You can reach me on WhatsApp if anything happens! Can't wait to see you."

    My body deflates as her voice note comes to an end. If there is one person I truly feel ready to see, it's my older cousin Ama. She's the only daughter of my mom's eldest brother and has made a deliberate effort to keep in contact with me after I RSVP'd for the party three months ago. At first, I was taken aback since I could barely put a face to the name, but Ama didn't care.

    She was born in Ghana, unlike me, but relocated with her mother to the U.K. as a child following her parents' messy divorce. She's only recently returned and lives with Grandma Lily while running Surplus Ghana, her tech startup that connects customers to restaurants with unsold food at the end of each day.

    My chest tightens at the thought of Ama not being the one to pick me up. I'm really not trying to freak out here, but I didn't mentally prepare to see anyone but her.

    The sound of laughter causes me to look up from my phone and I watch as a woman pushing a stroller walks through the automatic sliding doors and steps outside to greet an older man. He tightly embraces the woman and then bends down to toss the baby girl in the air. Her high-pitched squeals are the last thing I hear before the sliding doors close. Judging from their identical wide noses, I'm guessing he's her father.

Envy ripples through me as I take in the reunion. It is so unlike how my dad and I interact. I can't tell you the last time our limbs came near each other in something that even resembles a hug. Typically, our lack of affection is something I'm so used to that it barely registers, but today it kind of stings. The stinging is brief though as I'm interrupted by my phone vibrating with an incoming audio call from Chelsea. Tearing my eyes away from the duo outside, I answer my best friend's call.

"Girl, are you still in the airport? I haven't heard from you since you left Amsterdam," she says before I even get a chance to say hello.

"You won't believe the morning I've had," I sigh, then proceed to recount everything that's gone wrong. "Oh, and to make matters worse, I just found out my cousin won't be able to pick me up, so now I'm just standing at the exit like a deer in friggen headlights."

"Wait, what? Your cousin left you stranded?"

"Well, not exactly. Some boy, my grandma's neighbour, is picking me up instead. But that's not the point. Ama was the one who was supposed to pick me up. I was expecting to see Ama on the other side of those doors. Not some random guy!"

"Okay, calm. It's just a change of plans, Rob," Chelsea says calmly. I can imagine her lying down on our living room couch, filing her acrylics to her signature stiletto shape as she speaks. "You can ask him to take you to get a few items to hold you over until your bag arrives and pick up a local SIM card. I'm pretty sure my mom has bought one at the airport before."

Chelsea is Ghanaian on both sides and has been my best friend since we met back in the ninth grade. The same year, her eldest brother, Will, relocated to Accra to work at their uncle's law firm. Ever since he left, Chelsea, her parents, and her older sister, Whitney, haven't missed a December in Ghana. This year, they'll be flying in the week before Christmas to spend the holidays with him as usual.

I tilt my head upward, not wanting the unshed tears pooling in my eyes to stream in the opposite direction. *Tears are not an exaggeration.* Tears are a perfectly normal reaction to my current catastrophic circumstance, I tell myself.

"I'm not sure about this anymore, Chels," I say, my voice wobbling. "Coming out here is starting to feel like a bad idea. Or maybe I should have just come with you guys and not bothered with the whole 'reconnecting with my mom's family' thing."

"Rob, we talked about this. Going there two weeks before the rest of your family arrives makes sense for what you want to do."

A flicker of annoyance thrums through my veins. Of course, I'm besties with a girl who believes in holding her friends accountable. But deep down, I know Chelsea's right. My body relaxes as I force air through my lips.

"You're sick and tired of not knowing anything about your mom because your dad refuses to talk about her, right?" Her tone is blatant and final.

"I am," I say, trying to match her confidence.

"So let me remind you of what you told me when you booked your flight with the last of your summer job money. If your dad is unwilling to open up, it's time to take matters into your own hands. You are so close to the truth, Robyn. Don't turn back now."

two

MY EYES anxiously dart around the outside of the terminal for the umpteenth time, trying to ignore the countless taxi drivers whistling in my direction. A large crowd is gathered in the arrivals waiting area and people are waving posters in the air, but none have my name on it.

He's not here yet.

At this point, I don't care who picks me up, I just want to take a shower and change out of these clothes. While I'm used to Toronto's hot summers, they don't compare to Accra's smothering heat. A light film of sweat has already coated my skin, and my springy afro, which I've pulled into a puff at the top of my head, has shrunken by two sizes.

I glance back at the airport, my eyes scanning the signage; maybe I could seek refuge inside. Shit, no entry after exiting.

I don't want to text Ama while she's handling her work emergency, but if I don't feel a cool blast of air conditioning in the next five minutes, I may combust right outside Kotoka International.

"Robyn! Robyn Carter!" I whip around to face the person wheezing my name. The boy in front of me is hunched over, with a black backpack, panting like a primary school student after a track and field day. With his eyes focused on the ground beneath his feet, he doesn't see the way my mouth pops open at the sight of him. I know Ama mentioned something about him being a "great kid" but she mentioned nothing about a boy who looks like God took his time, and then some, while creating him.

I barely have time to register the toned arms that bulge from the sleeves of his plain grey T-shirt, when he snaps up to face me with a sheepish smile tugging at his lips. He watches me curiously as if he's trying to learn each detail of my face and my heart skips a beat at his assessment. Then as if he's certain he's collected all the data he needs, he smiles widely, revealing the slightest middle gap on the top row of his effortlessly white teeth. I step back slightly as I blink in the brightness. If I wasn't so dedicated to being annoyed right now, it would be a smile worth texting Chelsea about.

"Sorry again for being late."

"Oh my gosh, don't worry about it! It's totally fine!" I say in a way that's a lot more reassuring than I feel. What the heck, Rob? Just because you see a cute boy with glossy dark skin and facial features that are chiseled to perfection, doesn't mean you have to foam at the mouth. Have some decorum!

"But is it really?" His left eyebrow is raised as he asks this, and I feel my face heat up at the fact that it's so painfully obvious that just moments earlier I was ready to rain my wrath and fury on him.

What is happening right now? No one other than Chelsea is supposed to be able to read me this quickly and easily. But before I can provide a rebuttal, he's moving past me to pick up my lone suitcase and carry-on.

"Come on. The car's just over there."

I walk behind him, still a little dazed at everything that has just transpired. Who the heck is this boy and why does he have me, Robyn Carter, the girl who always has something to say, completely speechless right now?

I slow down a little to observe his lengthy frame from behind as he confidently strides toward the car. On a good day, the puff at the top of my head often meets most people's eyes before I do, and Osei is not an exception to the rule. He's at least six feet tall, with a lean, athletic build. But the thing that really catches my attention is the curls on the top of his low fade. They're springy and defined as if he just brushed it with one of those afro sponge brushes. Both this and a low-cut with waves are tied neck and neck for my favourite hairstyles on Black men.

"Is everything fine?" Osei asks, as he glances back at me. I tear my eyes away from his hair to focus on picking up my pace.

"Yeah, all good," I reply, my cheeks hot with embarrassment. I can't believe he almost just caught me checking him out.

As we weave through the car park, Osei declines the help of the men who linger around asking us if we'll need help loading my bags into the car. He effortlessly cracks jokes with them in this assured way, that makes me smile at the interaction. When we finally get to the silver SUV, Osei unlocks the car for me before stowing my suitcases in the truck.

Once I'm seated and my luggage is packed away, he slides into the driver's seat, leans over to place his backpack near my feet, then turns his key in the ignition. An R&B song I don't recognize starts playing where it left off and I have to sit on my hands to stop myself from reaching over and changing it. For the most part, I like all kinds of music, but I've never really taken to R&B. I think it's all that begging and pleading; it just feels so desperate to me.

We drive in silence for a while as Osei manoeuvres our way out of the Kotoka parking lot. Chelsea warned me that Accra traffic would be congested due to the influx of holiday travellers, but congested is an understatement for the utter chaos I am witnessing right now. I can feel Osei stealing glances at me, but I am too transfixed by the commotion on the road ahead to entertain him.

It's Monday morning, and the neighbourhood we're moving through is rammed with cars, motorcycles and vans driving to unknown destinations. Modern high-rises and office buildings tower over the pedestrians who mill in, out and around the ongoing traffic. The modernity is a sharp contrast to the women balancing wooden containers with small snacks on their heads.

My stomach grumbles as I watch the car in front of us hail one woman to their window. She rushes over, holding the container on her head with one hand before placing it on the ground and bending down to plop fresh bofrot into a white bag. The oily balls of fried sweet dough stick to the paper bag.

The entire exchange is so quick that before I can fully process if they've even paid, she moves on to another outstretched arm flagging her down from their car. The entire scene is an explosion of energy, captivating to my senses, and I hate that I have a sudden urge to capture it on camera. It's an urge that I thought I had removed from my life three years ago, but clearly, I did not yank it out from the root.

When we finally get to a point where the traffic is moving at a normal pace, Osei starts singing along to the song playing. It's 'Snooze' by SZA, something I actually do recognize thanks to Chelsea playing it back-to-back when it first dropped. But Osei's rendition is terribly off key. I turn away to stifle my laughter as his accent twists the lyrics in the most endearing way. It's almost as if God knew he would be too powerful if he could sing.

"What?" I hear him ask, amusement lacing his tone.

"Oh, nothing." I say rolling my lips inwards to stop myself from smiling too hard. Osei simply shrugs then belts out the chorus even louder than before.

He sings along loudly and I can't hold back my laughter any longer. As the sound leaves my body, I feel the tension from today's chaotic events leave with it. The annoyance from the airline losing my bag. The anxiety of being picked up by a stranger. My fears of not making a good first impression. The hesitation I have towards seeing my family again. Even my usual distaste for R&B doesn't seem to matter at this moment. The only thought at the forefront of my mind is that I think I might just like it here after all.

three

"HIP-HOP IS the best genre and it's not up for debate," I laugh, my body turned toward the boy who just a few hours earlier, was a complete stranger to me. But after being stuck together for over an hour and a half, on what was supposed to be a thirty-minute journey, we've become surprisingly friendly.

Typically, an untimely delay on a day as important as this would make me seriously anxious. But right now, I'm too distracted to care.

"Oh it's absolutely up for debate. You're just scared if we go head-to-head you're gonna lose."

I watch as Osei shrugs with so much nonchalance you'd think we were having two separate conversations. I'm all worked up and my chest is heaving as I try to plead my case, but he's leaning back in the driver's seat, one hand on the wheel, not minding my outbursts.

"I'll have you know Robyn Carter never loses," I huff, playfully crossing my arms.

"Oh, I don't doubt that," Osei replies. He says it so quickly that I almost miss the undercurrent of something that sounds a lot like flirting in his tone.

"Wh-wha-whatever," I stammer, feeling my face get flushed. "Why were you late to pick me up anyway?" I ask, trying to ignore the fluttering in my chest.

"Technically speaking, I was here before your flight even landed. It's just after a while of waiting; you weren't coming out, and I got a little distracted."

This piques my interest.

"Distracted doing what?" I ask as he slows down at another red light.

He nods toward the backpack that sits at my feet and it takes a moment before I register that a DSLR camera is peaking out. Just a glimpse of the camera's familiar body makes my heart rate quicken, and my palms begin to itch.

"How did *that* make you late?" I spit out turning back to face him.

"I can show you better than I can tell you," he nods at the bag as the streetlight changes to green. "Take it out."

Slowly, I bend forward to lift it out of the bag and the weight of the camera in my hands instantly transports me to one of the worst night's of my life. A pang of jealousy strikes my core, and I force myself to speak so I don't have to relive it.

"Is that a Canon EOS Rebel T7i?" I ask as my hands slightly tremble, unable to mask my discomfort.

Osei perks up and trades quick glances between the road and me. If he notices the drastic change in my demeanour, he doesn't act like it.

"It is! Are you a photographer, too?" His eyes twinkle with curiosity as he asks this. Deep down I know his enquiry has no malice, but I feel myself becoming defensive regardless.

"What, do I have to be a photographer to know which

camera this is?" I scoff as if he hasn't asked a completely logical question.

"Uh, no, I guess not," he says hesitantly, his thick eyebrows now furrowed in confusion. "Turn it on, and press that little playback button," he directs as he sidles up behind a stretch of unmoving cars.

"I know how to review pictures on a camera," I retort, turning the camera on.

"Right, right. You're not a photographer, but you know all about cameras." His tone is light-hearted, but I roll my eyes as I click the image playback button.

The first photo is a candid of the woman I saw pushing her baby in the stroller earlier. From Osei's point of view, her chin is sitting on the shoulder of the older man, a mixture of joy and relief swirling in the tears running down her cheeks. Even though you can see other people milling around in the background, it somehow feels like they're the only two in the terminal, as if nothing matters more than being in each other's arms. It's a beautiful display of a family being reunited, and if I look at it any longer, I will flood this car with tears.

My finger jabs the power button, and the screen goes black.

"What, is it that bad?" Osei asks, sneaking a perturbed glance my way before looking back at the curving bend of the roundabout ahead of us.

"It's okay. The composition could be a little better though," I sniff, turning my body toward the window. The overwhelming sense of envy and bitterness I'm starting to feel is too much to bear.

Don't you dare break down in this man's car, Robyn. Pull yourself together!

"You know what, you're probably right," he admits, and I snap back toward him in shock. "I wanted to catch them as authentically as possible, so I moved quickly and caught too many people in the background. Nothing a little photoshop can't fix, though," he chuckles. The hearty sound unfurls a sense of warmth in the pit of my stomach, but I convince myself it must be from something I ate on the plane, and refuse to think about it any further.

When the cars in front of us slow down again, he turns to study me. His dark pupils seem to pierce through mine, and my breath catches in my throat.

"You know, you said you're not a photographer, and at first, I believed you. But now, I'm not so sure. Only someone who knows their way around a camera would say something like that."

"I've taken a class or two," I shrug, fidgeting in my seat. "'Photography is also an open course at my university so anyone can take it." There's no need to mention it's the one class I'm not completely bombing this semester. It's just an elective, after all.

"And I bet you're good at it too, huh? Is that what you study at university? Do you want to make a full-blown career out of it?"

His words take me back to the conversation I had with my photography professor, Dr. Beal, before I left for Ghana. I had just finished my last exam and was handing in my final assignment for her course, a self-portrait study. She wouldn't let me leave until I listened to her talk about a one-year photography fellowship she claims will change my life. I had to kindly let her know that I liked my life the way it was.

"First of all," I start, feeling myself winding up to go off on a tangent. "Just because you're good at something doesn't mean you have to study it. And if you do, then what? How many people actually 'make it' as a photographer? As in, it's their sole source of income, and they don't have to chase down unpaid invoices to make ends meet. I just don't think it's worth going to university for."

I'm practically heaving once I finish my rant, and I'm omitting the fact that I, myself, haven't exactly figured out if the program I'm currently in—Life Science at the University of Toronto—is worthwhile either, but Osei doesn't need to know that.

"Look, I know we just met, but there's no way you expect me to think you truly believe that," he scoffs. "That's such an archaic train of thought."

We stare at each other in silence, a prolonged moment passing before the light changes to green and he tears his gaze off mine. Suddenly, my blood pressure is spiking, matching his acceleration speed.

Who does this guy think he is? Not only did he have me waiting out there for him while he was running around doing God knows what, but now he thinks he can tell me about myself. Nah, forget that. I haven't travelled all this way to be psychoanalyzed by a stranger before I've even met my family.

"You know what," I exclaim, whipping my body to face him. "You don't know anything about me or what I believe. Not all of us can be senseless dreamers. Some of us live in reality. A reality in which we don't run off and take secret pictures when people are counting on us to be there!"

The words gush out in a huff, and it takes me a moment to steady my breathing. I'm sure my body temperature has surpassed the weather by now, but Osei doesn't seem to care. His eyes never leave the road as a playful smirk dances across his full lips. It's almost as if he's just caught a preview of my very own Netflix stand-up special instead of witnessing me telling him off.

"I'm sorry, was something I just said funny to you?" While I can admit that ninety percent of my frustration stems from letting this stranger get so comfortable under my skin, the remaining ten percent is a valid reaction to all of the morning's nonsense combined.

"Oh no, no." His body shakes as he stifles a laugh. "Don't worry, Robyn. I've learned my lesson. Moving forward, I promise I will always be on time when it comes to you."

At this, I scoff loudly. "Oh, you do not have to worry about picking me up ever again. Not from the airport or anywhere else for that matter," I declare as the car slows down and we enter a residential neighbourhood.

"Are you sure about that?" A mischievous look in his eye makes me immediately slump with defeat in my seat.

"Please don't tell me my grandma asked you to show me around or something while I'm out here," I groan. Visions of Osei finding cunning ways to ruin my trip flash like a highlight reel in my mind.

"Fine. I won't tell you then," Osei replies while tossing me a grin so dazzling that I have to force myself to look away.

four

WHEN WE PULL up to Grandma Lily's, Osei blares his horn, and after a few moments, the iron gate slowly retracts into the cement wall that borders the property. The car rolls onto a stone driveway that cuts through a neatly manicured landscape, and my jaw drops when I notice the house. Shrubs embedded with bursts of bright pink blooms sprawl wildly against its white exterior, and multiple fan-shaped palm trees sit low around its base. The cream coloured colonial-style two-storey sits nestled amongst the front yard's lush greenery. I don't know what I was expecting, but an oasis smack in the middle of this big city was not it.

"It's beautiful, isn't it?" Osei asks, turning off the car. "Wait till you see the inside. Your grandma has outdone herself with this place."

"It is," I breathe, forgoing my aversion to him to soak it in. It feels surreal to be in the very place my mom once called home. Did she read up on the veranda above the entryway or prefer playing on the front lawn with her two siblings? Maybe my mom was more of an indoor person and never ventured outside unless she had to–like me. Was she anything like me? Well, the real question is, am *I* anything like *her*?

The chestnut door swings open and I blink rapidly in an attempt to air out the liquid sloshing through my tear ducts. A petite woman floats onto the porch, draped in an airy fuchsia dress that sweeps the ground. A halo of white curls surrounds her dark brown heart-shaped face, and she walks down the steps with her arms stretched wide. The oversized sleeves spread out like wings in flight.

"You are welcome," cries Grandma Lily as I climb out of the car. "You are welcome!" Her dark skin, though moisturized, is a testament to her full age. Each line and fold looks as if it carries its own significant story. But in her face, I see my own. Identical inky orbs in brown almond-shaped lids. A plump bottom lip that juts out marginally more than the top and a rounded nose resembling a compact car's side profile. I feel tempted to reach out and touch her to make sure she's not a work of my imagination.

Her hands tremble as they stretch to my face, briefly pausing as if to ask for permission. I nod shakily and feel drops of moisture splatter my shirt as she gently takes my cheeks in her palms. The contact warms my skin as if I've snuggled next to a fireplace, and I shut my eyes to relish in her comfort; every fear, anxiety and concern drifts skyward in her loving embrace. When I open my eyes, her eyes gleam with fresh tears—a bittersweet expression flitting across her features.

"Oh, Robyn," she whispers. "You look so much like your mother."

At this, I break down. My chest rises and falls vehemently as I sob into Grandma Lily's arms. I've dreamt about this moment, this reunion, for years. I thought about what it would look like. I practiced the lines I'd say. But no amount of rehearsal could prepare me for the tempestuous wave that crashes into me. Like wet clothes heavy with the weight of water, grief clings to my body, weighing me down as I try to walk back to shore.

"Don't cry, my child. *Bra ha.* Come, it's alright." When she pulls me in, I bury my damp face into her neck, breathing in the shea butter kneaded into her skin.

"It's okay, my child. It's okay. All that matters is that you're here now." Her voice is gentle as she rubs small, continuous circles into my back. Acknowledging my inner thoughts without me having to say them out loud. "*Ɛyɛ*, it is well."

When I finally pull myself together again, my mind instantly remembers the boy who brought me here, and I swivel toward the car to find that both Osei and my bags are nowhere in sight.

Grandma Lily reaches out and squeezes my hand. "Don't worry. He's still here."

My cheeks burn with embarrassment. I want to let Grandma Lily know I couldn't care less if he left, and I was just wondering where my bags went, but I know better than to argue with my elders.

She nods toward the house. "He's bringing your stuff to one of the empty rooms upstairs. Come now, let's get out from under this sun and get you something to eat."

The inside of her home is as beautiful as its exterior, just accented with modern finishings. The multi-pane windows flood beams of light into a spacious foyer where the botanical theme continues throughout. I follow Grandma Lily's lead as she slips off her sandals, my bare feet padding across the cold beige tiles. She guides me through the first floor, providing an oral history of her changes over the years. My late grandfather, Grandpa Isaac, inherited the house, but when he passed away while my mom and her siblings were still in university, he left it to Grandma Lily, much to the dismay of his siblings. A lengthy legal battle ensued in and out of court for over two decades, and two years ago, the court finally ruled in her favour. She has been working on developing the house into her dream home ever since.

"You see, I grew up in my grandfather's compound home in Kumasi and loved it immensely. All his children and their families living within a single complex meant my cousins were always just a few feet away. After I married your grandpa and we moved to Accra, so he could launch his company Antwi Family Printers, living in this house, so far away from my family, was a big change for me." Her hand strokes a white beam supporting the winding staircase as if she is reliving her first memories in her new home. I know from Ama that our family owns one of Ghana's largest printing companies. Uncle Emmanuel, my mom's younger brother, now runs the day-to-day operations, and clearly, it still provides for Grandma Lily and her lavish lifestyle in her old age.

"Eventually, I adjusted for the sake of my growing family, but deep down, I craved the community I had grown up with. When I lost your grandfather, it was my people that kept me sane. My siblings, neighbours, and even the children looked out for me, especially throughout the trial. After all these years, I no longer desire to live in a shared space, but having a home that can be a pillar for my community is still important to me. Whether it be for weddings, funerals, outdoorings or just a place to escape; my space is always available to my community."

We're at the back of the house now and through the window, I catch a glimpse of an overgrown tree in the corner of the large backyard. The vast space is the perfect size for any event.

"That's beautiful, Grandma," I sniff. I can't help but wonder if I belong in that community.

Her eyes are soft as she reads my mind. "This house belongs to you like it belongs to Ama and the rest of your extended family."

Given the verbal reassurance I need, I straighten my posture confidently.

"Thank you, Grandma. You don't know what it means to hear you say that."

She winks at me before twirling toward the kitchen. "Now come and eat. I've prepared something special for you."

As we enter the cooking space, I realize I recognize the scent that has been lingering throughout the house. On the counter, dozens of freshly fried plantain slices sit on a paper towel lining, grease seeping through to the ceramic plate. A pot is simmering on the stove and Grandma Lily waves me over as she uncovers it. My heart soars as I peer inside. Black-eyed beans submerged in a stew made with glistening palm oil.

"Red red? How did you know this was my favourite?" I ask. It's a dish Chelsea's Mom, Aunty Linda, makes when I spend evenings at their house after school. Even when her girls would rather eat something else, she always gives me a Tupperware full of it to go.

"It's all you used to eat when you would spend your summers here. I'm glad you still love it. Sit. Sit. Let me prepare you a plate." The new tidbit of information oozes warmth inside my belly as I plop into a chair at the kitchen table.

"This is a lot of food for two people," I chuckle, taking in the wooden surface covered with dishes. It all looks familiar, thanks to Aunty Linda and the Ghanaian hall parties she would drag Chelsea, Whitney and me to. Mounds of banku individually wrapped in plastic; a tray of fried tilapias with thinly sliced peppers and onions sprinkled on top; a mountain of fried rice next to grilled chicken; and a colourful garden salad topped with sliced boiled eggs.

"It's not only for us. Ama will have some when she gets home from work, but Osei is joining us now for lunch," she clarifies, setting my plate on the table. "Such a nice young man, isn't he? He's just a year older than you, you know. He's in his second year at Ashesi University."

Earlier today I would have agreed that 'nice' and Osei may belong in the same sentence, but after our little showdown in the car, I think the word 'nuisance' works better.

"Yeah, very nice," I mumble grudgingly. Why is this uni boy hanging around a nearly seventy-year-old woman anyway? I mean, sure, Grandma Lily doesn't appear to be a stereotypical African grandmother, but what on earth could they possibly have in common?

"He's your neighbour, right?" My tone is nonchalant, as if it bores me even to ask.

"Yes, he is. The Mensahs have lived across the street for the last ten years. He and his sister have always been such lovely kids, but when I noticed him always wearing that camera around his neck a few years ago, I asked him if he'd be interested in helping me document the changes I made to the house. Now that the renovations are complete, he's transitioning into my full-time event photographer," she coos proudly. "His first gig will be my joint Christmas/seventieth birthday party. From his work with the renovation, I already know the pictures will come out great."

Jealousy bubbles in the pit of my empty stomach and I fight the urge to roll my eyes. Of course, Osei used photography to stick his claws into my grandma.

"And we've been best friends ever since, isn't that right, Grandma Lily?" Osei chimes in, seemingly appearing out of nowhere. My body flinches as he slides into the seat next to me, his long limbs knocking against my shorter ones.

"You and I are not agemates, o," she laughs while waltzing

over to the stainless-steel fridge. I can't help but flash him the smirk plastered on my lips. Exactly, Osei, stay in your lane.

"But yes, I do enjoy your company and help around here. Thank you again for picking up Robyn today. I truly appreciate it."

My nostrils flare as he smirks in my direction. "No worries at all. You were right about us getting along. It feels as if I've known her my entire life." His voice is syrupy and sweet, and his gap reveals itself as his smile grows wider. I stuff my mouth with a forkful of plantain to keep from screaming.

"Oh, that's wonderful. Osei is just finishing up his classes for the term, but he has offered to show you around in the evenings and on the weekends when your cousin is unavailable. You know, to do whatever the young people get into during December."

"How kind of him." My attempt to be covertly sarcastic is poor, but Grandma Lily doesn't seem to notice.

"Extremely," she responds genuinely, handing us both bottles of chilled water before sitting across from us. "And I can trust you two will be on your best behaviour?" Her right eyebrow cocks up to her powder white hairline, and I feel myself physically shudder from the insinuation. After what I've learnt about him today, I can guarantee that Osei and I will never happen.

"You do not need to worry about me," I reply, meaning every last word. Sure, Osei is good-looking with his curly hightop fade or whatever, but he's far too pompous for me. Besides, if it hasn't been made painfully clear by now, not only does he live on a whole other continent, he and I have nothing in common. We would never work out.

"I'm *always* on my best behaviour, Grandma Lily." Osei summons the innocence of a small child to smile at her, and it takes everything in me not to tattle about him being late today.

Yes, I know it's petty, and while it no longer feels like such a big deal, I still think he deserves to be knocked down a peg or two.

"Great! I'm sure you two will have a wonderful time." She claps her palms together loudly. "Now, Robyn, have you called your dad to tell him you've arrived?"

My body tenses as I feel two sets of curious eyes surveying me.

"Um, I texted him at the airport. But I haven't talked to him yet," I admit, staring at my plate.

Even though Chelsea and I live downtown in an apartment near campus, which is more or less an hour away from my home in Brampton, Dad and I have barely seen each other lately. I could lie and say it is because he's been busy at his pharmacy and I've been swamped with midterms and assignments, but I know there's more to it than that. The reason I've been skipping Sunday dinners to stay on campus every weekend is because of his reaction when I first told him about the trip. He never told me I couldn't go, but his silence on the matter was deafening enough.

My dad doesn't have a relationship with Grandma Lily or Uncle Emmanuel and Aunty Naa, my mom's two siblings. And while he's never stopped them from reaching out to me, he's never proactively contacted them. It's the primary reason our connection isn't as strong. A child can only make and take so many long-distance calls on their own.

Maybe things were different before my mom passed, but this has been my norm for as long as I can physically remember. Though since being out here with Grandma Lily, I'm struggling to understand how things got to this point. If the rest of the family is anything like her, certainly the problem is him.

"Well, promise me you will. The last thing a parent needs is to worry about their child halfway across the world. Take my word for it." Her last statement has a micro-dose of sadness that is impossible to ignore.

"Okay, I promise," I utter, shifting the beans around my plate using my fork. The motion leaves little white streaks throughout the sea of orange oil.

My mind is far from the phone call. I already know how things with him go. What's presently running through my mind instead is that there's no way I'm leaving Ghana without finally uncovering what tore my family apart.

five

AFTER LUNCH, Osei drives me to Accra Mall to buy items that will last me the next few days; in case my missing suitcase doesn't arrive tomorrow. Luckily for me, he disappears to find me a SIM card, and I get to wander the halls of Shoprite unsupervised. By the time we leave, the traffic near the mall is unbearable, making the fifteen minute car ride home over an hour long but this time around, Osei lets me endure the slow crawl in silence. When we return to the house, there's a note on the kitchen island from Grandma Lily. She's gone to a Monday night church service with her friend but will return later tonight.

"Here," Osei says, leaning forward to hand me my phone with its new SIM card. I'm sitting on one of the three rattan and metal stools beside the island, and Osei stands on the other side. "I've already loaded some data on it for you, but if you need to buy more, Ama can show you how."

"Thanks," I grunt, scrolling through my notifications. Most are from Chelsea on various platforms, but one email is from Dr. Beal.

TO: Robyn Carter
FROM: Dr. Stephanie Beal
SUBJECT: Re: The London School of Film, Media and Design Emerging Black Artists' Fellowship (Open to Students Aged 18-25 Worldwide)

Hi Robyn,

I hope you are enjoying the warm weather! You just escaped a brutal snowstorm. Anyway, I know you said you weren't interested, but I wanted to send over the application just in case. The application deadline is January 14th, so there's not much time to assemble your submission, but it isn't impossible. Let me know if you want to talk more about it, and I'll be happy to hop on a Zoom call with you. Happy Holidays!

Dr. Beal

Reflexively, my finger moves to swipe the message into the trash, but then I stop. For a reason that I can't fully grasp, deletion seems too final. I'll archive it for now, that way it's out of my inbox but not permanently gone.

"So," Osei starts. I watch as he turns toward the fridge, pulls out a water bottle, then spins back to face me. "Is there anything in particular you want to do while you're in Accra?"

"Osei," I sigh. "My grandma isn't here. You don't have to continue with the charade."

He laughs heartily and then tilts his head back to drink from his water. It's hard not to stare at his annoyingly perfect neck. It's thick but not in a gross, meaty way. No, Osei's neck perfectly suits the shape of his big head.

"Who said I'm acting?"

"Okay, fine, maybe you're not acting. But you don't have to worry about me. My girl Chelsea will be here in two weeks, and she has a whole itinerary of things she wants us to do together."

"Chelseaaa," he drags her name out as if tasting it on his tongue. "She's Ghanaian? Cute?"

My eyes narrow into sharp slits and he bursts out laughing. I wouldn't even hook up my enemy with this menace. When his laughter dies down, he cocks his head to the side, twirling the half-empty bottle with his long fingers.

"And what will you do until she gets here?"

"Other things."

"Other things, like what?" From the expression on his face, it's evident that he receives immense pleasure from getting on my nerves.

I plan to use the next two weeks to learn as much as I can about my mom. If not through Grandma Lily, I hope to come across something that will help fill in the blanks in my mind. But most importantly, I need to build up the courage to ask what went wrong between Mom's family and Dad, before everyone else gets here. But there's no way I'm sharing any of this with a boy who struggles to take things seriously for longer than five seconds.

"Other things that don't concern you," I crack.

"Fine, fine. I'm backing off," Osei laughs, holding his hands up in surrender. "But just so you know, the offer still stands. And whatever we end up doing, it won't just be with me."

I follow him silently as he moves from behind the island toward the hallway and he turns to face me as he walks down the wide corridor.

"My twin sister Kuukua will probably tag along, and you can meet some of my friends, too. We're going out this Friday. It should be fun."

"Riveting," I reply, my tone void of excitement.

He laughs even louder at this, and I hate myself for instinctively wondering what else I can say to bring it up a decibel. Osei turns around to open the door, then spins back to face me.

"See you later, Miss Carter," he smiles, his body half-outside the door.

"Mr. Mensah." My lips twitch when I see the pleasant surprise in his eyes. You're not the only one who can get intel from my grandma, Osei.

Once I ensure I've locked the door, I venture up the winding staircase to my bedroom. I'm just outside the door when I see an incoming FaceTime call from Dad. Wincing, I momentarily think about declining but decide otherwise. There's no way I can get away with not speaking to him on my first day here.

"Hi, Dad," I say, pushing the door open. "Still at the pharmacy?" The wall behind him is blank, his black-framed degrees from the University of West Indies and the University of Toronto the only decor pieces.

"Hi, Robyn. Yes, I am. It's only four o'clock here. How was your trip?" His slight Bajan accent strings the words together like a song.

"Good," I reply, falling back onto the queen-sized bed. The guest room is one of four on the second floor. The bed frame sits against the back wall with two natural oak nightstands on either side. Grandma Lily has styled the entire space with soft yellow, beige and brown decor to make it look like something straight out of a coastal boutique hotel. There's even a basket of neatly rolled cream coloured towels on the armchair by the door.

"That's great," he says, nodding his head firmly as if he's

speaking to one of his customers about the unfortunate side effects of their medication. The phone is close to his face, and under his office's bright lighting, I notice silver hairs sprouting from his bushy eyebrows. That's new. When did those come in?

"And did you get your final grades back yet?" he asks, drawing my attention from his brows. "I want to know how well my future pharmacist did in her first semester of university."

"No, not yet," I reply hurriedly, not liking the direction this conversation is heading. "Remember I told you eMarks is still down?"

Dad kisses his teeth.

"I'm paying all this money for you to get an education at one of the best universities in Canada, and yet they can't afford working technology to keep their students informed of their grades. Seems like they need to resort to pen and paper if you ask me!"

I chuckle nervously at his rant but the blood drains from my face as I feel my lie start to catch up to me.

My first semester of university hasn't been easy, to say the least. You know that first-year learning curve guidance counsellors warn you about when you're a senior in high school? Not only is it very real, it's steep as hell. While I'm not failing out or anything, I'm not getting the kind of grades either Dad nor I are used to. I've managed to keep him off my back with a tiny white lie about eMarks, the university's grade submission system, being down all semester, but even I know that lie won't be able to save me for much longer.

"Don't worry Dad, it should be fixed by the end of the year," I assure him, avoiding eye contact. In the weeks leading up to this trip, I've practically lived in the library. I'm just hoping those final assignments will be enough to boost my

GPA so that he doesn't disown me completely. Besides, the last thing I need for him to see right now is that my highest grade is in an elective he doesn't even know I'm taking.

"Good, good. You need to make sure you're at the top of your class if you want to get into the pharmacology program when it's time to apply at the end of your first year. It has limited enrolment, remember? You need to stay on track, Robyn. Don't lose sight of the plan."

How could I lose sight of the plan when it's been obstructing my vision from anything else since the start of ninth grade?

When I decided I would follow in Dad's footsteps to become a pharmacist, I never once questioned it, because not only was I naturally good at science, I had also seen firsthand the success it brought him. All throughout high school I excelled in every course necessary to get accepted into one of the best schools in the province. My GPA was one of the highest in my graduating class, and my application was damn near flawless, but evidently none of that is enough when you're no longer the big fish in a small pond. In university, being the best doesn't matter when everyone else is just as good or even better than you. I need to do a lot better than 'best' if I want to get into pharmacology next year.

"The plan hasn't changed," I murmur, shifting the phone from my face and to the ceiling so he can't see the anxiety pinching between my brows.

"And once you're done with undergrad, you will get into my pharmacy school, no problem. Like father, like daughter, remember?" Dad grins, all thirty-two of his pearly whites on display.

It's been over twenty years since Dad traded sea breeze for frigid winters to attend the University of Toronto's pharmacy school and he never lets me forget it. The story of how he arrived on a full scholarship and graduated at the top of his class is one I've heard on several occasions, even though he always conveniently leaves out a massive part of his graduate school chapter: meeting my mom.

The sound of knuckles rapping against wood catches my attention and pulls me out of our conversation. Thank God. Saved by the knock.

"Sorry, Dad, I have to go. Someone is at my door," I blurt out, springing to my feet.

"That's fine. I have to get back out there anyway," Dad states, rising from his seat. "Can't leave those interns by themselves for too long, or they start recommending laxatives for appendicitis."

For a moment, he stares at me intently. I wait wide-eyed, hoping for something more, but his final words are brief as he ends the call.

"Be safe out there."

Sighing, I toss my phone onto the canary-coloured duvet before walking to the door.

Why did I let myself believe, for even a second, that dad would ask anything more about my trip? By now, you would think I know him better than that.

When I unlock the door, Ama squeals as she enters the room.

"Robyn! My goodness! I knew from our FaceTime calls we resembled each other, but this is freaky," she laughs, her thick British accent coming through with the sharp pronunciation of each syllable. Even though she's almost a head shorter than I am, we look more like sisters than cousins with our matching dark skin and almond-shaped eyes. Ama scoops me into a hug so tight my body has no choice but to relax in her petite arms.

"Hi Ama, it's so nice to finally meet you in person."

"Oh, come on now. This is not our first time meeting," she

laughs, pulling away from me before plopping down on the bed. She's dressed in a navy blue, long-sleeve wrap dress that slides up her ample hips as she sits. "The last summer we were both here was before I left for London. I was ten, and you were only four, but we were inseparable." Her long, copper-tinted microlocs are pulled back in a low bun, emphasizing how her eyebrows playfully wiggle at me.

"And now look at you. A fine babe, with your glossy skin and banging figure. What happened to those chubby cheeks all the adults used to squeeze?" She asks, then covers her mouth quickly in disgust. "Oh goodness, I'm sounding awfully like an old aunty, innit?"

"A little bit," I chuckle, sitting next to her. "I'm sorry it's been so long since I've been back," I confess, the familiar itch returning to my right palm.

"Nonsense. None of this is your fault, babe. Take it from me. I've been back in Ghana for over a year, and I've seen my dad less than three times. Mind you, I'm literally staying with his mother." She laughs as she says this, but her smile doesn't reach her eyes. Instead, disappointment flickers within them. "It's not solely our responsibility to maintain relationships with family. When we're younger, parents play the biggest role in ensuring we stay connected. But as we get older, what we *can* do is mend the relationships with those who are willing. So I'm so proud of you for coming out here, Robyn," she proclaims, reaching to squeeze my hand. Her hand grips mine tightly, and the itching in my palm stops, her sincerity soothing my nerves.

"Thank you, Ama. That means a lot coming from you."

"Of course, cuz," she beams. "I've managed to make some time in my schedule tomorrow morning, and I want to make it up to you for not being there to pick you up from the airport."

"Oh, it's no big deal," I lie, my hand flying up to nervously tug at my curls.

"Babe, please," she snorts. "You didn't even reply to my voice note."

"I did, too!" I squeal.

"Liking the message hardly counts, hun," she counters, lightly elbowing me in the rib. "Regardless, I still want to treat you. We also need to get your measurements for your dress for the big party."

"My dress? But I already have a dress." Before I left, Chelsea and I ventured to the Eaton Centre to look for something light enough to withstand the heat, long enough to be appropriate, yet stylish enough for IG. I ended up choosing a satin black midi with adjustable straps and a chic cowl neckline.

"Save your dress for a night out, love. Your Type A grandma has a precise vision for what she wants her children and grandchildren to wear, and yes, it involves matching kente."

six

AMA'S TREAT is a trip to a nail salon called Polish'd in Labone, an upscale neighbourhood in Accra. As we walk inside, I look up in awe at the three-tier chandelier that hangs above the nail stations. Giant, grey suede thrones serve as pedicure chairs and floor-to-ceiling mirrors line the wall with bright fluorescent bulbs surrounding them. But it's not the beauty of the high-class salon that leaves me speechless; it's the beauty belonging to its patrons that truly takes my breath away.

A cheerful, plump woman with a low-cropped haircut smiles at us brightly as we wait. She's holding a tray topped with glasses of champagne in her right hand. "Please, can I offer you ladies something to drink?"

"I'm going to pass because I have to drive, but she'll have one," Ama winks as she passes me the flute. Back home, I don't drink much. The possibility of losing control over myself has always seemed unappealing to me. Also, there's the not-so-subtle indoctrination from dad, whose only experience of alcohol is drinking sparkling apple juice at his church's end-of-year banquet. But during my time in Ghana, Chelsea and I decided I'll be making an exception to the rule, but before I can even put the glass to my lips, darkness submerges the salon. With the power cut, the nail drills come to a grinding halt, and the ceiling fans stop spinning above us. The only sound that remains is a collective outburst of frustration.

"Eiiiiiiiii!"

"O! This country is not serious!"

"Ei! Ghana!"

"Dumsor again?"

"Please, don't worry! We have a generator," the lady who gave us our drinks shouts over the commotion before hastily dashing to the back of the room. I nervously glance over at my cousin, who doesn't look the least bit surprised.

"You'll get used to that happening real soon," she laughs.

As Ama backs her car out of the nail salon parking lot, I admire the shiny black polish coating my lengthy natural nails. I used to bite them religiously, until Chelsea realized she wanted to go into cosmetology and begged me to stop so she could have someone other than herself to practice doing nails on.

Feeling around in my tote bag, I pull out my phone to send her a picture of the new set. It's still early back home, but she's most likely up and on her way to Humber College where she's getting her diploma in Cosmetic Management.

CHELSEA

Damn Rob! You never let me do acrylics on you.

ROBYN

These are my natural nails! You're the one helping me retain length, remember?

THE FULL PICTURE

CHELSEA
IKYFL! Wow, I really did that!

"Just a heads up," Ama says, drawing my attention away from my phone and on to her as she reaches over to turn down the Amaarae song blasting from her car's speakers. It's still quite busy outside, but traffic has calmed down significantly from when we went to pick up my suitcase earlier this morning. "The seamstress can be a bit much, but she knows her way around a sewing machine. Grandma Lily swears by her"

"A bit much?" I ask, tossing my phone back into my bag.

"Oh, she's just your typical Ghana aunty. Comments on your weight, nags you about getting married. The usual."

"Fantastic. Gotta love the aunties," I huff, rolling my eyes. Back home, my run-ins with them are limited, but I've heard enough from Chelsea to know what to expect, and Mrs. Botchway doesn't disappoint.

The first thing that flies out of her mouth when we arrive at the small shop is how we are too beautiful to be single. When she finally gets around to taking measurements, she works slowly, squeezing in as many related and unrelated questions as she can.

"Please, what kind of dress style are you thinking of?" She questions. My body flinches as she tightly wraps the measuring tape around my bust. Is she making me a binder or a dress?

"Uh, nothing too fancy. Maybe something form-fitting and strapless?" I suggest, trying my best to breathe from under the tightness of the tape.

A loud clicking noise escapes her mouth as she removes her hand from my body. "Oh no, no. Your chest is far too large for that. How about some straps? Two fingers wide, maybe?"

Two fingers wide? What is this, Sunday school?

"Um." My eyes anxiously divert to Ama, who is sitting on the only chair in the small room, flipping through a photo album of Mrs. Botchway's designs. Without even looking up, she comes to my defence.

"Aunty, that sounds nice and all, but I think Robyn can pull off any style she wants just fine."

"*Herh*, you young people just love to show your skin, but fine. Strapless it is."

Mrs. Botchway pulls a pen from behind her ear to jot down my measurements before scurrying into the back room. When she returns, she's holding three yards of kente in each hand. The base colour is a deep violet, while a zigzag of shiny threads forming gold and lilac diamonds repeat across the cloth to create an intricate pattern.

"It's gorgeous," I rave, running my fingers across the thick fabric.

"What if we add some gold beading on the top half? Not too much *kraa*, but just enough to make the colours more vibrant."

From the way her eyes glimmer as she envisions her next creation, it's clear to see how much she loves what she does. I wonder if she's always felt this way about designing. When she was my age, did she know this was what she wanted to do for the rest of her life? My mind struggles to understand how an eighteen-year-old is supposed to know for sure that choosing a passion over something stable and guaranteed will be worth the risk.

"Gold beading will be the perfect addition," I smile, forcing myself to shift my focus back to the kente in my palms instead of the uncertainty of my future. Under all her layers of Ghana aunty-ness, I can see why Grandma Lily still patronizes Mrs. Botchway's business after all these years. The woman knows what she's doing.

* * *

"So he's your grandma's friend?" Chelsea's face is pixelated thanks to my room having the worst connection in the house. But even with the poor quality, I can make out the familiar background of our two-bedroom apartment. With its crisp white walls, cement columns and ceiling to floor windows that give us a breathtaking view of the iconic Toronto skyline.

"He's her neighbour," I correct, while using my fingers to fluff out my wash'n'go with leave-in conditioner.

After spending the day with Ama on Monday, the rest of the week has been slow but intentional. I haven't been out much, but I've enjoyed spending time with Grandma Lily during the day and Ama after she gets off work in the evening.

They share detailed stories about my mom without me having to ask and answer every follow-up question I throw their way. *What was her favourite food?* She loved Grandma Lily's award-winning waakye. *Did she get along with her siblings?* Ama vividly remembers my mom and her younger sister, Aunty Naa, teasing her dad for being cheap during the holidays. *What was her temperament like?* She was a happy baby and an even happier adult. She never left a room without making someone smile.

With the help of their memories, I no longer have just an unfinished outline of the woman I don't remember. She's transforming into a picture bursting with colour right before my eyes. But now it's Friday night, and with Grandma Lily at a retirement party and Ama on a blind date, I'm being forced to go out with Osei and his friends. According to them, a young girl like me has no business being inside on a Friday night in Accra.

"The neighbour. Got it." Chelsea taps her chin with her

index finger as if it helps to download the new information. "But he's her photographer?"

"Something like that."

"Hm, looks like you two have that in common then." There's a sly grin on her glossy lips as she tosses her auburn knotless braids over her shoulder. One thing Chelsea's hair will never be is plain black. Since learning how to do her own hair, she's constantly trying out new colours and styles. I, on the other hand, like to keep my hair up or knotless braids in the only colour you'll find me in: black.

"Girl, you know I'm not a photographer."

"The portfolio you shot for me begs to differ," she counters, and I roll my eyes. Last month, Chelsea decided she wanted to start offering hair and makeup services, and asked me to shoot content for her Instagram and website launch.

My initial response was a resounding 'hell no'. Outside of class, I don't take pictures. But she persisted, and eventually I caved. So while Chelsea loves the end results and has the pictures up on all social media platforms, I on the other hand, still feel indifferent toward them.

"That was a one-time thing, and you know it," I proclaim, jabbing my finger at the screen.

"Well, *I'm* just glad my bestie is finally getting out of the house and with a boy who's fine as hell at that," she exclaims.

"I should have never sent you that man's Instagram," I whine as I bend over to pull my hair into my signature puff.

"And how did you find his Instagram again? I doubt you asked for it directly."

"Can't a girl do some research on her nemesis? Damn," I say, shaking my head once I'm upright again.

"Sure, that's what it was," she laughs.

"Yeah, yeah," I dismiss her, stepping away from the camera so my entire body is visible. "What do you think?"

I twirl in the bodycon dress I found collecting dust in my closet while packing. Chelsea forced me to buy it back in September for an Afrobeats themed Frosh Week party, but by the time the first week of classes rolled around, I was already up to my eyeballs in course readings and never made it out of the apartment.

"See how good you look when you're not trying to hide your body with oversized sweaters," she squeals. "Ouuu, Osei is gonna eat you up!"

"Goodbye, Chels," I laugh before ending the call.

I head downstairs to wait for Osei, but the back view of someone I don't recognize causes me to shriek upon entering the kitchen.

"What the—"

The girl leaps up from her seat next to the island and turns around to face me.

"Hi! You must be Robyn. I'm Osei's sister, Kuukua."

"Oh wow," I exhale as I take her in. "You're gorgeous!"

Her dark skin is luminous under a fiery red minidress, and her long legs are probably the length of my entire body. Complete with pouty lips and cat-shaped eyes hiding under thick strip lashes, she's a photographer's dream. Not that I would know anything about what they dream of though.

Kuukua laughs off my compliment in a way that makes it clear that she's used to being gushed over.

"Thanks! They say I stole all the good looks from Osei in the womb," she snorts as she picks up a gold clutch sitting on top of the kitchen counter. "Are you ready to head out?"

"Oh, is your brother not coming anymore?" I reply, sounding hopeful as she struts to the door. Tonight is already looking up, and we haven't even left the house.

"Actually, he's going to meet us there! Osei got roped into picking up our cousin from the airport. So I called us a Bolt instead," she says, referring to the rideshare out here that Ama claims has way better rates than Uber.

"Well, I hope he doesn't make him wait as long as he made me," I mumble, bending over to slide on my black heels.

"What was that?" Kuukua asks, turning to look back at me.

"Nothing!" I cheese, popping back up. "Let's get out of here."

* * *

Our driver, Dela, keeps the air conditioning on high while we giggle at his endless but harmless flirting.

"I hope you are enjoying your stay, Robyn," he yells as he turns onto a busy street littered with partygoers. He's trying to be heard over the music, which is more static than sound, but we don't have the heart to tell him to turn it off. "You are welcome in Ghana anytime. Anytime!"

"Oh, thank you, uncle," I smile at him through the rearview mirror. There's an extra layer of sweetness in my tone. It's my best attempt at Chelsea's infamous 'speaking to Ghanaian elders' voice.

"Oh, come on! I'm not your uncle! Do I look like an uncle to you?" He exclaims, making Kuukua and I shriek with laughter. Dela may not look exactly like an uncle, but he's definitely close. I'm sitting behind him, so I have a clear view of the shiny round spot on the top of his head.

"You girls are laughing, but I'm serious, o! It was not too long ago I was boogying with you people at Purple Pub, you know!"

"We've heard," Kuukua laughs. "*Ma bre*" she repeats in Twi. We're still laughing as Dela brings the car to a halt. I look up and read the name of the club, 'Front/Back'.

"Nah, this is crazy," I yell, observing the mob of people

once we pay Dela in cash and exit the car. "Is it always this busy? Or is this because it's December?"

"Definitely because of the holidays. It feels as if the clock struck twelve on November 30th, and the population doubled in size. Just wait until it gets closer to Christmas." We hold hands as we bypass a long line of people waiting to enter. "The last couple of Decembers have been insane," she yells into my ear. "With the influx of tourists, everything has doubled in price, and you can't even go out without sitting in at least two hours of traffic."

Hearing this makes my mouth feel dry and all I can taste is guilt on my tongue. I know I'm not exactly who Kuukua is referring to when she says tourists, but I can't help but feel like one anyway.

"Damn, I'm sorry. It must suck to be pushed out like that."

"Nonsense," Kuukua says, waving my apology away with her raised palm. "It's not you people that we're upset with. It's our useless leaders' fault for inviting all these people but not having the infrastructure to sustain it. A broken system is a broken system, with or without tourists. But enough about this country and its never-ending issues. My brother's friends are waiting for us inside."

As we head through the open-air venue, I can't help but smile as we pass a gorgeous group of girls singing at the top of their lungs. The air is electric as the crowd vibes to a mix of hip-hop, music from across the diaspora and Ghanaian classics.

"Is that?" I gasp, pointing at the man in shades sipping champagne while nodding to the song in what I assume is a V.I.P. section. Hanging tea lights and greenery shimmer above his head as he nods along to the bassline of a familiar Nigerian hit.

"Sarkodie," confirms Kuukua, laughing at my fangirl-ish

outburst. Next to Ghana's biggest rapper, others who I assume are even more famous than he is – judging by the size of their entourage – pop bottles in a cloud of hookah smoke.

When we finally reach the table, Osei's friends, Jojo and David, jump up to greet us. As we exchange introductions, I pretend not to notice David's hand briefly lingering on the small of Kuukua's back. Secretly hooking up with your twin's best friend? Oh, I absolutely love this girl.

"Come now. You people sit and have something to drink," David insists as he ushers us into a seated area at the back of the club. A platter of mouth-watering kebabs, crisp fried yam, and charbroiled sausages sits next to a steel bucket full of ice and drinks. Once we've all picked up our glasses, Jojo reaches for a glistening champagne bottle and pops off the cork.

"Let the enjoyment begin!"

seven

"IS THAT OSEI?" I yell over the music to Kuukua, watching the tall figure make his way toward us.

"Huh," she shouts while swaying to the beat beside me.

"Your brother! Is that him over there?" The crowd seems to part as I say this, making it clear that it is indeed Osei in all his six-two glory. He's just a few strides away from our table when a short woman reaches out to hug him. She's gorgeous, with proportions that probably aren't humanly possible without Ghanaian DNA or a really good surgeon. I plop down in the cushioned seat and pull out my phone. Just because I don't care for Osei like that, doesn't mean I want to watch him all hugged up with some girl. When I hear hands next to me sliding and slapping one another, I scroll through Instagram, not bothering to look up. It's been a few days since we last saw each other and the thought of facing him again in this setting is making knots tangle in my stomach. I don't know why though. It's not like I care about what he thinks or anything. I guess it's just new territory for us.

"Yo, Jojo, David, how far," Osei greets them.

"*Chale*, wassup," says one of the two boys in a cheer. It's hard to tell who as I can't make out their voices yet.

"Sis," his tone is playful, and I can sense a movement shift in front of me.

"Hey, watch it," Kuukua cries. The sound of her palm connecting with his skin follows.

"Relax. Your HD frontal looks fine," Osei teases, and I wonder if Kuukua has ever dreamed of being an only child. Knowing I'm not the only one he likes to annoy makes me want to join forces with her and take him down.

I keep my eyes glued to my screen, but it's hard to miss his blue-and-black Jordans approaching before the couch I'm seated in sinks from the weight of his body. Despite the scent of sweat, alcohol and shisha lingering in the air, his cologne still manages to find its way to my nostrils. It's clean and crisp and reminds me of freshly washed laundry.

"Hello, Miss Carter. You clean up nice."

Against my better judgment, the corners of my lips turn upward at the compliment.

"I hope you didn't make your cousin wait too long," I smirk and finally bring myself to take him in. Up close, he looks as good as he smells. He's dressed simply in a black graphic T-shirt and slightly distressed dark-wash jeans, but he manages to make it look like he's just walked off the runway. I won't be telling him any of that though. He doesn't need me to point out the obvious.

"Oh, trust me, I've learned my lesson," he chuckles, popping a piece of fried yam into his mouth. His easy response surprises me, but I fight the urge to push it further.

"So where is he?" I question, looking around the crowd for someone who resembles the Mensah twins. Maybe if I'm lucky, he'll be the alter-ego of his male cousin. Deliciously handsome, but with a personality that doesn't make me want to yank my puff out strand by strand.

"Who?" Osei asks while pouring orange Ceres Fruit Juice into a plastic cup full of ice.

"Uh, your cousin," I say, bringing my own cup to my lips. "I thought you went to pick him up."

"Oh yeah," Osei says, licking his lips as he nods toward the entrance, and I awkwardly avert my gaze. Why is this boy always drinking something around me?

"He saw some old friends when we came in and went to say hello. Also, he's not our cousin."

"That's not what Kuukua said," I say, glancing over at his sister. I watch as David whispers something in her ear, and from the way her head snaps back as she giggles, I just know sis is down bad.

"We just say we're cousins because it's easier than explaining that our dads are just best friends," Osei explains, his eyes following mine. When he spots the two giggling, he immediately hops up, his knee knocking over the unclosed carton of Ceres in the process.

"You have got to be kidding me," I shriek as the orange liquid seeps through my dress, but Osei has already wedged himself between David and Kuukua and doesn't seem to notice.

"Where's the bathroom?" I yell over the music to Jojo, who is dancing by himself with his eyes closed.

"At the back," he shouts back without opening them.

After locating the bathroom and squeezing past a group of girls taking pictures in the mirror, I pat down my dress with a wet paper towel. I've removed the stickiness, but the fabric is thin, so a big wet splotch remains.

"Well, at least we're in an open air club," I mutter while

looking down at my dress as I leave the bathroom. I barely make it two steps out of the door before I walk directly into a firm body entering the area. Two large hands swiftly grab me as I'm about to hit the ground, and we both break out in simultaneous apology.

"I am so sorry!"

I lean back to look at my saviour's face as he steadies me on my feet. Although the sun set several hours ago, amber eyes gleam down at me from behind tinted brown lenses, and his intense gaze sends a chill down my spine.

"Hi," he breathes, slowly releasing me from his grasp.

"Hi," I whisper back, taking him in.

A linen, short-sleeve button-down hangs loosely off his defined upper body and on his exposed chest sits a thick gold Cuban. In his earlobes, round diamonds sparkle, and his haircut is so crisp, I could probably slice my palm from just brushing against it.

"Wow, you are stunning," he breathes, his eyes dancing across my face. My cheeks heat up at the compliment, then cool down as I register his familiar accent.

"Wait, are you from Toronto?" I laugh, my nose scrunching up in surprise.

"I am. Well, technically, Brampton. But it's all the same thing," he chuckles. "Is it really that obvious?"

I laugh loudly. "I can pick out my people in any crowd."

"I literally just landed today," he beams. His smile lights up his entire face, and his skin, a warm shade of brown, appears golden.

"What are the chances that two people from the GTA would meet for the first time halfway across the world?" I joke as we move out of the way of passing bathroom-goers.

"The probability is definitely not high," he remarks, his eyes soft with wonder. "But who am I to question my good fortune? I'm Kelvin, by the way. I'm guessing you're Ghanaian."

"Robyn," I reply, pressing my palm to my chest. "And I'm only half-Ghanaian."

"Oh yeah? What's your other ha—"

The shrill sound of a record scratching cuts him off, and the tease of the next track causes the bar to roar.

"Oh my gosh, I love this song!" I cry, recognizing the beat drop. Spinning towards the music, my body sways to the familiar sound. Before I can register what is happening, the dancing crowd pushes me into Kelvin, closing our gap. His hands swiftly slide around my waist as we collide, and the motion causes my body and brain to freeze.

Think, Robyn, what would Chelsea do right now? I can almost hear her kissing her teeth in my head. *Dance, stupid!*

Taking a deep breath, I allow my hips to sway against his firm frame slowly. He guides me to follow his tempo, and we simultaneously ride the beat. Pressed so closely together, the sound of his heavy breathing trickles from my ear to my heart, causing it to thrash against my chest. The intimacy is daunting and foreign, yet I don't want it to end. I squeeze my eyes shut, wanting to savour every second, but a teasing voice infiltrates the moment.

"I see you've met Kelvin."

My eyes pop open to see Osei grinning down at me. Oh, you have got to be kidding me! Is Kelvin their family friend?

"You two know each other?" I hear Kelvin ask from behind me. I swear there's a tinge of jealousy in his tone, but I'm too shocked by this revelation to turn around and confirm if it shows on his face as well.

"Remember I was telling you about the girl from Canada staying next door? This is her. Anyway, Jojo got another round of drinks. You people coming or what?" Osei asks, looking down at me expectantly.

"I think we're good right here," I answer promptly. Osei chuckles, but doesn't reply as he pivots back to the table, not giving us a second glance.

Just as I'm about to press Kelvin about his relation to Osei, the D.J. cuts on a fast-paced beat. It makes him slightly tighten his grip on my waist in preparation for the swift change in dancing styles.

"And this, right here, is where I tap out," I laugh, pressing my palms over his hands and twisting to face him. "I'm not the girl for all that."

Slow wining, I can manage, but fast wining is the easiest way to set myself up to be embarrassed. My West Indian genes did not come through in that department.

"Aww, come on, you were killing it," he grins, removing his sunglasses, and I'm nearly hypnotized by the hazel flecks floating in his irises.

"Oh, please," I scoff.

"Honestly. I've been to my fair share of house parties and encountered a lot of bad dancing. That," he says, focusing on my lower half, desire flashing across his eyes. "Wasn't bad."

I playfully roll my eyes, ignoring the heat spreading across my cheeks. "You're just trying to gas me."

"I'm serious. Maybe different, but definitely not bad," he winks. "But don't worry, different is good. I need that in my life right now. Here, let me see your phone."

He doesn't wait for my response before leaning forward and pulling it from my hand. He holds it to my face to unlock it, and I watch his fingers tap across the screen.

"Kelvin *Williams*?" I ask, reading the new name in my contacts out loud after he hands it back–my nose wrinkles in surprise at his last name.

"Yeah, I'm Fante."

"Ohh, you're a Fante boy," I tease. "You know I'm Ashanti, right?"

Beyond the names of the largest tribes, Ashanti, Fante and Ga, I don't know much about tribes in Ghana. But I know enough that people across cultures typically prefer to be with their own people.

"Well, I've always thought Ashanti women were the most breathtaking women in Ghana, and clearly, I was right about that," he states, staring down at me intensely. "Well, I'm glad the odds have been in my favour today. Not only are we from the same city, but we get to spend this trip living next to each other."

"Wait, you're staying with Mensahs?" I know my voice is unnecessarily loud right now, but I'm too shocked to care.

"Yeah. This trip is my first time back since my parents and I left Ghana eight years ago, so they suggested I stay with the Mensahs. We have a place, but it's not in the city. It's more of a holiday spot if anything."

I bite down on my bottom lip as I process this information. I should be excited that Kelvin is guaranteed to be in close proximity for the rest of my trip, but knowing Osei will be there right next to him seems to taint the joy I should be feeling. But before I can process why I feel that way, the crowd goes ballistic as the D.J. plays a viral song, and I can feel the surge of collective effervescence course through my body. It runs through my veins and streams through my bloodstream, making me forget about anything other than this moment. Yanking Kelvin's hands back around my waist, I merge my body into his and together, we move as one.

eight

AFTER THREE MORE SONGS, Kelvin guides me to the bar to take a break from all the dancing. He orders us two lemonade-and-vodkas and turns to face me while we wait for the bartender to make them.

"I still can't believe that we're both at UofT in the same exact program and we've never crossed paths before," he yells over the music, his head shaking in awe. I'm both tickled and flattered at his dedication to holding a conversation in such a loud environment. "I know you're a year younger than me, but I'm just surprised I haven't seen you around campus or at the Black Science Students welcome week event. I'm a part of the committee so I should have seen you by now for sure."

For a brief moment, I consider telling him that I've been buried between readings, playing a perpetual game of catchup, and have no extra time to mix and mingle with the members of UofT's Black caucus.

Maybe if I tell someone who's been in my shoes just a year prior, he'll be able to give me some advice on how to stop feeling like I'm forever in sinking sand. But almost as soon as the thought crosses my mind, I decide against it.

From just this initial meeting alone, it's clear that Kelvin is someone who stays on top of his shit. From the way he dresses to how he carries himself. I mean who willingly joins a committee if they don't have their life all the way together?

"Yeah, it's crazy isn't it," I mumble instead, then divert my attention to the cocktails the bartender is sliding towards us. "Oh wow, those look delicious!"

The tall glasses are frosted, full of ice and have a curled lemon peel hanging off the side. We each take one, then walk side by side to a less crowded area of the club. He directs me to a two-seater velvet couch in an area that is covered with greenery. The potted palm trees and bushes keep the area mostly out of view from the rest of the dancers we were just immersed with.

"So tell me about yourself, Robyn?"

I snort. Good question. Just a few months ago, I feel like I would have been able to answer that with ease.

"What do you want to know?" I ask, taking a sip of my drink.

"Everything." His reply is so earnest I almost choke on an ice cube.

"Wow, okay," I cough. "I guess, um, I'm an only child. Raised by a single dad and I've lived in Brampton my entire life. Well, up until this past fall when I moved to Toronto for uni with my best friend Chelsea. What else, what else? Oh, I love chocolate fudge and horror movies, and I can't stand R&B. Sorry, it's just so cringey! And, yeah, this is my first time in Ghana since my mom's funeral, sixteen years ago."

"Oh, I'm sorry to hear that," he says quietly, his hand stretching out to squeeze mine, which rests in the space between us.

"Thanks. I don't remember much about her, but it's been

nice being here. I'm hoping to put together some of the missing pieces, you know?"

"That must be nice. I hope you get the answers to any questions you may have."

I smile up at him feeling grateful that his calm and assured presence makes discussing something so sensitive feel so easy.

"Thanks Kelvin. But, enough about me, tell me some things about you."

"Well, I'm nineteen. I'm in my second year of university and I used to run track. A sprinter to be specific."

"Okayyy, we have Usain Bolt in the building!" I jokingly pull at the part of his shirt that covers his shoulder with my thumb and forefinger.

"You know, just a small OFSAA record-holder. No big deal," he grins, stretching his arms into Bolt's signature pose and we both double over with laughter.

"I also live in downtown Toronto, but on campus with my boy Leo, and I definitely agree with you about R&B music. Turn that shit off around me!"

"Finally, somebody who gets it!" I exclaim.

He laughs before continuing. "I think Kendrick is the greatest rapper of our generation and it's my dream to become a neurologist."

I let out a long whistle.

"Neurology? You sure ain't playing around."

Kelvin shrugs off my compliment in a way that tells me not only is he used to hearing this, he is also in no way concerned that he won't achieve this dream.

"It's definitely not light work, but my dad is a neurologist and I've seen how many lives—especially Black ones—that he's been able to save by simply just believing his patients. I want to be able to contribute to my community like he does."

He's so assured in his response that the envy I've been feeling lately when it comes to people knowing themselves, is nowhere to be found. Instead I just feel seen. This was me just last year. Whenever anyone would ask what I wanted to do after high school, I could list out my whole life plan and the path that I was going to take to get there. UofT for undergrad and pharmacy school. Work side by side with Dad and then eventually take over his pharmacy.

"Wow, I can definitely relate to that," I start, feeling uncontrollably vulnerable. It's 1 a.m., we're in a sweaty-ass club in Accra, and we're here talking about saving lives when we probably should be dancing, but everything about this moment just feels so right. "My dad is a pharmacist and my whole life I've always noticed the look of surprise, quickly followed by relief when the customers that looked like us realized he owned the pharmacy. It used to be a no-brainer to me that I would follow in his footsteps and be that kind of inspiration to other little Black girls, but now I'm not so sure," I admit, the words spilling out of me in a rush.

At this point I don't know if it's all the alcohol running through my bloodstream or the butterflies going apeshit in my belly, but I feel like Kelvin is someone I can be honest with; so I'm not holding back.

"Why not?" He asks considerately. There's not an ounce of judgment or confusion in his tone. He's simply just curious, and I can feel myself resting in his comfortable presence even more.

"I don't know. I guess I just feel like I'm drowning in schoolwork and no amount of studying or reading is keeping me afloat. It just doesn't make any sense, because school has always come easy to me. I mean I was my class' valedictorian for crying out loud. But for some reason, everything is just ten times harder in university. Problems I used to be able to solve with ease, I'm second-guessing and concepts that I could regurgitate in my sleep no longer make sense to me."

As the words keep tumbling out, it hits me that this is the first time I've said any of this out loud to someone else. Not even Chelsea knows how bad it's gotten, because every time she sees me staying up too late or spending long hours at the library, I assure her everything is under control.

"I mean I'm not on academic probation or anything," I admit, recognizing I'm being a tad dramatic even for me. "But it's all been such a big change for me. I guess I'm just struggling to find my footing right now and I hate how uncomfortable that feels."

My heart thuds against my ribcage as Kelvin nods slowly, seemingly absorbing my confessional with every bob.

"I've been there before," he replies.

"You have?"

"Why do you think someone who obtained a provincial 100 metre record just two years ago isn't still sprinting?"

"Oh," I say, as his words settle around me. It didn't even cross my mind when he first brought it up—but that does make sense. Even Chelsea's boyfriend Jalen, who won OFSAA with our high school soccer team still plays right now at the other major university downtown, TMU. Most high-performing athletes don't just stop, unless they get injured or something else, something more pressing, pulls them away from their sport.

"I wanted so badly to have the best of both worlds. Being a student-athlete at one of the best universities in the country was my dream for years. But it didn't take long before I realized sometimes you just can't have it all. I decided to choose to focus on school. School was something I knew wasn't a gamble. It was safe and sustainable, and I knew with the right help, I would have a guaranteed future—unlike with sprinting. I started attending the Black Science students peer-tutoring sessions and got my GPA back on track by the end of my second semester. So, please Robyn. Don't think you're the only one struggling with that transition from high school to university, because trust me, you're not."

"Wow," is all I can say. I'm in complete disbelief that someone as well put-together as Kelvin experienced something so similar to me. With the way he carries himself, he just gives off this calm and collected vibe, but I guess there's more to him than meets the surface.

"Thanks, Kelvin, it means a lot to hear you say that."

The relief from opening up and being accepted so easily, feels like a hit of dopamine. For the first time in a long time, it feels as if the weight I've been dragging behind me all semester has been cut loose. Who knew, being honest about your feelings could be so freeing?

"Don't worry," he says, lacing his fingers with mine. His eyes are bright and focused on me. "You have *me* now and I won't let you fail."

nine

"SO TELL ME," Ama starts, standing up from her seat at the kitchen table. "How has your first week in Ghana been?" She scrapes the remains of her waakye in the trash, then moves to wash her plate at the kitchen sink. Last night, Ama mentioned how she was craving the rice dish, and Grandma Lily promised to have it ready for us this morning before leaving to meet up with her birthday party planner.

"So far, it's been great. Everyone and everything has exceeded my expectations," I admit, my right hand still deep in the smoky rice and peas. Well, everyone except Osei, that is.

"And when you say everyone, you really mean Kelvin, innit?" Ama jokes, drying her hands with the towel hanging off the stove. "I can't believe you've been here for one bloody week, and you're already boo'd up! *My* dating pool is infested with the exes of my childhood friends. Gosh, I hate how everyone is connected in this city."

"Ama! We only met three days ago! I am not cuffed yet," I squeal. "But, I won't lie, Kelvin has absolutely been a treat," I cheese, unable to stop my excitement from stretching a smile across my face.

Kelvin and I have been texting non-stop since the night we met at Front/Back and even though it's still so early, I can't deny how much our lives could go together. How much our paths already seem to converge. Chelsea always says: us girls need to know early on when a guy meets the requirements to ride the ride, so we can try our best to avoid heartbreak and so far Kelvin doesn't appear to disappoint. The two of us just make sense.

"But you're right about everyone knowing one another," I agree, standing to rinse my empty plate in the sink. "I can't believe he's the first person I met out here by myself, and he was *still* linked to Osei."

"What's up with you two anyway? Every time he comes around, you look as if you want to strangle him for simply breathing," Ama giggles. "Based on the conversations you and I had before you came out here, I was so certain you two would be a perfect match or at least good friends."

Her admission makes me feel hollow inside. My mind races through our conversations over FaceTime these past three months. We shared bits and pieces about our childhoods and teenage years, and she also told me why she started Surplus Ghana. When she asked me why I was studying Life Sciences, I gave her the same generic response I give everyone else: to follow in Dad's footsteps. So what could I have said that made Ama think Osei, the carefree dreamer, and I were alike?

"Really? What made you think that?" I ask while wiping down my plate with a kitchen towel. I try to keep an air of curiosity in my tone, but even I know I sound unreasonably defensive.

"Now that I think about it," she starts, squinting as she ponders our past conversations. Her work bag is now on her shoulder, and she spins a set of keys around her pointer finger. "I guess it was quite brief, but the way your eyes shone as you described a grade you got on a photography assignment, I was so sure I'd seen that exact look on Osei when he talks about his work."

Damn it! I know which assignment she's talking about. The stupid 'emotions' assignment Dr. Beal assigned. We had to create a story that conveys a journey of emotion in five photographs without showing faces. The focus was to express feelings through body language, so I worked with some members of the contemporary dance club and took pictures of them in motion. My goal was to display the range of feelings one experiences after loss through close-cropped shots of human bodies in movement. I didn't realize I had gone above and beyond until I finished presenting and noticed Dr. Beal and several others wiping streams of tears from their faces.

I got my grade back while on a call with Ama, and she wouldn't drop it until I told her why I was grinning as if I just won the lotto. Her ecstatic response to my grade was so overwhelmingly supportive that it induced the painful memory of the night I decided to stop sharing work outside of class three years earlier. I quickly changed the topic and pushed past her response so I didn't have to endure the feeling again.

"Oh, that was nothing," I drift off, reaching up to put away the dry plate that suddenly feels like cement in my hands. The words I typically say whenever someone brings up photography refuse to form, no matter how hard I try. I can't articulate that the excitement Ama thought she saw on my face was simply because my prof was an easy grader. It's a bird course after all. Something light to bump up your GPA. Nothing more, nothing less.

As my silence stretches on, she eyes me inquisitively before setting her Louis Vuitton tote bag on the island and tossing her keys inside.

"Come with me," she commands, spinning on her black pumps while waving for me to follow her into the hallway.

"Wait, aren't you going to be late for work?" I call after her. As I skip to keep up with her brisk pace, my hand scrunches around the waistband of the oversized sweatpants I wear to lounge around the air-conditioned house.

"I may have to work in December, but I never said I have to be on time," she says, throwing a loud cackle in my direction. When she finally stops walking, we're outside a room at the back of the first floor that I've never noticed before. As she reaches out to turn the handle, we lock eyes, and it's impossible not to see the look of hope that flashes across her face.

"Robyn, I think it's important that you see this," she says before letting us inside.

I blink slowly in the utter darkness, but when I hear the flick of the light switch, a loud gasp escapes my lips at the change in lighting. The entire room floods with a soft red glow.

"Oh my gosh, is this a darkroom?" I ask, my hand flying to cover my mouth. A stack of rectangular trays sits next to a bulky machine on a long table that leans against the left wall. On the right, a wide sink is installed at the back and above it, a laundry line is strung from corner to corner, but no clothes are hanging from the wooden pins. Instead, floating above our heads are several photographs.

"It is." I can't see her, but Ama's voice sounds shaky behind me. "Grandpa Isaac had it built before he passed."

I slowly step further into the room, taking in the museum of pictures chronicling the life of my mom and her family. The never-before-seen sepia and black-and-white images stare back at me, each with their own story to share. Ignoring the dust accumulating on my fingertips, I trace each hanging photograph, admiring the angle choices, the lighting and the focus. But when I get to a picture of two young girls standing outside a building, I pause. A sign in the background reads: Wesley Girls' High School. My mom is standing hand in hand with her sister Naa, who looks no older than four years old. Her hair is cut low, and she's grinning from ear to ear, and that's when I notice the bulky film camera hanging around my mom's neck. No. No. No. This can't be possible. There's no way this is possible.

"He built this room for her," Ama whispers, before placing something light in my hand. The feeling of glossy photo paper against my palms causes a sudden onset of goosebumps to blanket my skin from head to toe.

My fingers tremble as I look down at the photos in my hand. Carefully, I bring them to my face, trying to discern every detail. In one, Grandma Lily is captured from the side while looking off into the distance. Dark brown curls cascade around her delicate facial features. There's also a portrait of Grandpa Isaac where he is staring straight on, his moustache almost as thick as the afro on the top of his head. The following image is of Uncle Emmanuel in his late teens. He cheekily smirks up at the camera while lying on a bed with arms crossed behind his head. In the last one, Aunty Naa is sitting on what looks like the steps at the front of the house. She's smiling delicately, with her chin resting on her knuckles and her elbows digging into her thighs. Even under the red lighting, I can tell the photos have a warm finish. All four subjects are in perfect focus, while their backgrounds are a soft blur of colours and grain—a flawless bokeh.

"They were all taken by your mom," Ama says, blissfully unaware of the tightening in my chest and the panic taking over my body.

My mom was a photographer? How is that even possible? Not after everything Dad said to me that night. When he shattered every inkling of the dream I dared to conceive.

A knot of betrayal forms a lump in my throat, making it difficult to speak.

"W-when did she stop shooting photography?" I croak. "Tell me she stopped before she left Ghana, Ama. Tell me!"

Through my blurred vision, I can see Ama wince at my raised voice, but I'm far too distraught to dial it back. I'm too distraught to ask politely.

"Oh, Robyn. I am so, so, sorry." Her voice is a whisper, but the regret is resounding. The photographs slowly slip from my hands as the secret unfolds, gently floating to the floor.

"This is the reason she left Ghana in the first place. She went to the University of Toronto to obtain her Master of Visual Studies in Studio Arts."

The final confirmation swells the lump in my throat, causing a burning sensation to seize the few words I have left. The only thing running through my mind is how much I need to get out of here.

I stumble backwards trying to feel for the door behind me as I struggle to breathe. I can see Ama's lips moving, but my brain is too busy trying and failing to focus on breathing to process the words leaving her mouth. But once I feel the coolness of the brass handle against my palm, I spin on my heels, bolt down the hallway, and dash out the front door.

ten

OUT ON THE porch I desperately try to gasp for air, but a gust of dry wind constricts my throat, making me cough uncontrollably. Thank you *so* much, Accra. Harmattan is exactly what I need right now.

I bend over, trying to steady myself, and my lungs feel as if they're two stress balls being squeezed by someone in deep anguish. Amid my panic, I don't hear the sound of the gate creaking open, but Osei is in the front yard and he's sprinting toward me at full speed.

"Robyn," he yells, climbing the front steps two at a time. Once he reaches me, he grabs my face without hesitation and pulls me up to look at him. A sense of calm blankets his expression, but his grip on my cheeks is taut with fear.

"Take a second and breathe, okay? I need you to breathe for me, Rob. Copy what I do, okay? Just like this." He begins to breathe out slow gusts of air, and I mirror him. We stand on the porch, our eyes locked, exhaling until every last hiccup is gone. His large hands cup my cheeks, grounding me with his firm touch.

"Do you feel better?" he asks after a few long moments of just breathing. He's hesitant to remove his hands; I get the feeling that if I told him not to, he would never let go. I nod shakily, my breathing returning to normal as he lowers his hands. Osei examines me thoroughly and the intensity of his scrutiny makes a fuzzy feeling ripple within me.

"Um, thank you for that," I mutter, staggering down to sit on the first step. While my breathing may be steady, my legs are starting to feel as if one is a few inches longer than the other. "I'm kind of shocked at how good you are at that breathing stuff," I tell Osei as he plops down beside me. "I wouldn't take you for that kind of guy."

His smile is soft yet guarded. "I was stopping by to say hello to your grandma, but when I saw you out here, I immediately recognized what was happening," he explains quietly. "Breathing like that is what helps me whenever I'm experiencing an anxiety attack."

As he says this, I realize how serious he is right now. It's my first time seeing him in this manner since we've met, and I don't quite know how to feel in the sedated version of his presence.

Anxiety is not foreign to me, but mine has always been fleeting. It comes in waves and then passes. It reveals itself through itchy palms or sweaty armpits, before disappearing again. I've never had a full-blown panic attack like this before. The thought alone increases my heart rate expeditiously, causing my foot to tap in sync with the quickened beats.

"Hey, Rob. Look at me," he says, placing his palm on my knee. The bouncing falters under his touch. "We don't have to talk about this if you don't want to. Let's change the subject, okay? What do you plan to study next year?"

Of course, he unintentionally picks a topic still connected

to my panic. I search my mind, looking for something to pivot the direction our conversation is heading, but all I can muster up in response is, "What do *you* study?"

"Oh, me? I'm in Computer Science," he shrugs.

His response catches me by surprise. The way he goes on and on about photography, I was sure he was getting a degree in the arts.

"What, no photography?" I ask, my voice doused with more bitterness than I intend.

"Um, yeah, no photography," he confirms, sounding wounded by my tone. He removes his hand from my knee, and I try my best not to flinch from the sudden shift in his demeanour. "The school my parents wanted me to attend, Ashesi, does not have an arts program. It's cool, though, because I don't mind CompSci, and there's a really dope student-led photography and film club on campus. I've only been in school for a semester, but I've been able to contribute to some insanely cool projects, so honestly, I still feel quite fulfilled."

Fulfillment. I've never thought of it like that. It's the perfect word to describe how I feel whenever I hand in an assignment to Dr. Beal. It's one of the reasons that I didn't quit photography when dad made it clear that I could never explore my passion outside the four walls of my high school's media lab.

"And what about your parents?" I ask shakily. "They don't mind?"

"That I shoot photography?" As he asks this, confusion flits across his features.

"Not just that you shoot photography, but because it's what you want to do long-term. That's what you want, right? To be a photographer full-time?" I'm throwing the question at him, but the words fly toward me, bouncing back with nothing but pure vim.

"I mean, yes." He gently scratches his jaw as if thinking about it for the first time. "They definitely prefer that I set my sights on something guaranteed, hence the Computer Science degree, but other than that, we don't talk about it much. At the end of the day, I just feel like the choice should be mine. I don't want to live a life I didn't pick for myself just because I was scared to take a risk, you know?"

"When I was in the tenth grade, I was placed in digital photography class because the communications course I initially selected was accidentally overbooked." I start, the words coming out shakily. His words have seeped deep into my recollection, releasing the memory I haven't dared to share with a soul.

"Before this, I had no previous interest in the arts since I was strictly a science student. Science was all that I had known, thanks to my dad, who is a pharmacist. I didn't think photography would be for me, but I could do nothing to get out of it, so I buckled down and tried to do my best. I wasn't going to let an arts class mess with my stellar GPA after all," I sniff, trying to add a fake smile to lighten the mood, but from the unwavering serious expression on his face, I can tell Osei doesn't buy it.

"Anyway, nothing could have prepared me for the feeling of being behind the lens. Pure exhilaration. The thrill that came with being able to freeze time with a click of the button."

"I understand that completely," Osei nods fervently. "Photographers have the ability to immortalize legacies long after their subject is gone. Even when memories fade, pictures don't. Photos are timeless. Photos last forever."

"Exactly," I agree, a faint smile on my lips. "I got really into it and applied the same work ethic my dad taught me to study math and science to photography, and it paid off. Like, *really* paid off. The first assignment was shooting studio portraits."

Osei nods, familiar with the task. Getting into pairs, shooting portraits of the other person using the three-point lighting setup. Key light, fill light, backlight—the whole works.

"I was the only student in the class to get 100% on that assignment. Afterwards, my teacher pulled me aside to tell me how much raw potential she thought I had and that there was a school with a special arts program in our district she thought I'd be perfect for."

For the first time in my life, I had something I was good at on my own. No one drilled it into me or made me memorize how it should be from early on. I was simply a natural, and for a little while, it felt great. Until it didn't."

"I'm guessing you didn't transfer into the program," he summarizes. The tenderness in his tone causes waves of anxious energy to flutter through me.

"You see, up until then, my dad had never raised his voice at me. After my mom's passing, the line between parent and child was blurry because I had to pick up the slack that was left behind. I always knew I had to do my share around the house, but it was much more after that. I helped with the cooking and cleaning, and he provided for me financially. But that night, it became crystal clear who was the child in our house. Before I could even mention the specialist school, he exploded at me for the first time. All it took was for him to see my signature in the corner of the portrait." I squeeze my eyes shut as I remember the way he tore it into pieces. The sound of my violent screams filled the kitchen as he went off on his tirade.

That night, I learned that the Bajan slang he rarely allows himself to use comes out the most when he's upset. I drop my voice an octave to mimic Dad's accent.

"So ya really tink ya cyan turn a hobby into a career, huh Robyn? Many before ya have tried and failed so what makes ya tink you'll be the one to succeed? Ya tink foolish fantasies will fund your life lil' girl?"

Clarity seems to descend on Osei, and I can see his mind putting it all together: our initial meeting, our interactions in the car, and my apprehension of him in general. It all comes back to this.

"That was the end of it. My dream died that day on the cold tiles of our kitchen floor," I shrug. How could I argue with the person who cared for me by himself? Someone who achieved what I–at the time–believed to be the pinnacle of success without support from anyone else. Who was I to question his decision?

"Eventually, I guess the parental brainwashing seeped in, and it became harder to sift between his stance and mine. While it was too late in the semester to drop the class, I convinced myself I was taking it because it was a bird course. I've taken it every single year since then and even enrolled in the first-year course at my university by telling myself the same lie. 'It's just something easy to boost my average'."

"I am so sorry, Robyn. You didn't deserve any of that."

I try to keep my eyes from dampening as sincerity drips from his voice, but it's useless.

"I've missed so many opportunities because of the fear *he* instilled in me. Just for me to find out the woman that he loved, married and had a child with was a photographer herself." I'm full-on crying at this point, snot streaming out of my nostrils and all.

"I'm guessing you saw the darkroom, huh?" Osei whispers. From the look on his face, I can tell he feels guilty that he knew about it before I did, but even I know I can't blame him for this.

"Yup. Ama showed me." I shake my head indignantly. "God, how could I have been so stupid to let him shut down something that is practically ingrained in my DNA? This is probably why he has always been so apprehensive about me coming out here. He knew I would find out." My hands are flailing as I speak, my anger running rampant. "We never talk about her, you know? We move around like she's a ghost in our own home, and I'm so sick of it!"

Osei peers at me quietly. This lamb-like version of him is so foreign I almost want to reach out and shake him to see if he still has it in him to annoy me.

"So what are you going to do about it?" he finally asks, his voice getting worked up as if this was his own family discovery.

What *am* I going to do? Do I call Dad and confront him? Nah, he'd probably just come up with more excuses for why he never told me. I must do something to compensate for all the lost time. For every minute I've spent denying my creativity and passing up on opportunities of a lifetime. Then it suddenly clicks, slamming into me faster than the quickest shutter speed.

"I'm going to London," I exclaim, jumping to my feet.

"You're going to London?" Osei repeats back, dumbfounded. He takes his time to stand, eyeing me as if I'm a ticking bomb just seconds away from going off.

"Well, I still have to apply, but my professor, Dr. Beal, has been begging me to look into this program." I pull my phone out of my sweatpants pocket and swipe to find the Gmail app. Once I'm in, I scroll through my archive folder until I spot the email I'm looking for and read it aloud.

"The London School of Film, Media and Design Emerging Black Artists' Fellowship. Open to students aged 18-25 worldwide."

I smirk at the email, relief flooding my system. Thank God 'Robyn of last week' didn't delete it. Girl, I could kiss you right now!

"Oh nice, I've heard of that program," Osei nods approvingly, dusting himself off as he stands. "But don't you have to submit a collection of work for the application? Do you have something that you can use?"

A broad grin stretches across my lips as I look up from my phone and at the boy that I'm now grateful lives next door. "That, my new neighbour, is where you come in."

eleven

MY SUBMISSION MUST BE FLAWLESS. There is no way I'm getting into a global program with only two spots for photographers without an undeniably captivating submission. I want to showcase something relatable that doesn't feel performative. A topic that speaks to who I am yet doesn't feel exploitative. With today being December 11th and the application due on January 14th, I have just over a month to do this. The only problem is that every time I sit down to start, I can't decide what I want to shoot.

"What about Ghana in December?" Chelsea offers via FaceTime. "You can take portraits of different members of the diaspora visiting for the holidays. Highlight the rise in tourism since the Year of Return."

I'm sprawled out on Grandma Lily's living room couch as we brainstorm ideas for my submission. Since I won't be leaving Ghana until January 6th, I need to start working on my application as soon as possible. I need to develop a theme, take the pictures and start to edit the project all while I'm in Accra, which is why I needed Osei's help. While getting him to lend me his camera was easy, it's what he wanted in return that I'm quickly starting to regret.

"I think we can do better than that," Osei retorts, shutting down Chelsea's idea in the same blunt manner he used to kill our first ten suggestions. He's leaning back on the matching recliner to the left of the couch, his laptop discarded at his feet.

He's supposed to be preparing for his final exam, which takes place in a few hours, but instead of brushing up on last-minute notes, he's here, acting as if the spirit of America's Next Top Model's greatest photographer, Nigel Barker, has taken over his body.

"You know what, I give up," Chelsea announces. My phone screen goes dark, and I can hear the sound of a car door opening. When the door slams shut, she puts the camera back on her face.

"This is my only break between classes today, and instead of watching makeup tutorials on TikTok while I scarf down Timmies like I usually do, I'm here getting my feelings hurt," she cries before taking a long sip of her daily Tim Hortons coffee. "Robyn, I'm sorry, girl, but I'm leaving you two to figure this out. Osei, you better watch your back when I land in Accra."

My bottom lip sticks out in protest as she waves to the camera, but still, I wave back. I know I can't hold my friend captive to come up with an idea for *my* fellowship application. It's not up to her. This is solely on me.

"See you soon, Chels," Osei yells before the call cuts off. Rolling from my stomach and onto my back, I prop my elbows into the buttery tan leather to get a good look at him. He's acting as if they didn't just meet thirty minutes ago. My glare is searing, but he blinks back at me cooly.

"Really?"

"What?" Osei asks innocently, through fluttering lashes.

"When I agreed that you could help me—"

"You agreed that I could be your assistant."

"When I agreed that you could *help* me," I repeat through clenched teeth. "It was because you promised not to get in the way. Yet, all you've been doing since I started working on my submission is exactly that."

The fellowship application is similar to any university's, but the art submission piece is the main difference. For photographers, that means shooting a ten-image photo essay. If accepted, the chosen fellows will get the opportunity to live in London to conduct an independent creative project for the one-year fellowship. Fellows will immerse themselves in the program's community through six months of training provided by the university, followed by a six-month paid internship in their respective fields. The fellowship promises to give experiences, connections, and relationships with art institutions, media companies and professional artists in and around London.

If anyone should understand how big of an opportunity this is, it should be Osei. But from the way he's been moving, I can't help but wonder if he wants to apply to the fellowship himself. I mean, he totally can if he wants to, but I feel like that would be worth mentioning, no? Or maybe he's trying to sabotage me? Nah, that can't be it. I swallow the bitter thought, hoping for his and my sake that it doesn't upset my stomach down the road.

"Robyn, it's been four days since you decided that you wanted to apply, and you still haven't come up with a theme for this photo essay," he leans forward to pick up his laptop, then slides it into his backpack. "I may be the one verbally disagreeing, but if you liked any of the ideas that have been thrown around, you would have chosen by now."

My neck is hot with irritation as he zips up his bag. What is with this guy and his constant need to call me out?

Through slitted eyes, I watch as he slides one backpack strap over his toned shoulder. He's dressed more formally than usual today. A crisp white golf polo tucked into perfectly straight khaki slacks. Even after sitting, there are hardly any creases or wrinkles in sight. I shift in my seat to sit upright on the couch and turn to face the mounted television. I'd rather look at the blank screen than witness how annoyingly handsome Osei looks right now.

"Look, Rob, I'm sure you don't need me to point this out, but time is not on your side. The closer it gets to the holidays and your grandma's birthday, the harder it will be to shoot with everything happening." He walks into my line of vision and crouches in front of me so I can't avoid his serious gaze. With less than a foot between us, I'm suddenly painfully aware of my thudding heartbeat.

"If you want to impress them, I suggest you stop being afraid to dig deeper. You have one opportunity to tell a story, Robyn. Let's make sure it's one that truly matters to *you*."

Osei stands up and then retreats to the archway that separates the living room from the hallway. Pausing momentarily, he shoots me a goofy grin as if he didn't go all Coach Carter on me just seconds prior.

"We'll talk more about this after my exam. Don't forget to wish me luck," he chimes before disappearing out of view. "Not that I really need it."

Ugh, I cannot stand that boy. I cannot stand him! There has got to be another way to get this done without having to depend on pretentious Osei and his stupid camera.

It's not even because of *what* he said. I *want* to submit work that evokes a response so strong it will be impossible for them not to choose me. It's just how pushy he's been about this that rubs me the wrong way. The last thing I need right now is another person trying to rule my life. I have to make it clear through my work and to him that I'm doing this solely for me.

Sounds of muffled vibrations rumble behind me, and I shift through the couch's decorative pillows in search of my phone. Once I retrieve and unlock it, the name that pops at the top of the screen makes my heart swell three sizes.

> **KELVIN**
> How's the brainstorming going?

> **ROBYN**
> It's not. I'm still in a creative rut 😒 And your 'boy' was no help 🙄 No surprise there.

> **KELVIN**
> I'm sorry I couldn't be there. 😔 My dad has me running around like crazy doing these errands for him.

> **ROBYN**
> Aww, it's okay, I understand. Next time. Actually, no, scratch that. Hopefully, there won't be a next time if I pick a subject soon.

> **KELVIN**
> Okay, but just in case, how does brainstorming tomorrow over dinner sound? 👀

Not caring if Grandma Lily can hear me from wherever she is in the house, I squeal in my seat, kicking my legs with glee.

> **ROBYN**
> Sounds good.

"Ei! Who is shouting in my house," Grandma Lily cries from upstairs.

"Sorry, Grandma!" I shout back, bursting out into a fit of giggles while sending messages to Ama and Chelsea about the impending date. I'm going to need all hands, both virtual and in-person, on deck to get me ready for it.

"Herh, Robyn. Who knew someone so small could make a noise that loud," Grandma Lily groans, strolling into the living room. She's donning another signature house dress that gracefully drapes from her small frame. The tie-dye batik is dyed bright orange, rich in colour like the inside of a papaya, with a pattern of white adinkra symbols I can't recall. A piece of the same shimmery fabric, twisted into an intricate headwrap, covers her hair.

"Sorry, Grandma," I blush, tugging the coils that droop at the back of my puff. As she approaches, I notice her arms tucked behind her back.

"What's that?" I ask, straining my neck to get a better view. An amused smile tugs at Grandma Lily's lips.

"Patience is a virtue, my dear," she teasingly scolds as she sits beside me. Once seated, she reveals the small cardboard box she was hiding.

"So I hear Ama gave you a tour of your mother's special room." There's a pained expression on her face as she says this. I nod slowly, unsure of where this conversation is headed.

"You know, everything in that room is exactly the way she left it the summer you both last visited. I always have the room dusted, but other than that, there's been no changes. That summer, Nana wanted to develop old rolls your grandfather had taken. But she was constantly being distracted, that daughter of mine," Grandma Lily adds with a subdued laugh.

"Each time she started working on it, she'd get through a few rolls before disappearing to do something else. The day you two were supposed to leave, I told her to let the last photos dry, and when she comes back the following summer, they'll be exactly where she left them. But as you know, your mom never did come back. Well, not to this house anyway."

Unable to form words, I stare at Grandma Lily, years of unspoken grief hanging in the balance. Gently, she places the box in my lap, and I rush to pop open the bent flaps to see what's inside. A bulky plastic case in the shape of a camera stares up at me.

"The year your mother moved to Toronto was the beginning of the digital age. She insisted she wouldn't need this, and even though I urged her to take it, she turned out to be right," she smiles fondly at the memory. "Anyway, I overheard you talking about the program you're applying to. The fellows—"

"Oh, that?" I cut her off. "It's nothing serious. Don't worry about it," I insist, my head jerking up sharply. I wasn't necessarily trying to keep the fellowship a secret, but I didn't think it was worth mentioning unless I got in. Given my last experience with a parental figure regarding this topic, I'm afraid my aspiration will be snuffed out before I even get the chance to set it ablaze.

Her head tilts slightly, marvelling at me momentarily. "You really are your mother's daughter."

Curiosity drifts up from within me, as I wonder what I've done to make her respond like this. It hits me that despite all these newly unlocked memories, there's still so much about her that I don't know, but Grandma Lily shoos the thought away before I can press for more information.

"Ah, well, whether that fellowship is serious or not, something tells me you need this camera." She takes her time to stand, carefully rising to her feet while stretching. Her batik spread widely. "Don't ask me if it still works, because me *dier*, I have no idea. But it's all yours now, so feel free to do whatever you want with it."

When she leaves the room, I carefully unsnap the case's buttons and free the camera. The Praktica PLC3 is hefty in my palms. It's a lot heavier than the DSLR cameras I'm used to. I'm not familiar enough with film to know if it still works, but the camera's body is void of dents or scratches. Applying pressure with my fingers, I pinch the cap up to reveal a clear lens, free of any cracks. My thumb runs across the embroidered strap, circling each word written in raised blue thread, 'Property of Nana Antwi.'

As I read the inscription, Osei's words leap to the forefront of my mind. *Photographers have the ability to immortalize legacies long after their subject is gone.*

Suddenly, potential storyboard ideas spring to life in my mind. My mom may not be alive, but her legacy surrounds us. It breathes through her relatives, lives in the walls of this home and hangs from the clothing line in her darkroom. But most importantly, it's in this very camera that sits in the palm of my hand. A grin slowly spreads across my lips as it begins to dawn on me that I know exactly what I need to do. I may never be able to photograph her myself, but that doesn't mean I can't still make her the subject of my submission.

twelve

THE GOLD STRAPPY heels I have on tonight are the highest pair I own, yet Kelvin still manages to tower over me. My forehead just misses his chin, as we embrace on the road outside Grandma Lily's gate.

"You look incredible," Kelvin says, admiring my appearance under the glow of the lone streetlight. I've let my hair down tonight, evenly parting my tightly coiled curls so that my fro flows wildly from each side. My hair stops just above the thin straps of the black slip dress I bought for the party and caresses both sides of my iridescent cheeks.

Thanks to Chelsea's step-by-step guide on makeup for Black girls in hot climates, my skin tint–a shade deeper than I usually use–melts seamlessly with my newly sun-kissed complexion, which is further accentuated by the shimmering gloss that coats my lips. Kelvin's right. Tonight, I've outdone myself.

"Thank you. You look quite handsome yourself," I reply, dragging my gaze over the newly-acquired waves that ripple across the surface of Kelvin's low, black fade.

"I know how to put something together when it matters,"

he smirks, running a palm over the haircut. A lighthearted scoff escapes my lips. You don't have to be around Kelvin long to know he's almost always the best-dressed guy in the room. Tonight's outfit is a cream plissé shorts co-ord that screams his effortless sense of style.

Typically, this street vibrates with passing traffic and roadside sellers around this time, but tonight, it all seems to have disappeared with the setting sun. The only remaining sound is a faint highlife melody that serenades us from an idling car outside the Mensah's gate. I carefully unweave my arm from around Kelvin's thick torso to face him, and my body tingles as if I'm a sparkler that's just been lit, as I look up at him from under my feathery lash extensions. Just the sight of him is enough to set me off.

He takes my hand, and the warm contact transforms the tingling sensation into full-blown fireworks. I tighten my grip on him to keep from falling as we walk the short distance on the gravel road to the waiting Uber. Once he's sure I'm safely inside, Kelvin shuts the door and jogs over to the other side of the car. Notes of oak and cinnamon drift off his frame as he settles beside me and I lean into him, mesmerized by the smell.

"So tonight," he starts, facing me as the driver begins the trip. His voice is animated, and I perk up anxiously at the edge of my seat. An electric current seems to circle his warm irises. "I'm taking you out of the country without having to leave Ghana."

"Well, I didn't expect a baecation for a first date," I admit, squinting one eye as if I'm weighing my options. "But you've intrigued me. Tell me more." I grin, sliding closer to him.

Fifteen minutes later, we're seated in an elegant outdoor garden that seems to transport us miles away from the heart of Accra. Kōzo, a Pan-Asian fusion restaurant, is aglow with warm ambient lighting and tropical decor. Above us, clouds stretch like freshly spun cotton candy in the inky blue sky, and bright green trees of varying sizes encircle the property.

"Wow, this place is breathtaking," I gush, admiring the minimalistic Asian-inspired decor. Both the outdoor and indoor seating areas are swarming with diners. Two bartenders are buzzing hurriedly behind a canopied bar that overlooks the lounge—mixing, pouring and shaking brightly-coloured cocktails to keep up with the demand.

"It is nice, isn't it?" He takes a small sip from the water he pre-ordered to the table, and his eyes lock with mine over the rim of the glass. "Kuukua recommended it to me when I said I wanted to take you somewhere special."

"Well, remind me to thank her later, because consider your mission accomplished," I say, holding his smouldering gaze.

It's been a minute since I last dated, my first and last 'relationship' was the summer after the tenth grade with Devon Hurst—the best friend of Chelsea's, then and now, boyfriend Jalen. But that was back when 'dating' meant aimlessly walking around the mall for an hour or two. It took us less than a week of roaming our local shopping complex to realize that, unlike our best friends, we had nothing in common. The following school year was critical for locking in my post-graduation path, so naturally, I became consumed with maintaining my GPA and haven't dated since.

But even though it's been so long, by the time the waitress brings our drinks, we barely notice her setting them down because Kelvin makes me feel as if I've never left the game. Between sips and giggles, we fall into sync easily, gliding comfortably from topic to topic without missing a beat.

"So let me get this straight. Osei and Kukuua's Dad is *your* dad's best friend?" I ask, using my chopsticks to pick up a piece of the California roll we've ordered.

He's chewing on a mouthful of udon noodles as I ask this

and nods in response. Our table's covered with food. A variety of sushi rolls, two bowls of steaming fried rice, a hot plate of Korean beef and a large serving of udon noodles. It's far more food than we can eat, but Kelvin insisted we order anything we thought looked good, so who was I to disagree?

"Yup. Our dads grew up in the same small town and went to all the same schools growing up," he starts. "The only time they were apart was when my dad left to study medicine in Toronto, and Uncle Mike went to medical school in London. They had a dream to open a clinic in Accra once they were both done with school, but my dad didn't factor in the possibility of meeting the love of his life in Toronto."

There's a far-off look in his eye as he says this. One that tells me everything I need to know about the Willams' family dynamic. His Dad is a man who adores his wife, and Kelvin won't settle for anything less than a love as pure as his parents.

A seed of jealousy takes root in my gut, and I shift in my seat, trying to unearth it. The motion causing my exposed thighs to dig uncomfortably into the metal ridges of the lounge chair I'm seated in.

"My mom, who is half Ghanaian and half Canadian, needed a lot of convincing to move to Accra," explains Kelvin. "But eventually they took the plunge, and a year later, I was born. So with our dads being business partners, the twins and I grew up as staples in each other's lives."

"Excuse me," our waitress interrupts, setting a small lamp at the centre of our table before disappearing again. Kelvin shoots her a smile, and the soft glow from the light illuminates the fullness of his lips. It takes everything in me to drag my focus back to his eyes as he continues where he left off.

"But as you can imagine, adjusting to life in Ghana after growing up in the West is not always easy. Eventually it got too hard on my mom, and after ten years of trying, my dad decided to sell his share of the clinic and move us back to Canada. Over the years our parents remained close, but us kids? Not as much. As far as I'm concerned there's no bad blood between us, but I think living thousands of miles apart made us realize how much of our lives have been woven together by proximity instead of actual friendship. It didn't take long before we lost touch and I know this probably isn't cool of me, but I just got too caught up with my life in Toronto to care."

I take a moment to absorb his words, chewing quietly on a spoonful of fried rice. My memories of my time in Ghana are practically nonexistent—a hazy recollection at best. So, while I initially thought this would make it harder to be back, it's been the exact opposite. Not remembering my mom's family has made it easier to relinquish expectations—since I have nothing to compare it to. I can't imagine what it feels like for Kelvin to step back into the life he once knew, and nothing be the same.

"Is it hard?" I ask quietly. "Being around them when you no longer have that bond?"

"It was at first," he says, as if he's choosing his words carefully. "I know this probably sounds stupid, but I don't think I realized that the version of the twins I knew would no longer exist, which is an unfair expectation because I've changed too. So yeah, it took me a moment to recalibrate, but I'm trying to get to know them for who they are now. With Kuukua, this has been easy. Which is not shocking since she's always been less . . . how do I put this nicely?"

"Combative? Obnoxious? Annoying?" I blurt out without restraint.

Kelvin roars at this, and his face scrunches up in the most delightful way. The reaction seizes my heart with a tight squeeze, and I can't fight the smirk tugging on the corner of my lips.

"Osei's not combative," he chuckles lightly once he calms

down. "Obnoxious and annoying, maybe, but he's not a fighter. I think it's just harder because our dynamic has shifted the most between the three of us. We just don't seem to care about any of the same things anymore. It's just kind of funny though, since Kuuks used to be the odd one out."

"Boys sticking to boys, typical kid behaviour," I chime in, clucking my tongue.

"Exactly. So, within the first few days of being back, I think it became uncomfortably obvious that Kuukua and I have more in common now. With the big things—following in our dads' footsteps to study medicine, for example. And the little things, like our taste in music and food. Osei would have never recommended a place like this," he laughs, throwing his arms wide as he looks around the open-air restaurant. "He'd probably say the place is overrated and overpriced or some shit."

I sheepishly nibble on my bottom lip as he says this. I, too, was side-eyeing a few prices I saw on the menu, after mentally converting the amounts to Canadian dollars, but Kelvin doesn't need to know that. I reach across the table and place my hand on his, and he turns his attention back to me. His hand is warm to the touch. Like the fresh hand towels you get once you've finished eating at a bougie establishment such as this.

"Well, I don't think this place is overrated," I proclaim, my thumb tracing small circles into the back of his hand. "I think it's perfect. Thank you for bringing me here tonight."

His gaze never leaves mine as he flips his hand over to squeeze my fingers gently, and I allow myself to get lost in his glistening eyes.

thirteen

"SO WHAT DO YOU THINK?" I ask eagerly, my cheek nestled against Kelvin's chest. His arm is sprawled across the back seat behind me and our bodies are meshed together. While his upper body is firm—most likely due to several hours spent at the gym, there's still a comforting tenderness to him that makes it hard not to completely sink into him.

Kelvin slowly repeats the title of my photo essay that I just shared with him, but instead of matching my excitement, the words come out as if he's trying not to cut his mouth against their rough edges.

"The Life and Death of Nana Antwi?"

I partially wiggle myself free to look up at him, and as the headlights from a passing car spills in through the window, I catch flickers of his pensive expression. Detaching my body from his completely, I scoot backwards so I'm at the edge of the middle seat and he's in full view. In my ears, the sound of my heart quickly beating drowns out the noisy crunch of gravel beneath the car's moving tires.

"What, do you not like it?" I ask, folding my arms against my chest. Until this moment, I was certain I had finally landed on the perfect subject for my photo essay. I was here in Ghana to learn more about my mom, so it only makes sense to take it a step further and document the process for my submission. I texted it to Osei earlier and was excited to share it with Kelvin tonight, but his response, or lack thereof, has doubt swirling in my mind.

"No, Robyn, it's not that I don't like it," he spits out rapidly. "It's just from what you've told me, everything you know about your mom, her life and even her death, is all new information that you are still processing. Are you sure you want to use such a sensitive subject for something as *small* as *this*?"

The hint of dismissal lacing his words sends my head flying back so far I'm surprised I miss the window. "What do you mean something as *small* as *this*?"

Four rows of wrinkled lines form on his tawny forehead as his expression contorts with genuine confusion.

"Well, this is just a summer program, right? How deep do you need to go? Shouldn't some things be kept between you and your family?"

"A summer program? It's a one-year fellowship, Kelvin. A fellowship that has launched the careers of Ro Marley and Stanton Greeves," I exclaim, listing off two of our generation's most famous Black photographers.

You don't have to be into photography to know the two Forbes 30 Under 30 photographers taking the industry by storm. Ro Marley, best known for her eclectic style, made history last September as the youngest photographer to shoot a cover for Vogue. While sports photojournalist Stanton Greeves, went viral for his ethereal shot of the 2022 NBA Finals MVP he captured on film.

The picture was on every major news outlet for two weeks straight, sparking heated debates on whether it trumped the photo of Michael Jordan hugging the championship trophy after defeating the Lakers in the 1991 NBA Finals.

This fellowship isn't some small summer initiative. It's a launchpad for Black artists, providing us with access and leverage in an industry that we may never otherwise be able to enter on that scale.

"Oh wow, Stanton Greeves?" Even with the car's limited visibility, I can spot the colour draining from his face as he realizes what he's just done. "I had his 2022 NBA Finals picture as my phone wallpaper for months. Damn, that *is* huge. Shit, I'm so sorry. I didn't mean to downplay it. I guess I just misheard you when you first told me about it. I could have sworn you said it occurred during the summer. Something for you to do before you start your second year."

"Yeah, well, it doesn't," I huff, my body slightly shaking. This conversation has struck a chord, and I hate that I can't shake how annoyed I am by it right now.

"Well, in that case, your idea is great, Robyn. It makes sense to go all in for something of this magnitude. When the stakes are this high, what is there to lose, right? Besides, you would know better than me. You're the photographer, after all."

"I guess," I mumble begrudgingly. I can't lie, the whiplash from our conversation's sharp turn has slightly rattled me. What difference does it make if the fellowship runs throughout the summer or for the entire year? Shouldn't I go all out regardless?

An awkward silence fills the small space like a toxic fume, and I know we can both feel that the energy in the car has shifted. As the driver turns onto Grandma Lily's familiar street, my shoulders drop, and my heart rate settles as I recognize my surroundings. Once the car comes to a complete stop in front of her gate, I yank my door open before Kelvin can even pull out the cash to pay the driver.

Just breathe Robyn. Slow breaths, remember? Kelvin didn't know. It was an honest mistake.

Quite frankly, it was dumb of me to assume he would even get this. Truthfully, this type of conversation is best suited for someone who understands right off the bat. Someone who knows that art is a medium of self-expression and actualization. Someone like...

The sound of the car door closing pulls me out of my thoughts, and I spin to face him. My smile is tight-lipped and my thoughts—that maybe we should just call it quits before we get any further along—perch patiently on the tip of my tongue.

"Kelvin—" I start at the same time he says, "Robyn—"

We pause momentarily, then chuckle in unison, reminiscing on our first encounter and I instinctively reach for my neck, gently kneading the tension knotted in it.

"We've got to stop doing that, huh," Kelvin smiles at me softly.

"Yeah," I chuckle. "You can go ahead," I offer, curiosity outweighing my desire to go into complete flight mode.

"Look, Robyn, I am sorry for ruining our night. We had such a good time until I put my big foot in my mouth."

"It is quite large," I mumble, looking down at the length of his crisp white Air Force Ones. They're spotless, so I know they're fresh out of the box. White shoes do not last more than a few days in a city as dusty as Accra.

Kelvin chuckles as he steps toward me and laces his fingers with mine, drawing my attention back upward.

"All you wanted in that moment was someone to share your joy with. I'm not a photographer or an artist, so my two cents weren't needed. Whether it's a summer program or a year-long thing, at that moment, my only concern should have been how to be your biggest hype man."

My jaw drops open, then shuts firmly close as he finishes his apology. Before I could even articulate my feelings, Kelvin knew exactly what I wanted to hear. Once again he's proven just how much he gets me, and I can feel my frustration wearing off.

Releasing his hand from mine, I move forward and entwine my arms around his torso, and the last remains of the car ride's tension dissipates into the night as he presses his lips into my temple.

"Thank you, Kelvin. I appreciate your apology. I really do," I say, snuggling into his chest. "This project means a lot to me and I've already experienced what it feels like to not have support with dad. If we're gonna do this, I really can't have anything less than a champion right now."

"I hear you, Robyn. From here on out, I'll always be your biggest fan," he whispers, and the fuzzy feeling from dinner returns as I tighten my grip around his waist.

I know it's still so early, but his words reaffirm my belief that Kelvin is a good fit for me. The way we met, the ways in which we connect: none of this can be a coincidence. Besides, if I don't get into the fellowship, my future will continue to unfold in the city where he lives. I really think that we can make it beyond a holiday fling and that alone is enough to curb any sinking feelings.

fourteen

THE FRONT DOOR creaks loudly as I try—and fail—to quietly slide back into Grandma Lily's house. It's half past twelve, and other than the motion-sensor spotlights that brighten as I step onto the porch, I'm surrounded by darkness. Once inside, I lean my back against the door, pushing against it with my body weight. When I hear the familiar click, I lock the door behind me, then tiptoe down the hallway, my gold heels dangling in one hand and my phone in the other. When I reach the bottom of the staircase, I notice that it is not actually pitch black and a light is shining from the back of the house.

Hmm, that's odd. I wonder why Ama isn't sleeping?

Retreating from the steps, I head toward the direction of the brightness. Before I was even finished getting dressed for my date, Ama had gone off to a blind date with the grandson of one of Grandma Lily's good friends. Unfortunately for Ama, while Kelvin and I were getting closer, she suffered through her date's non-stop boasting. She'd texted me whilst Kelvin and I were at Kōzo, telling me how she'd ended up paying for her drink and leaving before the appetizers came out, to spare herself from the painful details of his distant relation to President Nana Akufo-Addo. So unless that horror of a date had induced some kind of insomnia, by now she should be fast asleep.

"Ama, what on earth are you still doing up?" I hiss as I enter the kitchen. At first glance, I find the room empty. No one is sitting at the island, and no one is poking around the fridge. Then I notice the red glow from the stove's hot surface indicator and hear the all-too-familiar voice coming from beyond my peripheral vision.

"Isn't it past your bedtime, Miss Carter?"

"Don't you have your own house, Mr. Mensah?" Kissing my teeth, I stalk over to where he's seated at the kitchen table.

"I like to come over here to think," he beams, his brown lips glistening with grease as if he's just lathered a year's worth of beauty supply lip gloss on their surface.

"Think or eat?" I clarify, grimacing down at the jollof that contains more beef pieces than it does grains of rice. The white ceramic bowl he's eating from is so wide that he might as well eat directly from the pot sitting on the burner.

His eyes light up as he smiles, flashing me with his signature front gap.

"The latter helps with the former."

"You do know that sneaking meat out of the pot in the middle of the night in your own home is practically a criminal offence?" I ask, bending down to place my heels on the kitchen floor before sitting in the seat across from him. "And here you are doing it at someone else's? Have you no shame?"

"Shame is overrated," he quips. Osei opens his mouth wide to shovel a spoonful of rice into it, and I roll my lips inward to hold back my laughter. His commitment to being unhinged is so ridiculous it's comical.

"Why are you like this, Osei?" I ask, shaking my head as I lean against the seat.

"Childhood trauma." He shrugs, and my mouth pops open into a small 'o'. But before I can even press him for more details, he swiftly changes the topic. "I got your text, by the way. *The Life and Death of Nana Antwi*." I watch as he licks his lips and breaks out into a wide grin. "I think you got something special with that one."

"Wait, really?" I ask, leaning forward. My elbows dig into the table as I get a good look at him. I need to make sure he's not pulling my leg. "Are you serious?"

"Yup. I think it's brilliant. Well, almost."

"Oh, come on," I plop back into my seat, exasperated.

"What?" He laughs. "I think we can still go deeper, I just don't know *how* yet. But don't worry. We're on the right path, though. It's a great start."

I make a big show of rolling my eyes but don't bother to hide the smile that reaches my eyes. I'm not going to front and act like Osei's feedback doesn't mean anything to me. Based on the work he's shown me and what I've seen in the portfolio linked to his Instagram bio, the boy knows what he's talking about. Coming from Osei, 'a great start' is a hell of a compliment.

"So when do we start shooting? You know we're running out of time," he points out.

"I know, I know. Now that I have everything planned out, my first subject, Grandma Lily, said tomorrow is the only day she'll be free. Does that work for you?"

Osei nods.

"Great. Chelsea lands tomorrow morning, she's gonna help with hair and makeup. So, aim to be here around two in the afternoon. We're gonna shoot out in the front yard."

"That's good with me. I'll bring a reflector too—because we will need it with the sun."

His face is contemplative as if he's running through a

mental checklist of what else we may need. The way his thick eyebrows meet in the middle of his forehead makes me realize that he isn't just saying 'we' to tick me off. He truly thinks of us as a team. The realization makes blood rush to my face.

"Why do you keep saying 'we'?" I ask quietly. The suspicious feeling I felt earlier—that Osei may desire full creative control of my entire submission makes me uneasy. Under the table, my palms prickle with nerves, and I brush them against my dress. My hands glide across the smooth texture, then drop onto my bare thighs, and I try to focus on the contrast between the soft fabric and the bristles of hair already sprouting from my freshly shaven legs.

"Huh?" Osei asks, looking up from his bowl. I wince as an orange rice grain flicks from his mouth and lands before me.

"You keep using the word 'we' like it's *our* application or something," I stress. "You know only one name can go on the application, right?"

"Trust me, Robyn, as bright as you shine, it's impossible to forget you're the star. I'm just happy to be part of the supporting cast, but I'm sorry if I've gotten a little carried away. I guess I want this for you like I would want it for myself."

I throw his words back at him. "But why don't you want it for yourself? I've seen your work, Osei. You're more than good enough to apply and even get accepted. And no, I'm not buying your whole " 'I'm satisfied with computer science as long as I can do photography on the side' act."

"And here I was thinking I was a convincing actor."

"Pfft, maybe in Ghallywood," I snort.

Osei erupts into a laugh so soulless that it makes it immediately clear that none of this is actually funny to him. Dejection floods his dark eyes as he gently slides the half-finished bowl into the middle of the table, no longer having the appetite to stuff his face.

"You've known me for not more than two weeks, and you're the only person able to see past that facade, you know? Or at least, the only person who's brought it up to me directly."

"Hey, Pot meet Kettle." I wave at him with a small smile. "I mean, I'm not shocked about your guys not noticing. Male friendships are not exactly known for their adept observance of their friend's feelings, but Kuukua? That surprises me. I assumed you two were close."

"Most people think that," he says, standing up to turn off the burner that's been warming the remaining jollof on the stove. Once it is off, he sits back down in front of me. "And in some ways, I guess we are. But living in my sister's shadow doesn't exactly breed room for closeness."

My mind flashes back to my first encounter with Kuukua and how I was instantly drawn to her. While both Mensah twins are a sight to behold, there's a magnetism about Kuukua that is hard to ignore. The thought of unknowingly adding to his insecurity makes me feel guilty and I fix my gaze on my white toenails instead of his sad eyes.

"Don't worry, you're not the only victim who's fallen under her spell." He chuckles, and my mind instantly flashes to his friend David. "My parents have been spellbound for nineteen years. Kuuks just has that effect on people. She's always fallen in line. She never gave them any trouble while we were in JHS or boarding school. She isn't swayed by her emotions or riddled with behavioural issues that detract from who she is. No, Kuuks is the golden child of every Ghanaian parent's dreams. The one who allows them to flex their bragging rights. A living, breathing, reminder that all their sacrifices have paid off. Then there's me."

"Oh, come on. You can't be that bad. You got into a

Computer Science program, and I know that's not easy. Trust me, I struggled to make a website from a template on Wix for my dad's pharmacy."

He laughs loudly. "It took a lot for me to become this Osei you see now," he admits, making me remember the breathing techniques he showed me on the steps after I found out about my mom.

"Does this have something to do with your anxiety? You mentioned having attacks when I was having mine."

He nods. "It wasn't until recently that I even knew what they were. It had always been 'Osei being dramatic again' or 'Why can't you be more like your sister?'. Someone who never sweats under pressure. Never folds when tasked with something new. Kuukua always rises to the occasion. Having anxiety attacks in Ghana is one thing, but letting your twin sister constantly outshine you as the technically 'older brother'? It was as if I was asking for shame to descend on our home."

"No!" I say, in mock horror.

"The shame of it all, right?" He shakes his head playfully. "I mean, we're twins, right? How can two people be so different?"

"I mean, aren't you guys fraternal? You're not exactly split from the same DNA," I offer sheepishly.

"Unfortunately for me, my parents aren't too concerned with the particulars of genetics. Anyway, I eventually realized that if I could mask as much of the Osei they didn't seem to want and mirror my life to my sister's, being around them would be much easier. So I did just that. It was around the same time my dad's younger brother visited from London and brought us both cameras as gifts. My parents were not thrilled about this as they were quite expensive, but my dad had a soft spot for Uncle Ekow. He had practically raised him and sponsored him to go to school in London, so we were allowed to keep them as a token of his appreciation to his elder brother." His smile is genuine now, reliving the memory of getting his camera.

"Only God knows what Kuukua did with hers, but I saw mine as an escape. Taking pictures around our area felt like a chance to be myself whenever I wasn't playing the role of dutiful son and perfect twin."

"And that's how Grandma Lily spotted you," I say, finally drawing the conclusion.

"Yup. She's the only adult in my life who actively pushes me toward pursuing photography. Unlike my parents, who tolerate it as long as I don't lose sight of their end goal."

"And what about Kuukua? How does she feel about all this?"

"I'm sure Kuukua feels the same way my parents do."

"But have you asked her this directly?" I push, and he pulls back momentarily.

"Well, no, but there's no point in asking. Kuukua never spoke up for me when we were kids and I was getting berated for showing too much emotion. So I know not to expect too much from her now."

I can feel my heart crack a little as he says this. I don't know what it's like to have a sibling, let alone a twin, but my sisterhood with Chelsea is something that I seriously cherish. I can't imagine what it would feel like to have shared so much of your life with someone and yet still feel so far away from them.

"But don't you see that you're doing the same thing you're getting at me for? You were so pressed about me not studying photography, and here you are doing the same thing."

"Why do you think I've been rooting for this as hard as I have? It's easier for you, Robyn. My environment doesn't allow me to dream as big as you can. Even if I wanted to study photography in university, where would I do that at a high level? You have a privilege I can only dream of."

"But the fellowship is open to applicants our age around the world, you know? You can apply, too." I insist. An additional applicant means one less chance for me, but as much as I want to be the one the fellowship committee chooses, it wouldn't feel right if I didn't bring this up.

"Maybe next time," he says, rising from his chair. The scraping sound of the chair skidding across the tile signifies that the conversation is over. I watch him cover his bowl of remaining rice with plastic wrap and move the pot into the fridge. He floats around the kitchen in the same effortless manner Grandma Lily does, and it sinks in how much this place is a safe haven for him. When the kitchen is back to how he found it, he moves toward the light switch, his bowl in hand, and looks back at me as if he's just remembered I'm there.

"Come on, it's late, and you need to get some rest before your big shoot tomorrow." His tone is brimming with its usual cheeriness as if we didn't just have a heart-to-heart over Grandma Lily's dining table. Bending down to scoop up my heels, I scoot my chair back with my bum before walking toward him.

When I'm just a few feet away, he raises his hand to flip the switch, and darkness submerges the room. In the archway behind him, the glow from the night sky floods into the unlit hallway, but the kitchen remains pitch black. As my eyes adjust, I realize his tall figure is lit up in the most ethereal way even though I can't make out the details of his face. And for whatever reason, not being able to see his usual lingering gaze makes it easy for my true feelings to roll off my tongue.

"Osei, I want you to know that I don't take any of this for granted. You're letting me borrow your camera, helping me brainstorm and pushing me out of my comfort zone. Even if it's just my name on the application, this photo essay will be just as much yours as it is mine. After how I've treated you, I don't deserve your kindness, but for whatever reason, you've shown it to me anyway. So for that, I want to say thank you."

"For you, Robyn? Always."

As his words suspend in the unlit space between us, it begins to hit me that Osei's face is not the one I'm worried about being seen right now.

fifteen

"WHAT DO YOU THINK GRANDMA?" I ask, as Chelsea and I peer over her shoulder to get a good look at her reflection in the bathroom mirror. Chelsea arrived in Accra just a few hours earlier, and was still able to pull off the most stunning makeover in under forty-five minutes. She's managed to highlight Grandma Lily's best features, from soft pink eyeshadow on her lids to highlighted cheekbones, while still making her look like herself.

"Ei, Chelsea. You've done well o! I'm impressed!"

We laugh as Grandma admires her beauty in the mirror, swivelling her head around to capture every angle.

"Aww, Grandma. I'm so happy you love it," Chelsea coos, leaning over to hug her from behind. "If only I had more time, I would have really beat your face." She gives me a pointed look in the reflection.

"Ehn? Please, no beating is necessary." The serious manner of Grandma Lily's words makes us break into a fit of giggles.

"Don't mind her Grandma, she's just being silly. Why don't you head out front to see if Osei has set up the lighting? We'll be right there with you."

Once Grandma Lily leaves, I turn to squeeze Chelsea's arms with an apologetic smile. "Sorry, for making you work under pressure. I'm in a rush to get these photos taken before the sun sets, so I really appreciate you coming through for me. I can't even imagine how jetlagged you must be."

"Oh you know I was just playing with you," Chelsea says while packing up all the products she used. "I am just so happy you're finally doing this! Once we got to Will's place, I made him bring me here immediately. You should have seen the way we were flying through the streets. He's so excited for you, Rob. He said after he saw how you captured my hairstyling, he always knew you were destined for the creative industry."

My heart smiles at this revelation, and I absentmindedly pull out the solid gold nameplate that has hung around my neck for the last four years. Spending time with the Ankrahs was my first real taste of what it was like to have an extended family. Although Will has lived out here most of the time Chelsea and I have been best friends, he's always gone out of his way to make me feel included. Whenever he returns to Toronto, he brings me something different from Ghana.

"I can't wait to see him later," I say, as I brush my thumb against my Twi name, 'Abena', written on the necklace's solid gold surface. It's the first gift he ever gave me. Whenever I'm at the Ankrahs' house, their parents call me by my Twi name like they do with their children. It took some getting used to at first, but I love it now. It makes me feel as if I've been around from the start. It's been a while since I've seen him in person, but we're all going out later tonight to celebrate my first December in Ghana.

"He can't wait either! But aren't you in a race against the sun or something?" Chelsea asks while looking down at her Apple watch.

"Oh shoot!" I exclaim, grabbing the notebook I've sketched

out my storyboards in from the bathroom counter. "Just make sure you come on out once you're done cleaning up here. I need my girl by my side!" For the most part, I feel ready for this, but it won't hurt to have my biggest cheerleader with me.

"Oh you know I won't miss this for the world!"

Once I'm outside, I spot Osei and Grandma Lily huddled together looking at an image on his camera's preview. Osei is explaining something in detail and Grandma Lily is nodding along encouragingly like it's the most interesting thing in the world. Seeing the two of them in complete rhythm like this makes my previously calm energy morph into apprehension. It's clear that Grandma Lily completely trusts Osei's photography skills; I just hope I can do her justice as well.

"All right, are you guys ready?" I ask, when I finally find my voice. I watch as both of their heads fly up and when I see the excitement on their faces when they spot me, I feel a sense of relief push my anxious thoughts to the side.

"Oh yes, my dear. Osei was just showing me what these do," she says, pointing to the circle reflectors that are resting against the steps. "God has really blessed the two of you and my Nana with such an amazing skill. She may not have been able to show the world what she was capable of, but God willing, you both will." Her eyes well up as she says this, and I feel my own start to sting with tears.

Osei playfully groans at our waterworks.

"*Yɛnko*! Let's get to work!" He hands me the camera and moves over to my laptop that's sitting on the porch, and starts playing a R&B song I know for sure I haven't downloaded.

"Really?" I ask, looking at him incredulously. When did he have the time to download songs onto my Apple Music?

"Ready when you are Miss Carter," he says, grinning as he grabs the reflector.

I take a deep breath, tune out the background noise and get

in the zone. I start by showing both Grandma Lily and Osei what I've sketched out in my notebook. It's a combination of the ideas Osei and I brainstormed earlier—along with a few more that I added later on.

"So I'm thinking, we'll start with Grandma by the bougainvillea tree. I'll take some portraits of her front and side angles. Then make our way to the stairs and the side of the house. The images will all be variations of ones my mom took of her over the years, but with my own twist. I want to get a shot of the full house in view as well so we'll do some wider shots as well." I want to capture Grandma Lily in a way that shows who she is. The matriarch of this family. Someone who is strong, supportive and kind, but also someone who has experienced significant loss. I want those selecting the fellows to be able to feel her presence, the way I do, even if it's just through the screen.

"Sounds good," Osei says, moving into position. I grab Grandma Lily's hand and walk her over to the tree. Once I've positioned her to face me head on, I take a few steps back and lift the camera to my eye.

"Okay, Grandma just act natural."

"You sound just like your mother," she chuckles and I take that moment, as the light from Osei's reflector catches the sparkle in her eye, to capture the first shot.

Later that night, Chelsea and I stumble out of Ace Nightclub as the sun slowly rises, the sky blending from indigo to orange to blue behind the club. Ghanaians and tourists from around the world have started to arrive in the city in droves, and despite it being early in the morning, they mill around the parking lot, not yet ready for their night to end. They're itching for the next party, desperate not to be the person who leaves before it eventually kicks off.

Since the Ankrahs landed, we haven't been able to go anywhere without Chelsea stopping every few seconds to squeal with people from Decembers past. She drags me to each greeting, making the same promise over and over that I'm more than certain she won't be able to keep. *We must link up this December!*

When we finally leave the crowded lot, a car comes speeding towards us, blaring its horn, and Chelsea yanks me to her side and out of the way. She unleashes a string of words in Twi that I can only imagine are as violent as they sound, before turning to me with a loud huff. Once we're out of harm's way, Chelsea turns toward me as if nothing just happened and squeals.

"I cannot believe we're both here right now. I've been dreaming of this moment since the year we first met."

"I know," I say, tightening my grip around her arm. "This trip has been amazing so far, but you being here has just made it ten times better." With Osei and Chelsea's help, the shoot went off without a hitch. Every shot I planned was created with ease, as if I had breathed life into it. When it comes to brainstorming, the three of us may not be a good team, but on set, we were unstoppable. Everyone fell into their roles and supported each other when needed. It felt freakishly natural—like the three of us had been working together for years.

"It looks like we're not the only ones having a good time tonight," Chelsea smirks, tossing her head toward where Will and Ama are closely conversing next to his car. They met earlier in the day when he picked Chelsea up, and after getting lost in conversation, I had to physically drag Ama away so she wouldn't be late to pick up our finished dresses for Grandma Lily's party from Mrs. Botchway.

"No, Robyn, you don't understand. Whit and I have been trying to get Will to come out with us during the holidays for four years. *Four years*! And every year, he tells us the same lame story about refusing to step outside in December when inflation is at its highest. One small mention from your cousin that we're going to Ace tonight, and suddenly, he's 'Mr. Nightlife' himself."

"Oh, leave him," I laugh, as we stop walking to observe them from a distance. "I think it's sweet. They seem like a good match."

"Oh, I'm not denying that! They have the whole 'expats surviving Ghana' thing in common, and they're both old—" Chelsea shrieks as a pair of hands adorned with long acrylic nails wrap around our bare shoulders.

"Who are you calling old Chelly?" Whitney barks, appearing out of nowhere and forcing her way between us. Whitney is the same age as Ama, who is twenty-three, five years older than us. And Will is a year older than them both. Chelsea, being the baby of her family, always finds ways to sneak diss her older siblings.

"Not my favourite big sister." Chelsea flutters her lashes at Whitney, who just rolls her eyes before turning to face me.

"Robyn. Long time no see. You've finally made it to Ghana, huh?"

In the same way that Will welcomes me like an older brother, Whitney has never shied away from treating me any differently than her little sister. But the Whitney we get on a day-to-day basis is dependent on whatever mood she's in. Some days, it's the Whitney who takes the time to show fourteen-year-old Robyn and Chelsea how to slow wine so we don't make fools of ourselves at our first semi-formal dance. But most days, it's the Whitney who couldn't care less about how we feel and sees us as annoying little sisters.

"Hey Whit," I mumble, taking her in. Unlike Chelsea who is short and has a warm brown complexion, Whitney is tall, with skin so deep she often gets mistaken for South Sudanese-American supermodel Anok Yai. "How's school?"

Whitney is in her final year of the Masters of Sport Management and Leadership program at the University of Windsor. Since it's almost four hours away from Toronto, she lives on campus and I haven't seen much of her since she left in September.

"You know how it goes. Just glad to be almost done with it." She clicks her tongue and nods in her brother's direction. "Is that your cousin over there with Will?"

"It is. Her name is Ama! Don't they look good together?" Chelsea answers for me, dreamily eyeing the pair. I know her well enough to know she's already imagining their traditional wedding, as extravagant as the ones she forces Jalen and I to watch on YouTube.

"Hmm," Whitney grunts, sizing up Ama from across the road. I can feel my body heating up in Ama's defence. Whitney and Will have always been quite close, even with the physical distance. While Chelsea and I haven't thought much about Will's last two girlfriends, and his parents want him to settle down, Whitney has always been the one to be quick to rule them out.

"They do look good together, Chels," I say. "Ama has been so sweet to me both leading up to, and during this trip, so it's not surprising that he's drawn to her. They both have that in common."

One of Whitney's freshly threaded brows cocks upward. "Is she from Ghana?"

"Well, yeah, but she moved to London as a kid. She just recently came back to work, like Will. Why does it matter?" I ask, confused as to where she could be going with this.

"Nothing, just curious," she replies quickly, continuing to eye my cousin. "Anyway, I heard there's another romance budding in town. Robyn Carter's first trip to Ghana and she's already all boo'd up. How cute." Whitney turns to smirk at me, and I find myself wishing she would lose her footing in the nearby gutter. I don't want her to fall in, or anything, but a close brush with whatever lurks in the underbelly of Accra would be satisfactory.

"I am not all boo'd up," I scoff, my eyes darting over to Chelsea. She mouths an apology as she winces under my glare. Note to self, Robyn: don't share everything with your best friend, who's known to spill piping hot tea with her snarky older sister.

"Righttt," Whitney sings, as she eyes my afro puff that I'm sure is a ball of frizz right now. Despite being in the same humid club with us all night, her smooth skin is covered in foundation as dark as molasses, yet there's not a crease in sight. I, on the other hand, have never blotted my face as much as I did tonight. Quite frankly, I think indoor night clubs in a West African city should be a human rights violation.

I step away from her, desperate to create space between us as she inspects me. After what feels like an eternity, her eyes flick back down to my face.

"Cheslea showed me a pic. He's cute. I approve."

At this, I instantly feel conflicted. Chelsea and Whitney may butt heads, but her older sister's approval means everything to her, and as much as I hate to admit it, that nagging need for Whitney's approval has rubbed off on me, too.

"Thanks," I mumble sheepishly, unable to hide the swell of pride forming in my chest.

Her brown eyes scan mine for a second, and her nose scrunches in disgust as she registers the look of hope on my face.

"Wait, don't tell me you're seriously considering dating this guy for real? Oh, come on, Robyn," she cackles loudly. "When I say 'approve', I mean for a holiday ting. Everybody knows falling in love during December in Ghana is a losing game."

"Relax, Whit," Chelsea says, stepping out to face her sister with her back to me like a defender in soccer. "Rob's not falling in love. She's just having fun! Plus, Kelvin lives in Toronto, remember? They can easily continue dating if anything were to go past this."

The way Whitney shrugs, seemingly over the matter, makes my irritation multiply even more. I don't even know why I'm entertaining her nonsense while my toes are throbbing from my heels, literally begging me to get in the car.

"Suit yourself," she chirps. "Just don't say I didn't warn you when it ends in tears."

As she walks in the direction of her brother's car, I shoot the sharpest daggers I can conjure up into the back of her head as I tell myself that her jet black hair looks more like a helmet than it does a wig. It doesn't, but thinking that it does makes me feel slightly better.

"I'm sorry for telling her about Kelvin. I was just so excited for you, and I guess I forgot she's still jaded from a past December fling gone wrong," Chelsea confesses, her hand squeezing my bicep. The pressure of her fingers against my skin causes my anger to slowly disperse from the pit of my stomach. Instead, annoyance furrows in its place.

"It's fine," I say curtly, turning to survey the line of cars parked in front of Will's. A small group of boys are idling a few cars ahead. I didn't see him inside the dark nightclub, but now, under the rising sun's rays, it is impossible to miss Osei's sturdy frame. He's leaning against the driver's door of his mom's car, and from the way he's moving his hands animatedly, I can tell he's talking about something he's passionate about in great detail. Against my will, my stomach does somersaults at the thought. Osei, in his element, is my favourite version of him.

"Hey, Chels," I say, my eyes never leaving Osei and his friends. It's hard to make out the others, but I know Kelvin isn't among them since he and Kuukua had gone to dinner with some of their childhood friends. "I just need a second. You go ahead with your siblings and Ama, and I'm gonna ride back with Osei." I gesture towards him.

"You sure?" She asks hesitantly, turning to look where his group of friends are loitering.

"Positive," I insist, wrapping my arms around her neck and pulling her body into mine. "I'll call you tomorrow. And don't worry, I'm not upset with you." I whisper, easing the worries I know are storming her thoughts. As she squeezes me back, I can feel her shoulders droop with relief.

"I love you, Rob. All I want is for you to be happy."

"I know Chels. I know."

sixteen

WHEN I WALK UP to Osei and his friends, I don't even have to open my mouth for him to know exactly what I need. One brief introduction later, and we're in his car on our way home with some old school R&B playing in the background. Or at least home is where I thought we were going.

"Wait, this is not our street," I cry as Osei parks next to a group of people mingling on the side of a road.

"Calm down." He laughs while turning off the engine and points to the street vendor we are in front of. The little handmade sign on the front of the stall reads 'Mama Afua's'. "You look like you could use something to eat right now."

As if it's conspiring with him, my stomach grumbles at the mention of food, making us both laugh.

Held back by my stilettos and impractically short, yet extremely cute silver sequin romper, Osei helps me out of the car and guides me to the stall, his palm resting on the lower half of my back. I try my best to ignore the shiver running down my spine from his touch but it's a pointless endeavour. Chivalry is always gonna do it for me.

Once we make it to the stall, he suddenly turns around,

leaping over the curb we just crossed, and pops open his trunk. When he springs back out, his Canon swings from his neck, and he's beaming up at me.

"Can't forget this." He holds his most prized possession toward me.

Highlife music is playing softly in the background, and the woman, I presume to be Mama Afua, is frying eggs behind the stall that faces the road. Next to the eggs, soft slices of bread are toasting on the grill. The scent of fried egg and fresh bread surrounds me, and I moan in delight. I watch as Osei laughs at something she says, then pays for two sandwiches and a green bottle of something called Alvaro.

"Wait, that didn't sound like Twi," I say as he leads me to a secluded area of makeshift tables and benches. Even though I don't understand my mom's native tongue, I've gotten pretty good at recognizing it when hearing it, and some of the words they were saying sounded like they had different inflections.

"That's because it wasn't. It was Fante."

"You're Fante, too?"

"Yes, I am. Is that a problem?"

"Absolutely not," I assure him. Of course, he and Kelvin are from the same tribe. Their dads grew up together.

"Great. Here, come and sit. I want to get a picture of you," Osei says when we reach the sitting area.

"No, wait. I hate when people take my picture," I protest, covering my face with my free hand. When there's no guarantee that the person behind the camera knows my angles better than I do, I just don't see the point. Chelsea's only just learned to take pictures on her iPhone that don't make me look like a garden gnome.

But Osei's not hearing any of this. "How else will you know how good you look when you're happy?" he insists, and I grin widely despite myself. "Just act as if I'm not even here."

Hearing the exact words I said to Grandma Lily not less than twenty-four hours ago causes me to throw my head back in laughter. As my body shudders with giggles, I feel the camera's bright flash illuminating me.

"It's perfect," Osei chirps, lowering his camera. I nibble on my bottom lip, unsure whether to believe him. Don't get me wrong; I think Osei is good at what he does, but very few people can produce an image that both the photographer and the subject will agree is undeniably perfect, in just one take.

Shooting up from the bench, I start toward him. "Let me see."

Up close, his face is luminescent from a light layer of sweat and the warm hues of the rising sun. If I had his camera, I would capture him just as he is. Instead, I take a mental image and hope my memory won't rob me of this moment.

"Trust me," he affirms with a toothy grin before handing the camera over to me. His fingers delay on mine, and my eyes dart to the point of contact. They move from the tips of his fingers to the thickness of his well-cut arms, until I reach his face. His skin is even in complexion and abundant in melanin, similar to mine. I watch his brown eyes fixate on mine, and my breath slightly catches. But before I can process why I'm waiting to exhale, a loud sound breaks the silence, causing our heads to spin toward the noise. A group of partygoers spill out of a white Nissan, singing Asake lyrics at the top of their lungs.

Their clamour fizzles out the remaining tension between us, and I laugh nervously as Osei moves to the bench on the opposite side of the table. When we're both seated and facing each other, I look down at his camera to see how he did. In the image, I hold the bread and egg with two hands, my head thrown back, and my dark coils gracing my bare shoulders. I've never seen myself captured by someone else like this. Eyes scrunched shut with elation. My mouth stretched wide and curled upward with glee. My joy is damn near palpable. He's right, it is perfect.

"Wow, Osei. This is beautiful. You are really good at this," I applaud, placing the camera on the wooden table.

"You already knew that, though," he jokes, before ripping off a big chunk of his sandwich. My stomach grumbles at the sight, and I take a bite of my own. As the combination of sweet bread and salty fried egg tickle my tastebuds, the corners of my mouth immediately turn upward.

"I'm not even trying to be dramatic, but I think this is the best meal I've had yet," I proclaim after swallowing my mouthful of egg and bread. "Eggs do not taste this good at home! Wow, this is so fresh! I never understood why you guys love eggs as much as you do, but I get it now!"

Osei laughs as I let out a muffled moan after taking another bite. "You guys? You say that like you're not Ghanaian yourself."

"You know what I mean," I reply, rolling my eyes.

"So now I'm curious," Osei's head tips to the side. "If some small roadside egg and bread is your best meal this trip, what in the world have you been eating?"

"I mean, Grandma Lily's food definitely trumps this, but outside of her cooking, sushi, burgers, hotel buffets, that kinda stuff," I shrug, listing off the various cuisines I've tried so far.

He teasingly shakes his head at me. "Tsk tsk. All things you can find at home."

Not paying him any mind, I place the bread and egg on my napkin to crack open the pear-flavoured drink. The malt beverage fizzes in my mouth, and I sigh in satisfaction, mentally adding Alvaro to the list of things I want to return to Toronto by the bucket load.

"What? No Alvaro in Toronto?" Osei questions as I drink from the green bottle with my head tilted back and eyes closed.

"Nope," I reply, popping the 'p'. I pull the drink from my lips and stare at the bottle like it's a long-lost friend. "Again, not to be dramatic or anything, but I would literally trade my entire life in Toronto for this drink right here!"

Osei chuckles and slowly shakes his head in response. "You Americans always come and make these bold claims about trading your lifestyle for this one. Vacationing in Ghana and living in Ghana are two very separate realities."

His usual amused face has shifted to a solemn gaze as he observes the young children, who look no older than four or five years old, asking for money from the ongoing drivers and pedestrians on the busy road before us.

"Excuse you, I'm not American; I am Canadian, thank you very much. Please don't confuse me with the ones who voted a reality television star into their White House," I tease to lighten the mood. As bad as it is, the joke causes him to snap out of his trance and turn to me with a slight grin.

"You know, the more I get to know you, the harder it is for me to understand what a girl like you sees in someone like Kelvin."

"What don't you like about Kelvin?" I ask, genuinely curious to hear what the origin story of their ongoing rivalry is.

"Wow, I'm surprised he hasn't told you yet considering how much time you two have been spending together lately."

This makes me roll my eyes. We've only been on a handful of dates and the rest have been group outings with Osei present, so I don't know why he's exaggerating like this.

"You're sounding a bit jealous to me. Have you been watching us leave from your window or something?" I tease.

"Jealous of who? Kelvin?" He laughs loudly, and his eyes are bright with humour. Gosh, I hate how much I love to hear that sound despite how annoying he's being right now.

"Come on, just tell me," I say, slightly shaking his arm.

"Kelvin said you guys drifted apart when he moved to Toronto, but you make it seem like there's more to the story."

"Drifted apart? Is that what he's calling it now?"

"I mean he didn't say it in those exact words," I say, careful not to misrepresent Kelvin.

"That's interesting. I didn't know sending emails every week for three months and him not replying was considered us 'drifting apart'." His fingers fly up to make air quotes and even though he's speaking in his usual comedic tone, it's clear to see how much this is really bothering him.

"Oh wow, I'm sorry Osei. It probably wasn't intentional on his part. I'm sure the move was just a big adjustment for him. I can only imagine how much of a culture shock it was, especially back then."

"That's what I told myself for the first month or so, but after three straight months?" He raises his eyebrow at me. "It also didn't help that my parents were getting frequent updates on how well Kelvin was doing at his new school. 'Kelvin joined the track and field team, Kelvin is at the top of his class, Kelvin discovered the cure for cancer."

I roll my eyes at his exaggeration, but I'm starting to see where he's coming from. I faced enough pressure from Dad as an only child. If I was being compared to a twin *and* my best friend, I probably wouldn't like them very much either.

"Maybe he lost access to his email or something? Did you ever ask your parents to check for you?"

"I can admit now that that was probably the logical next step, but back then I was so embarrassed by being so easily forgotten I couldn't bring myself to ask them. Eventually, I moved on and forced myself to forget all about him, but when my parents told us he was coming this December I guess I kind of thought it would be a chance to start fresh. Maybe even pick up where we left off. But from the moment I picked him up at the airport I knew Kelvin and I had nothing in common anymore." Osei kisses his teeth loudly as he recounts their reunion. "He's all rigid and by the book now. A proper straight arrow, that guy. Not at all like how he used to be, and nothing like me."

"Wait a second," I say, in complete disbelief. "Let me get this straight. You are seriously holding Kelvin to a memory of him that is over eight years old? Give me a flipping break! Do you think it's easy for him to be back? Do you think you haven't changed too? At least he's trying to get to know the new you. Things will never go back to how they were when y'all were kids. Accept that, adjust accordingly, and get over it already!"

I'm out of breath by the time I finish my rant but Osei just peers at me with an incredulous look on his face.

"You really like him," he says, in disbelief.

"What?" I ask, completely thrown off by how he was able to get that from me telling him to give Kelvin a break.

"I'm just realizing this isn't just some December hookup for you."

"Why does everyone keep asking that," I cry, throwing up my hands in frustration.

"Who else said that?" His tone is surprisingly gentle.

"Chelsea's older sister, Whitney," I huff, folding my arms across my chest. "She kept going on about it when we were outside of Ace."

"Ah, I see. That's why you were upset when you came to my car."

I nod. "Like, obviously, I know it's still new, but why does the fact that we met in this specific place and at this time of the year dictate that there can't be something more between us? Was there a 'Dating Rules for December in Ghana' guidebook at Kotoka that I didn't see or something?" I ask, tightly pursing my lips. "And besides, I haven't had one before, but I highly doubt I'm a vacation romance kinda girl."

Osei softly smiles at me. "Well, if it makes you feel better, you're not the only one who doesn't care for December romances."

"You?" I cackle. "Mr. Osei 'can't walk through a crowd without greeting a minimum of ten babes' Mensah?"

"'Babes'? Yeah, you've been chilling with Ama too much," he chuckles.

"Oh, come on. I know you're lying. There's no way there's not one girl walking around Accra who believes she's in a relationship with you right now."

"Please," he chuckles. "No, Robyn. There's not one."

"In Kumasi?" I ask, throwing another Ghanaian city out there just in case he is being technical.

He laughs louder. "No!"

"Wow," I breathe, leaning back in shock. "Now I'm the one who's surprised."

"Well, whether you believe it or not, it's true. All the drama that comes with dating is just too much of a headache. I've seen enough from my boys to know that unless I find a love like Kaz and Noni from *Beyond the Lights*, I'm not interested in all that."

I smack my palms against the table. "No way! *Beyond the Lights* is one of my favourite movies!" How in the world does this boy manage to continuously surprise me?

"Mine too," he grins, increasingly animated as he recounts scenes from the film. "Even with Noni's fame, Kaz was the only one who saw her for who she was. From the moment they first meet, he convinces her not to jump from the balcony with three simple words. I. See. You. That right there," Osei says, tapping the table with extra force to emphasize his point. "Is all I want."

We sit in a stretch of silence as his words float in the space between us. I have never looked at it like that. My love for the movie was based solely on the fact that when it came out, it had been years since a good black romance movie had been on the big screen. Seeing Kaz love Noni in such an authentic, modern way was refreshing. I never once put myself in their shoes or thought about if what they had was something worth having for myself.

"Well, look at you," I say, holding his gaze. "Osei Mensah, a whole romantic. Who would have thought?"

He smirks, leaning against the table as he rises from his seat. He doesn't bother to respond, but from his expression alone, I know he is unashamed to be a full-blown lover boy.

"Come on, let's get out of here before Grandma Lily sends out a search party. Ama has been back for a while, so she must be wondering where you are."

When we get back to the parked car, Osei opens the passenger door for me, and I can feel that his eyes are fixated on me as I slide into my seat.

"Can I ask you something?" He says suddenly.

"Um, yeah," I reply, grateful to be seated because I suddenly feel weak in the knees.

"You two aren't official yet, right?"

"Um, no we're not," I say hesitantly, trying to decode his unreadable expression. Where is this coming from?

"See, I told you."

Now I'm just confused as to where he's going with this.

"Told me what?"

"I can't be jealous of someone who doesn't have what I want." He shrugs, his face nonchalant as he closes my door gently.

My heart thumps in my ears as I watch him walk from my

door to the driver's side of the car. What is actually happening right now? There's no way he just said what I think he did.

Does Osei really want me? I mean, sure I find Osei attractive. Anyone who gets within ten feet of him can see that he's gorgeous, but do I think there could be something more between us? I don't know!

Osei and I may have a few things in common, but we're still such different people. Someone like Osei needs a free spirit who goes with the flow and doesn't care what others think. I'm doing this photography thing right now, but what if it doesn't work out? If they don't pick my submission, where do I go from there?

Will I still be this version of me after that? This girl I've become in Accra, does she exist beyond this vacation? If I return back to the girl I've been my entire life, the girl whose dad dictates her future and whose life is already laid out for her, would he still want me then? I doubt it.

The sound of Osei laughing pulls me out of my trance.

"Come on. You know I was just joking with you, right?"

"Of course, I do," I reply sharply, not wanting him to know that just seconds before I was considering the possibility of us. "Let's just go already. I don't want Grandma Lily to worry."

As Osei merges onto the main road, I steal one last glance at him from the corner of my eye and for a split second I'm transfixed by the sight of him. But as quickly as the moment comes, I force myself to let it pass. Get a grip, Robyn. There's no one more off-limits than Osei Mensah.

seventeen

THE WEEK LEADING up to Christmas is non-stop commotion.

Airport runs and party preparations. Going out with Chelsea at night, and spending time with Kelvin during the day. In between it all, Osei and I have been running around like chickens with our heads cut off trying to finish my photo essay.

Not only has the constant busyness helped me dodge Dad's phone calls, resorting to sending brief texts for proof of life, but it's also been a worthy distraction from any budding feelings for Osei. We've been so caught up in getting things done that there's been no time to overthink what is or isn't happening between us.

So far, we have a shot of the house square on; a picture of the oil painting Grandma Lily commissioned of Grandpa Isaac in his prime; and a close-up of Mom's camera in her dark room. I also got both of her siblings to sit for portraits, which is my take on the photos Ama showed me of them.

Finding time in Uncle Emmanuel's busy schedule to sit down for his portrait is like pulling teeth, but Ama so graciously used her 'you never come see me' guilt card to get him to drop by Friday after work. It takes some convincing, but Osei and I get him to recreate my mom's picture of him in his childhood bedroom. Once we start shooting, it's as if the hardened persona he spent years hiding behind melts off, frame after frame.

Behind the lens, I don't see the younger, squatter version of my grandfather that he's become. Instead, all I see is teenage Emmanuel. From his glossy eyes, it's clear to see how much he misses his younger sister. When we wrap, he pulls me into a tight embrace. He is not a man of many words, so he leaves it at that, but I don't need words to understand he is grateful that I'm keeping my mom's memory alive.

Mom's younger sister, Aunty Naa, flies in from Dallas with her husband, a Black American named Chris Dupont, on Tuesday morning. When they pull up to the house, Aunty Naa breaks into sobs the moment she lays eyes on me, but I understand her reaction. The relief, the regret, and the apologies flow like the gushing stream of a waterfall during the rainy season. But as soon as she's done letting it all out, she shifts into go mode.

A natural behind the camera, she effortlessly embodies her younger self, charming us as she poses on the house's front steps. Each picture comes out better than the last, and Osei continuously teases her by asking if she's really an engineer or a model in America. With her long limbs and cropped hair, Aunty Naa looks like a thinner, more athletic version of my mom before she died.

Now that it is Saturday and Christmas is just two days away, I'm itching to change my hairstyle for the big day. On Ama's recommendation, I patronize the small salon at the junction near the house, instead of one of the braiders Chelsea sent me on TikTok.

Within an hour, the shop's owner, Miss Martha, detangled,

washed and blow-dried my tight coils straight. Now she and her team of two other braiders are tucking and weaving my stretched hair into neat, tiny knotless braids that stop just above my bum.

"Please, will you have some water?" One of the girls asks, catching my eye in the mirror surrounded by collage art made of torn-out pages from different hair magazines. A tiny wide-backed television is mounted in the upper left corner, blasting African music videos and competing with the sound of the air conditioning unit that keeps the shipping container salon cool.

"I'm okay, thank you," I say, smiling back politely. It's the fifth time she's asked me, the language barrier not allowing our exchanges to go any further. Miss Martha, a fair-skinned woman with permed hair pulled into a small ponytail at the back of her head, laughs loudly behind me. She's stretching the 1B kanekalon hair for the last section they have left to braid.

"Efua, stop worrying the girl," she chimes as the front door to the salon swings open. We all turn to see a wigless Kuukua standing in the doorway. She's dressed casually in a grey, v-neck tank top and black biker shorts. It's my first time seeing her natural hair, a dark, voluminous afro surrounding her perfectly oval-shaped head, and it's as lovely as she is. What doesn't this girl have?

"Eii, Kuukua," Miss Martha cries, dropping a handful of black braiding hair on the arm of my chair to greet her. "Where have you been?"

"Hi, Aunty," she sings, her smile stretching from ear to ear as she removes her AirPods. Her smile is an exact replica of her brother's, front gap and all. "I've been so busy with school, but I'm finally done for the term. Do you have some time to wash and braid cornrows to wear under my wig?"

"Of course, of course. Come this way." She ushers Kuukua to the back of the salon, where the two sinks and chairs are.

"Hey, Rob," she says, squeezing my shoulder as she passes.

"Oh, um, hey, Kuukua," I squeak, adjusting my posture. My voice sounds painfully awkward, and through the reflection, I can tell she notices. In the mirror, I catch the confusion cinching her brows before she turns away, plopping into the seat at the sink. I wince internally at the interaction. It's not that I don't like Kuukua anymore, but I can't get my conversation with Osei out of my head whenever I see her. I know it's technically unfair to take his side without hearing hers, but my bias has already crept in.

By the time the two braiders finish the last section of my hair, snip off the flyaways and dip the ends in boiling water, Miss Martha is finishing pulling Kuukua's thick afro into several neat cornrows. We awkwardly get up to pay and leave the store simultaneously, having no choice but to walk the short distance to our residences together.

"So," Kuukua starts, slightly kicking her feet as she strolls. "How are things going with you and Kelvin?"

"Um, so far so good. I can't complain," I say, pushing my braids out of my face.

"That's great," she coos, sending a genuine smile my way. "I can tell he really likes you, so I'm happy to hear that." Then she laughs, her face twisting with mild embarrassment. "You know, even I had a crush on him growing up, so I get the appeal. He's a charming guy."

This news surprises me, but I'm more amused than anything. The revelation loosens our rigidity, and I relax in her presence.

"So you always have a thing for your brother's friends, huh?" I tease, gently sending my elbow into her arm. Kuukua covers her face with her hands.

"Is it that obvious?" She groans, and I laugh.

"You mean when Osei has to peel you and David apart

whenever we're together? No, it's not obvious at all," I smirk thinking about our night out at Front/Back. "Are you two dating?"

"Uh," she says, chewing on her left cheek. "Not exactly. David doesn't want anything serious right now."

I'm slightly shocked by this. Everything about Kuukua screams no-nonsense. Continuing to entertain a guy who doesn't care to be serious with you isn't exactly something I'd expect from her.

"Damn. Is that why Osei is so adamant about the two of you not being together?"

At this, she scoffs, kicking the ground. Dust particles fly high into the air, and I have to duck to avoid them landing all over my freshly done braids.

"Partially, yes. Osei and David have been friends for a while, so I'm sure he knows things about David I probably would hate to find out. But Osei's real issue with me dating is that he refuses to accept that I, too, have wants and needs. He thinks I'm some robot incapable of emotion, and whenever he sees me with a guy, he tries to shut it down because he thinks it's out of character for me. Sure, maybe when I was younger, I was more reserved, but as I'm getting older and more in touch with my emotions, dating—even if it's not going to end in some serious relationship—is something I'm open to exploring."

Woah. I stop walking, taken aback by her outburst. Kuukua continues ahead of me, then notices after a few moments that I'm no longer beside her. She turns to face me, regret etched all over her facial features.

"Sorry, Robyn. I shouldn't have dumped all that on you. I forgot you and Osei are like friends now, so I get if you don't want to hear about this."

"No, no," I say, quickly masking my shock. "Don't feel bad, it's okay."

"Really?" She asks, and in her eyes, I see how much she needs to vent about this.

"Absolutely," I nod, and we continue walking.

"Look, don't get me wrong. I love my brother. He's quite literally my other half. But the way my parents raised us, they've kind of unintentionally pitted us against each other."

I nod slightly, remembering my earlier conversation with Osei.

"As hard as it is for him, it's not fun for me either. He wants us to see him for who he is, but I promise you I do. I love who he is, and I accept him for that. All *I* want is for him to see me too."

The irony of this doesn't escape me. While Osei is looking for a love that truly understands him for him, he doesn't see how he's refusing to understand the one person who should be his first example of love in human form.

"I'm sorry, Kuukua," I say genuinely. We're in front of the houses now, the gates of both residences facing each other with their matching iron finishes.

Her eyes are moist, but tears don't fall. Instead, they lull in her eyelids like tiny ponds.

"Don't say sorry for things that are not your fault," Kuukua shrugs, the tears practically evaporating as she speaks. "Speaking of families," she says, changing the topic. "Are you looking forward to meeting your extended family at the party tomorrow?"

"I won't lie, even though everyone has been so welcoming, it's still so nerve-wracking. I'm not used to the whole big family thing. Back home, it's just me and my dad."

"Well, from the parties I've been to at your grandma's house, the only thing you have to worry about is making sure you'll have room in your dress to eat," she chuckles, moving closer to her gate to unlock the pedestrian entrance. "They've always been gracious to my family, so I'm sure they will extend the same to you."

"That's good to know. Thanks, Kuukua!"

"Any time," she smiles. "I'm glad I bumped into you today,"

"Me too! And Kuukua, you should tell Osei how you've been feeling. Both of you seem to believe the other person doesn't understand what you're going through, but if you talk, you'll see how similar your feelings are."

She stares at me momentarily, her gaze contemplative but not expressing what's on her mind. Instead, all she says is, "Thanks, Rob," before heading through the open gate.

* * *

Back at Grandma Lily's house, hundreds of partially-filled gift baskets topped with gigantic purple bows litter the living room floor. Ama, Aunty Naa and Uncle Chris have created an assembly line and are stuffing each of them with goodies.

"Robyn," Ama squeals when I walk in. "Your hair looks sooo good! Miss Martha never misses!" I nod in agreement while admiring Ama's own hair. Miss Martha has slicked her hair back and added a blunt ponytail extension that ends at the nape of her neck.

"I know, right?" I say, flipping the long black braids over my shoulder. "How has it been over here at party central?"

"Your grandmother has lost her mind," Aunty Naa jokes, rolling her eyes as she places a portion of plastic-wrapped peanut brittle into the basket before her. "When I was growing up, I used to think it was a lot when she'd hand out customized handkerchiefs as party favours. But those were nothing compared to these elaborate gift baskets for over seventy guests."

"Sorry, Aunty," Ama croaks sheepishly. "I think I got a bit carried away showing her inspo from Instagram when we were in the planning phase. Accra parties are no small ting innit."

I laugh as I sit beside her, pulling out a handheld fan by its wooden handle from an open cardboard box. Grandma Lily's smiling face is printed smack centre on the front of the white stock blade. 'Lily Turns Seventy' and 'Christmas 2024' are scrawled below it in a swooping cursive font.

"Don't let your aunt fool you," Uncle Chris drawls in his thick Texan accent. My cheeks grow warm as he speaks, and his hazel eyes twinkle at me. I'm so sorry, but Aunty Naa's husband is almost identical to Omari Hardwick, so it's hard not to notice how hot he is, especially with this tan. He's been here less than a week, and his fair skin has already deepened three shades. "She's just as extra as her mother. Why don't you tell them what you did for your fortieth, dear?"

"Oh, you keep quiet," Aunty Naa huffs, and Ama and I burst out into schoolgirl giggles.

"Robyn, is that you?" Grandma Lily calls from somewhere in the house. "Can you come to the backyard, please?"

eighteen

OUT BACK, Grandma Lily is seated in a white plastic chair with her feet kicked up in another. From under the tree's dense canopy, she's keeping a watchful eye on the team setting up the rental tables, chairs and tents for her party. I weave around the workers, flashing tight-lipped smiles at the ones who greet me with nods. The lawn has been mowed, and the scent of freshly cut grass mingles with Accra's familiar smog, creating an oddly satisfying aroma.

"Hi, Grandma. You called?" I ask, my hand shielding my vision from the harsh midday sun.

"Robyn," she smiles at me brightly. "Your hair looks wonderful. Please, sit next to your grandma." She pats the seat of the empty chair beside her.

"Thank you, Grandma. How is the party setup going?" I ask.

"It's coming along. There's still a lot to do. Though, I didn't call you out here to talk about me. How are *you*, dear? I know things have been crazy, but I hope you've felt at home."

"Yes, Grandma. You and Ama have taken good care of me."

"Good, good," she nods, returning to the ongoing party

setup. She yells out in Twi to a short woman with a braided bob and a clipboard tucked under her arm. The woman, who I assume is Jemima, the party planner she's been working with these last few weeks, yells back. The two women nod in agreement before she hurries back inside the house.

"And your project is coming along okay? I heard your uncle stopped by to help," her upper lip twitches with amusement, and I imagine she's trying her best to envision her stoic son modelling for his niece. "I hope he didn't give you too much trouble."

"Not at all. Uncle Emmanuel was a natural," I wink, making her laugh escape. Happiness swells inside me. I've gotten used to being a part of an actual family unit. I don't know what I'm going to do when I have to go back home, face Dad and confront our muddled past.

"And your dad?" She questions, reading my mind. My posture stiffens at the mention of him. "You have been keeping in contact with him like you promised, right?" Grandma Lily asks.

"Grandma, I'm not going to lie to you. I don't know if I can talk to him without blowing up right now, so I haven't been able to bring myself to do anything other than text." I peer at her from the corner of my eye, awaiting her disappointed reaction.

Grandma Lily sighs loudly. "I was afraid this was going to happen."

"Afraid what was going to happen?" I ask, inching to the edge of my seat.

"There's nothing I've wanted more than to reconnect with you, my child," she starts, reaching out to cup my cheek in her palm. "But not at the expense of your relationship with your father. We've all been through a lot in the years since your mother's passing. You may not fully grasp the decisions we adults make, but promise me you'll be open to trying to. Talk to him, Robyn. Call him. Make sure you wish him a merry Christmas, and if you're up for it, ask him about everything you've been too afraid to say. I know he may not have always been forthcoming with information, but I believe he will be ready to open up to you this time. From his truth, I think you will better understand us all, including your mother." Vulnerability seems to catch in her throat, and she clears it loudly.

Grandma Lily coming to dad's defence is something I never expected from her. All my life, I was so sure they were on two opposite ends of the spectrum when it came to the aftermath of my mom's death, but clearly, she sees something in him that I've never been able to find. Her honesty is the only thing pushing me to want to go and seek it out.

"I'll call him Grandma," I promise. And this time, I mean it.

* * *

The crow of a rooster way too close for my liking wakes me up on Christmas morning. Following the sound, I pull open the curtains behind me and instantly spot bright green palm leaves. Waking up on Christmas morning without snow is different, but it's a good difference; one that I'm loving getting used to.

Despite our best efforts, and believe me, we tried, Ama and I were unable to escape attending Christmas Eve church service. No matter what we came up with, Grandma Lily wasn't having any of our excuses. We did, however, manage to broker a deal with her instead. If we agree to attend the Christmas Eve evening service, she'll let us skip church the following morning. While I'm all for celebrating the big guy's son's birthday, back-to-back services just a few hours apart feels a tiny bit excessive. It took some convincing, but after many promises that our souls would not burn in eternal damnation and a promise to be up early to help Jemima put the finishing touches on the party instead, Grandma Lily eventually relented.

After returning from Christmas Eve service, Ama and I stayed up for hours as I debriefed my conversation with Grandma Lily and filled her in on my plan to talk to Dad today. I pick up my phone from the nightstand and check the time. It's still early in Toronto, and Dad is probably not up yet, so I quickly text him to wish him a Merry Christmas and let him know I'll be calling later in the day.

As I swipe out of the thread, I see Osei's name just under it but surprisingly, the only thing there is the thumbs-up emoji I sent him last night. I frown instinctively, a rush of disappointment hitting me at once.

Since we've started shooting, I've woken up to texts from Osei every single morning. They usually contain website links to different Black photographers' portfolios for inspiration or behind-the-scenes videos of me shooting. He's also been sending me a never-ending list of drinks he thinks I should try next—since he's determined to prove there are better drinks in Ghana than Alvaro. (That I highly doubt!) But this morning, there is no text, and it makes me feel as if my phone needs to be deeply submerged in a bag of rice.

My screen goes dark as I hold down the power button, but before I can bring my phone back to life, I catch a glimpse of the utter desperation on my face in the pitch-black screen. The foreign emotion sends me into absolute shock, and I dash my phone across the bed.

Get it together, Robyn! Osei is not the boy you're supposed to be pining over!

I feel around the duvet for my phone, and once I turn it on again, it vibrates with a text from Kelvin. It's as if he knows, from all the way in the Mensah's guest room, that I need him to fight for dominance in my mind.

> **KELVIN**
> Merry Christmas, Beautiful. I'm looking forward to seeing you later at your grandma's party. I'll be coming over a bit earlier than the rest of the house because my parents want me to spend some time with my mom's family in Aburi.

> **ROBYN**
> Merry Christmas Kelvin! Sure, no problem. Hopefully, I can sneak away from party duties so we can spend some time together.

Almost immediately, Kelvin reacts to my message with a heart.

> **KELVIN**
> That is the only thing I want for Christmas 😊

I peel the covers off my legs and slip out of the bed, trying to shake off my mixed emotions before scampering to the bathroom. Splashing water on my face helps to alleviate my sleepiness, but it does little to cool me off. I reach to turn off the running tap and place both palms on the cool white quartz countertop, trying to steady myself. My reflection sparkles at me in the massive backlit mirror, one of the many modern finishes Grandma Lily has installed in the bathroom I'm sharing with Ama.

What is wrong with you, Robyn? Kelvin is a good guy. He's kind, sweet, and lives in your hometown. What more could you possibly want?

For him to truly see you.

I narrow my eyes at the girl in the mirror who's allowed Osei's musing to infiltrate her brain. Robyn, don't confuse what Osei wants with what you desire. You're happy with Kelvin, so continue to explore it without all this self-sabotaging. Besides, today is about Grandma Lily. Neither Kelvin nor Osei should be weighing this heavily on my mind.

After I finish my morning routine, I head downstairs and follow Mariah Carey's signature whistle notes into the kitchen. Inside, Ama, Aunty Naa and Uncle Chris are at the island, rolling cutlery into thick gold cloth napkins.

"*Afenhyia pa*," I sing from the kitchen entrance, but the sound of the music and chatting drowns me out. I stomp over to the stereo and lower the volume before loudly clearing my throat. "I said, *Afenhyia pa!*"

"*Afe nkɔ mmɛto yɛn!*" Everyone, excluding Chris, cries in response without looking up from their tasks. A beat passes before Ama and Aunty Naa register who they're responding to. Their heads swivel toward me, knives and forks clattering against the island's smooth marble surface.

"Robyn," Ama laughs, and the mixture of delight and shock on her face matches Aunty Naa's. "Merry Christmas to you too, babes." She walks over to hug me. "I see you've been putting that Twi book to good use."

"You know I had to give you guys a little something for the holidays," I chuckle, winking at Aunty Naa.

"Your pronunciation was perfect! The boy from across the street must be really rubbing off on you, huh."

My jaw drops at the mention of Osei. Or is it Kelvin she was referring to? Shit, now I'm confused. A slight panic thrums against my veins.

"Ei, calm down," Aunty Naa snorts. "You're acting as if I said you guys got married. I think it's sweet he's helping you with your application for that fellowship. He seems like a good friend."

A shallow breath escapes my lips. "A friend, right." I nod,

relieved she hasn't misconstrued what is happening between us. All I have to do is get through the rest of this trip without overthinking, because overthinking leads to catching feelings. And catching feelings leads to checking your phone every few hours for new messages, something I have no business doing.

Through the window, I see the rectangular tables covered with white linen tablecloths arranged into three long rows under the covering of two tents. Jemima and the team from yesterday are fussing around, adding the finishing touches to the colourful floral centrepieces. The purple, pink and yellow flowers mixed in ceramic white vases of various heights compliment the kente we used to make our dresses, while thin strips of that same fabric serve as runners across the centre of the tables.

"Ama, did your mom and Sammy get in okay?" I ask. Her mom and half-brother were supposed to be flying in from London the night before and staying with their relatives.

"Yeah, they got in last night. Grandma Lily invited them to the party, so let's all pray that she and my dad can act normal for once," she says, sucking in a breath.

"Herh, my brother acting normal?" Aunty Naa snickers, then quickly changes her tune when she notices the pained expression on Ama's face and the frown from her husband. "Well, who knows, weirder things have happened."

By one o'clock, when the first guest arrives, the backyard is completely transformed. Even though I've been watching them set up over the last two days, I clearly underestimated their ability to make over the blank green space. Stepping inside one of the massive tents, I almost forget I am at a birthday party and not a wedding.

The guests that have trickled in are mingling on the wooden dance floor, while servers dressed in formal black and-white attire hand out small bites. The D.J., a childhood friend of Ama's, is in the far corner of the tent, blasting all the oldies and a massive buffet is set up next to him. The noise level increases steadily with each new arrival, and the party is in full swing by three o'clock.

Little children sit on the uncovered grass showing off their Christmas presents; men are hunched over someone's phone, yelling over a soccer game, and aunties loudly coo as they hug and sway on the dance floor. When Chelsea and the Ankrahs arrive, Aunty Lydia hugs me so tight I can barely breathe, and Uncle Fred gives me a handshake that results in a hundred-dollar bill ending up in my palm. Whitney heads straight for the bar, and it isn't long before Will and Ama find themselves under the shade of the big tree, swooning at each other in hushed voices.

"You clean up nice," says a familiar voice from behind me. I turn around and make a production of rolling my eyes while twirling to give a full view of my dress. As promised, Mrs. Botchway delivered a masterpiece. The base of the dress is form fitting and cinches where my waist naturally concaves, and the top half is covered in gold beading that shimmers across my chest.

"You've already used that line on me," I smirk at a grinning Osei while taking a step back to take him in. He's dressed in a khaki-coloured kaftan, which contrasts beautifully against his dark skin, and his camera is strapped securely around his neck. He looks so good I almost forget how bothered I was when I didn't hear from him earlier today.

"Well would you believe me if I told you that every time I see you I have to resort to using the same compliment, because I fail to find the words that accurately depict how I feel?" He asks, his mood taking a sudden shift. I gawk in response, completely off guard by the turn of events. But before I can even stammer a response, Osei collapses into laughter.

"Relax, Robyn. I'm just fooling with you," he winks.

"Even on Christmas, you won't rest?" I ask, kissing my teeth but feeling an immense wave of relief. This was nothing more than his usual banter. See, clearly we both recognize that we're better off as friends. Nothing to worry about here, folks!

"And take a day off from messing with you? Never."

"Yeah, I almost thought something had happened to you when I didn't hear from you this morning," I add, trying to sound as nonchalant as possible.

"Aww, were you worried about me Miss Carter? Don't be. I just slept in."

I scoff loudly, making a show of just how little I care.

"Please, nobody was worried about you, Osei," I laugh, as the sound of someone tapping on a microphone pulls our attention toward the direction it came from.

"Ladies and gentlemen, may I have your attention please," says the M.C., another one of Ama's friends. "It is time for us to welcome the guest of honour. Please gather by the door and form two neat lines on either side."

It takes a moment to get everyone arranged, but eventually, we figure it out and Osei stands in between both lines, poised to capture her entrance.

"Ladies and gentlemen, please join me in welcoming the newest seventy-year-old on the block. Liliana Antwi," he roars. A classic Daddy Lumba song blares as the back door swings open, and Grandma Lily glides outside in a white silk dress sewn in her signature billowing style. But this one is extra special. It's complete with a lengthy train that trails behind her as she moves, and it sparkles with hundreds of Swarovski crystals. The makeup artist Ama hired has dolled her up in a soft pink glam, and the hair stylist has transformed her short white hair with a mousse that defines each ringlet.

I watch her guests, dressed in the party's colours, take turns greeting her. They squeeze her hands and imprint her cheeks with kisses. Pride squeezes my heart seeing Grandma Lily being loved on like this. She is utterly adored and completely cherished by her community. I feel privileged to get to be a part of this.

"Hey, gorgeous. Merry Christmas," a voice whispers into my ear. I whip around and come face-to-face with Kelvin. He's beaming as he holds up two massive bouquets of fresh-cut roses—each individual flower wrapped with a shiny red fifty-dollar Canadian bill.

nineteen

"OH MY GOSH, KELVIN," I shriek, staring at him in bewilderment. He looks good. No, he looks amazing. But that's no surprise. His white dress shirt, tailored to perfection across his broad chest and shoulders, is tucked into a pair of slim-fit, light grey checkered trousers. Dark Cartier sunglasses conceal his eyes, and his signature Cuban link lies around his neck, sparkling under the sunlight, much like his diamond earrings.

But regardless of how good he looks; he's still holding two massive bouquets covered with money in one hand and they might as well be a bright red 'look at me' sign stamped on his chest. A knot tightens in my chest as a few guests nearby start to notice us. It feels as if the D.J. has turned down the music so their whispers can reach us without interruption. I gently shove Kelvin toward the house, through the back door and into the kitchen so we can be alone.

"Do you like it?" He grins once we're inside. "One for the birthday girl and one for my favourite girl."

Horrified, a flash of heat courses through my body, and I shove both bouquets into his chest before stepping away from him. The topic of money doesn't seem to be an issue for Kelvin.

He's casually mentioned being gifted a Tesla by his parents for getting accepted into UofT and is constantly name-dropping designers I've never heard of. Since it didn't concern me, I hadn't given it a second thought. Now, with his wealth on display before my eyes, I'm beginning to think that I may have downplayed just how well-off he is.

"What?" He pulls the glasses off his face, and I see confusion swirling in his amber irises.

"Kelvin! This is way too much."

"Wait, why?"

"Are you crazy? I can't accept this much money from you." I exclaim. "And neither will my grandma."

"Robyn," Kelvin reaches out to grab my hands and pulls me toward him, his eyes shining as he bats his long eyelashes at me. "What I feel for you, I've never felt for anyone else." His words speed in on me, squaring me into one spot. "To me, this is nothing more than a small token of my appreciation for you. I know it's still early, but I can't ignore how I feel when I realize you're the first and last thing on my mind each day."

"Kelvin, I—" I say, trying to cut him off, but it's useless.

"I don't want to make you, or your grandma, feel uncomfortable on a day as special as this, but I can't keep this to myself any longer. Is it okay if I'm honest with you?"

Under his intense gaze, my "yes" is barely audible.

"I know you may think this is too soon, but I'm falling for you, Robyn."

Kelvin is looking at me with so much yearning that my heart feels like it is beating outside my chest. While I'm conflicted by this over-the-top display of affection, I can't help but feel flattered. And even though this is probably more over the top than I could have ever imagined, I'm beginning to realize that I do want this. I *want* Kelvin.

"I appreciate the kind gesture, Kelvin. I really do. But I need you to understand that this is all so new to me," I say cautiously, trying to find the right words to describe the flurry of activity inside of me right now. "The money I will not be taking, but I accept the apology, and I think I'm catching feelings for you, too." I think about it briefly then shake my head. "You know what, let me not lie on the Lord's birthday. I *know* I'm catching feelings for you too."

Kelvin laughs, and I revel in the sound. He reaches for my hands again, closing the distance I've created.

"We can take it slow, Robyn. We can even crawl if you want to. All I want is to be exclusive with you. I have eyes for you and only you." His voice feels safe and sound. It's exactly what you'd want to hear before diving into the deep end for the first time.

"I'd love that," I whisper, and he leans down to kiss my forehead. At his touch, all thoughts of everything and anyone else instantly leave my body and I feel overwhelmed by an intense desire for his lips to travel down to mine. It's when he pulls away slightly, drinking me in, that I immediately know the urge has struck him, too.

Time seems to go still as his gentle lips land on mine, and warmth spreads throughout my entire body. I always thought it would be weird kissing for the first time, awkward even, but somehow my lips know what to do. Kelvin's soft touch makes me feel even more comfortable, and I begin to follow his lead. A poke from his tongue asks permission to deepen the kiss, and I let him. I don't care that Grandma Lily, or any other relative, may walk in at any second. I want to savour this moment right here, right now.

I force myself to memorize every detail before we pull apart. The sounds from the party filter into the house as one of his hands finds its way around my neck, his fingers kneading into my skin, the scent of his familiar cologne and the taste of his mint-flavoured mouthwash. When we come up for air, I squeeze my eyes shut, unable to hide my satisfaction.

It's hard to believe I'm not dreaming, but I don't want to wake up anytime soon if I am. At the sound of laughter, my eyes flutter open, and I look up from under my lashes to see Kelvin smirking at me.

"Not bad for your first time," he says, his laugh lines more defined than ever.

"Why don't you kiss me again, and let's see if I can outdo myself?"

* * *

After two—surprisingly uninterrupted—make-out sessions, we are both filled with glee, high off of our first kiss. We giggle as we remove each shiny red bill from the roses and stuff them into his pockets and wallet, and with one last peck, he's off to visit his mom's family in Aburi.

When I re-enter the backyard, I proudly beam as I cradle both bouquets like newborns. My eyes roam around the party for Grandma Lily, and I spot her, Aunty Naa and Uncle Chris standing next to a table where Uncle Emmanuel, Ama and a woman I don't recognize are sitting down.

"Robyn." Aunty Naa smirks. "Nice of you to join us again."

"These are for you, Grandma," I say, ignoring my aunt's teasing and cousin's snickers.

"Oh, how lovely," Grandma Lily says, inhaling their faint fragrance. "Who are they from?"

"My friend Kelvin. You know the boy who is staying with the Mensahs? He had to leave to visit family, but he said Merry Christmas and Happy Birthday."

"Oh, he should have at least come to say hello to me directly," Grandma pouts and everyone around her freezes, unsure whether she will turn this into a lecture about children respecting their elders. Luckily for us, Grandma Lily shrugs, in too good of a mood to care. "Well, I'm going to put these in some water. Naa, come and help me," she declares, whisking her last born away. Uncle Chris shoots the rest of us a small wave before trailing after them.

Ama laughs. "That was a close call, innit?"

"Your grandma may be all hip and cool now, but don't be fooled. She used to be a hardcore woman," says the woman I don't recognize. "The first time Ama's dad brought me to meet her, I accidentally used my left hand to greet—because my right was full—and it took your Dad two weeks to convince her to get over it. Isn't that right, Emmanuel?" She asks shaking her head with a reminiscent smile.

Uncle Emmanuel only grunts in response, but a similar expression is on his face.

"Mum, you remember Robyn, right?" Ama asks, standing up to pull me closer.

"Of course I do," she says, facing me. Ama's mom has fair skin, a relaxed pixie cut and Ama's smile. She is wearing a peplum dress made of the same purple, gold and pink kente the immediate family members are wearing. "You probably don't remember me, but you can call me Aunty Ellen."

"Hi, Aunty," I wave with my free hand.

"Look how beautiful you are," she coos, surveying me from head to toe. "She's a spitting image of her mother!"

At this, my uncle speaks. "She is, isn't she? I've always thought Ama favoured Nana as well."

"That's the thing about life, ladies," Aunty Ellen tuts, leaning toward Ama and me. "You carry your child for nine months, and when you push them out, they'll look nothing like you." She shakes her head playfully as she pats down the hairs escaping Ama's ponytail. I smile as Ama leans into her touch, blissfully content to be reunited with her mom after spending so many months apart. "But if my baby has to look like anyone other than me, I'm glad it's your mum, Robyn. She was such a beautiful person. Not just on the outside but on the inside too."

"Aww, thank you, Aunty Ellen. That's so kind of you to say."

After an introduction to ten-year-old Sammy, who is called over from playing with the other kids, Ama and I leave her parents to themselves, and walk away with our arms linked together.

"Well, it looks like you got your Christmas wish. Your parents seem to be getting along great," I say as she steers me toward where the mobile bar is. I know she was nervous about how they were going to act around each other since it's been a while since her mom and dad have been in the same place.

"I know. My inner child is so gassed right now. Come, let's celebrate, yeah? Drinks on me?"

"Ama," I snort. "It's an open bar."

"Oh yeah," she giggles, her eyes laser-focused on the edge of the yard. When I see Will standing there with his sisters and the Mensah twins, I immediately understand her eagerness.

"Okayyy, Robynnn. I see you with the roses," Whitney cheers as we approach them, and I roll my eyes. Someone's in a good mood today; it must be all the free booze.

Ama and I take turns hugging each person and wishing them a Merry Christmas.

"Kuukua was just telling us that Kelvin invited everyone to his family's beach house in Kokrobite for New Year's weekend," Chelsea says, wiggling her pencil-filled brows at me after Ama and I grab the party's signature cocktail. The drink combines gin, crème de violette, orange liqueur and fresh lemon juice and is named after the birthday girl herself—the Water Lily.

"Yeah, he just told me, too," I say, smiling down at the flowers in my arms. "I was coming out here to tell you all."

"Uh-huh? Before or after you and 'pretty boy' started going at it?" Whitney smirks, her index finger rubbing the area above her top lip. I quickly wipe the smudged lip gloss off mine with the back of my hand, embarrassment crashing down on me.

Like a bad habit, my eyes flash to Osei taking mindless sips from his glass of orange juice. It's clear that he's taking a break from his duties as an event photographer, but other than that, it's hard to decode the expression on his face. Is it annoyance or disinterest that has him twisting his lips like that?

"Whit, leave Rob alone," Will barks. "He sounds like a good kid, and a weekend away from Accra would be fun. I'm down if you are?" He locks eyes with Ama, who nods eagerly in agreement. Like most Ghanaian men, Will is not tall by usual standards, but he may as well be Shaquille O'Neal next to Ama's tiny stature.

"If I can bring my girl Mo, I'm down, too," says Whitney.

"Sure, why not? Kelvin said there's room for one more," I shrug. Whitney having a plus one means she'll be distracted, and I'll have to deal with a whole lot less of her. So that's a win-win for me.

"And everyone has their tickets for Detty Rave?" Kuukua asks, looking around the circle to confirm if we're attending the annual one-day music festival hosted by Nigerian-born, Ghanaian-raised artist Mr. Eazi. We all nod.

"Great. Since it's on a Friday this year, we can drive straight to the beach house after the show, ring in the New Year on Sunday night, and leave the following Monday."

"Sounds good to me," Ama says, and everyone joins in, agreeing like a choir. As Chelsea asks what everyone plans to wear to the festival, my phone vibrates in the pocket Mrs. Botchway sewed into my dress. I pull it out to see I've just missed a call from Dad. Excusing myself from the group, I walk down the path that leads to the front of the house, where it's less noisy. I sit on the steps and set down the roses to call him back. I wait as the phone rings, but he doesn't pick up: FaceTime unavailable. I swipe up to check my messages and see he sent me one shortly after I missed his call.

> DAD
>
> Sorry, we've been playing phone tag. There was a sudden flu outbreak in the neighbourhood, and I've been at the pharmacy all day. I will call back when things die down. I've sent you some money via e-transfer. Merry Christmas, Robyn.

Sure enough, there is one new email.

TO: Robyn Carter
FROM: TD Canada Trust

SUBJECT: INTERAC e-Transfer: A money transfer from Marvin Carter has been automatically deposited.

Hi Robyn Carter,
Marvin Carter has sent you $400.00 (CAD) and the money has been automatically deposited into your bank account at TD Canada Trust.

Reference Number: CASxJhIK

Please do not reply to this email.

Just great. More money that I didn't ask for. I sigh, stuffing my phone back into my pocket. I was genuinely ready for this long overdue conversation, but I guess I'll have to wait a few more days.

ROBYN
Thanks, Dad. Merry Christmas to you, too.

twenty

GRANDMA LILY'S PARTY, quite literally, goes out with a bang. Fireworks burst into the night, colouring the sky in the party's signature colours to close out the festivities. Shortly after, the guests file out of the backyard with their gift baskets in tow. Now, the only people that remain, other than my family, are my friends and their parents. We're all tipsy from the alcohol and holiday cheer as the cleanup crew works hurriedly to take down the party around us.

My grandma, aunts, uncles, the Mensah and the Ankrah parents have taken their party inside, and we kids–minus Osei, who followed the adults–are outside.

Will and Ama have disappeared to the front of the house, but Kuukua, Chelsea, Whitney, and I are on what remains of the dance floor. We've convinced the D.J. to stay for an extra hour to play all the songs he couldn't when the adults were still present. We're in the middle of belting out Kendrick's latest hit, when I feel someone tug my arm.

"Hey, Rob, I'm about to head back to my place," Osei yells in my ear, his backpack hanging off one shoulder. The way he's wincing at Kendrick's rapping makes me giggle.

Besides African music, this boy really doesn't listen to anything besides R&B. Feeling bold, courtesy of the countless Water Lilies flowing through my system, I throw my arms around his neck, and Osei pauses momentarily. For a brief moment, his hands hover in the air before he allows himself to relax and wrap his hands firmly around my waist, gently bringing me toward him.

"Thanks so much for coming today. I know the pictures will come out great," I say, trying to ignore how giddy I feel. Gosh, why does he have to look so good in this kaftan?

He flashes a grin at me. "It's my pleasure. Do you mind walking me back to my place?"

"Sure," I nod, not thinking much of it. When I turn around to let the girls know where I'm heading, I realize they've stopped rapping with Kendrick and are giggling at us instead. Heat rushes to my face, instantly sobering me. Oh no, was I doing too much?

I'm not sure, but I don't want to stick around to find out. I turn on my heels and speed walk to the front yard, not bothering to look back.

It takes no time for Osei's long legs to catch up with mine, and we pass the front porch, where Ama and Will are sharing a deep and passionate kiss. My hand flies up to my mouth, and Osei shoots me a knowing look before grabbing my hand. We dash to the front gate, trying to avoid interrupting their moment.

"Your face," Osei laughs once we're on the other side of the gate.

"I just wasn't expecting it," I say, trying to catch my breath.

"You didn't expect that? What, did you not see them during the party? I'm surprised it's even taken them this long to kiss," he smirks.

"I mean, duh! I just didn't think we'd catch them mid-make-out session," I shriek.

"It was cute. Even though it's early, from the way he looks at her, it's obvious they're meant for more," Osei adds, with a soft smile and longing look in his eye.

"Yeah, I guess you could say that," I breathe, and silence falls over us. I can't help but wonder what Osei's thinking right now.

"Anyway," he says, shrugging off his backpack and unzipping it. "I wanted you to walk me out so that I could give you this and avoid all the *konkonsa*."

He hands me a white plastic bag. The square box inside is much smaller than the bag, so he's wrapped the remaining plastic around it like bubble wrap. "Merry Christmas, Robyn. It's small, but I know it's something you've been looking for."

It doesn't take long for me to unroll the bag and take out what's inside.

"Osei," I gasp, twisting the yellow and purple box around in my hands. It's a roll of Kodak Portra 400 Colour Print 35mm film. The exact kind I need for my mom's camera. "Oh my goodness! How did you find this in Accra?"

I've been looking everywhere and haven't been able to find any. Even when I initially asked Osei about it, he told me it would be a long shot finding any in the city.

"Ah, you know I have my ways."

"Tell me," I beg, lightly pushing against his chest with my free hand.

He laughs loudly, catching my hand in his, and my heart skips several beats from the heat of his palm.

"A friend was coming in from the States for Christmas, so I sent him money to bring a roll."

I pull my hand out of his grip to smack my forehead. Why

didn't I think of that? Chelsea could have easily ordered the film from Amazon and brought it when she came.

"Wow, thank you so much," I say, looking in awe at the little box.

"You still have four images to shoot for your photo essay, and I thought you'd like to take them on your mom's camera."

My bottom lip trembles as he says this. I was thinking about doing just that when we started working on my submission, but since I haven't been able to find any film, I didn't bother mentioning my idea. But of course, Osei managed to pull this off and help make my dreams come true again.

My shoulders fall with a sinking realization. I didn't get Osei *or* Kelvin anything. I mean, in my defence, I didn't think they'd get *me* something, but still.

"I am a terrible, terrible person," I say. "This is the second time today that someone has gotten me something, and I've had nothing to give them in return. I am so sorry, Osei."

Unfazed, he waves away my apology as he re-zips his bag.

"Don't even worry about it, Robyn. It's a Christmas gift, but it's also a thank you. Thank you for talking to Kuukua for me. I don't know what you said, but we had a candid conversation about our childhood and family for the first time, and we understand each other a lot better because of it. So, again, thank you. None of that would have happened without you."

My heart soars as he tells me this. Both he and his sister deserve it. They were reading the same book but were just on different chapters, so I'm glad I was able to help them get on the same page.

"Besides," he continues. "Knowing you didn't get anything for the guy you're catching feelings for either makes me feel slightly better. Now I know it's not just because you hate me or something," he teases.

"I'm sorry..."

My voice catches in my throat, and I look down at the pink rhinestone-covered heeled sandals I've been wearing all day, conflicted about what I'm apologizing for. I know it should be for not getting him a gift, but it's hard to ignore my nagging guilt for falling for someone who isn't him.

"It's okay," he says, when he realizes I'm at a loss for words. "As long as you're happy, I'll be okay. As your friend, your happiness is all that matters to me."

The f-word comes out sharply, piercing me a lot deeper than I expect. I know that's what I've been telling myself this whole time but the crushing weight of disappointment doesn't escape me.

Osei and I *are* better off as friends, and there is so much evidence to prove it. So why does it feel like the ultimate betrayal to hear this confirmed out loud?

"Our friendship," I say, hesitantly, as if I'm saying the word for the first time in my life. "Yeah, that makes sense. We are friends after all."

"Well, isn't that what you want?" He asks, staring at me. Behind his steely gaze, I see a glimmer of something more, but it disappears before I can draw it out, making it crystal clear that this is all we are destined for.

"It is what I want," I nod, bobbing my head vigorously as I accept our reality. "You're a great friend, Osei. You've been there for me these last few weeks, and I'm thankful to have someone like you. Helping you and Kuukua is nothing compared to what you've done for me."

"Great," he smiles. It's not hard to tell that he's forcing it to reach his eyes, but I don't mention this aloud for his sake and mine. "Then it's settled."

He pulls me into a stiff side hug, his arms awkwardly

draping around my shoulders as if we're in church and nosey aunties are watching our every move.

"Friends," he says, not looking at me.

"Friends," I agree, not looking at him.

… # twenty-one

MR. EAZI'S voice booms throughout the grounds at Untamed Empire as Ama, Chelsea, Whitney, and I make our way toward the Detty Rave main stage. The last few days have been a non-stop blur of partying, eating, sleeping and partying some more. We've attended as many events as we can physically manage, and now we are at our third and last festival for the season, Detty Rave.

"I don't know who I thought I was agreeing to go to all these events back-to-back," complains Ama as we walk one behind the other through the muddy grass. We are trying to find the boys and Kuukua in the multitudes of people, but our collective lack of height makes it challenging. Thick crowds swarm around us as we try not to get separated.

"I'm starting to wish I tagged along to that wedding with Ma and Pops instead," agrees Whitney. "It's a big one too! Ma said the bride's mother was handing out iPad minis in the gift bags! I could have found my future rich ex-husband!"

"Oh, come on, guys. My girl Doechii is performing tonight," I say, still in disbelief that the organizers were able to snag one of the hottest women in rap to headline their festival.

"You're just giddy because you'll finally know the lyrics," laughs Chelsea, reminding us of my embarrassing front-row moment at Afrochella when the Ghanaian superstar Ofori Amponsah shoved the mic in my face to sing along to his major hit 'Otoolege'.

"She was just standing there smiling till her cheeks swallowed her eyes whole," Ama cries.

"Then Whitney grabbed the mic and started singing it confidently word for word while being completely off-key," cackles Chelsea.

"Guys, you know that I know the song! I just don't know how to sing it in Twi word for word," I whine, playfully shoving Chelsea, who's closest to me. "But, yes, I am excited," I agree, laughing with them.

Toronto Robyn would be mortified to be the odd Ghanaian out, but Accra Robyn can laugh about it. This version of me feels unapologetically comfortable in her skin, and even when she's different, she still feels as if she belongs.

"Fans! Fans! 25 cedis! Get your fans!"

"Ouu, I want a fan," proclaims Ama, leading us to one of the vendors who have set up shop on the outskirts of the festival. They're selling everything from fans to fresh coconut water, kebabs and little paper plates of jollof rice. The fans the man is selling have a cloth blade made of eclectic *ntoma* styles and wooden handles.

"Now this is a fan," sighs Ama, manually fanning herself so hard her ponytail flaps in the wind. Chelsea, Whitney, and I quickly exchange our cedis for fans and merge our way back into the crowd.

"Hey," Ama says, tugging on my arm when we stop moving again after being met with a sea of people who won't let us pass. She smiles, eyeing the Praktica hanging around my neck, and I smile back. It's a silent gesture letting me know she understands its importance.

"Honestly, this is not it," declares Whitney, sighing in defeat. "I want to head back out where there are fewer people. Mo just got here and said she can get me into V.I.P."

"I'll come with," chimes Ama. "I don't need to be in V.I.P., but I do need air."

From how Chelsea looks at me and then back at Ama and Whitney, I know she'll enjoy the experience from where she can see.

"It's fine, go," I say, reassuring my best friend.

"Are you sure?" She asks, her eyes wide as she searches mine.

"Positive. I want to see Doechii and don't want to be too far back when she comes out. From what Kelvin texted, they shouldn't be too far from here. I'll text you if anything happens."

"You better," she says, squeezing my arm.

I watch as the girls turn and walk away until I lose them in the crowd. Fanning off the overwhelming heat, I continue my journey and eventually spot Kelvin's distinctive frame. I weave through the crowd to get to where he, Kuukua, David and Jojo are standing, each holding bottles of Smirnoff Ice. Thankfully for me, Osei is nowhere in sight.

"Hey you," he says, bending down to peck me on the lips. I blush as we pull apart, and lick his pineapple-flavoured drink off my lips. I'm still getting used to the public displays of affection, but it's hard to resist kissing back when his lips look as good as they do.

"*Chale*, get a room," David yells as we pull apart. He's standing behind Kuukua, his chin lodged into her right shoulder. She grins at me as she brings the glass bottle to her lips, and I wink back. Someone is ecstatic to be openly embracing her man.

Kelvin laughs and ignores him as he hands me an unopened bottle of Pineapple Smirnoff Ice.

"You okay? Where are the girls?"

"They're here," I say, nodding in the direction I just came from. "They just decided to hang back."

"Oh, okay," he says, then spins me around so my back is to him. I loudly squeal as he pulls me against his body. "You look beautiful, as always," Kelvin murmurs into my ear.

"Thanks, love," I say, leaning my body into his and raising my head to peck his cheek. I relax into his grip as his hands explore my body, grateful that I let Chelsea convince me to wear this sheer black bodysuit and my 'too short' jean shorts. After several seconds of him feeling the softness of my waist and hips, he moves a finger to the strap of my mom's camera, tracing it up and down. His gentle touch sends a shiver down my spine.

"I have no idea why you want to be behind the camera when you clearly belong in front of it," he breathes into my ear.

My entire body tenses in his arms, and the scent of alcohol on his breath seems to attack my nostrils. I know he means that as a compliment, but the words still rub me the wrong way. Is it possible they were even slightly condescending? But before I can fully process how I genuinely feel about them, the crowd breaks out into a collective roar.

"Are there any Doechii fans here?" The M.C. asks the crowd from under the glow of red and green strobe lights. The screams in response are ear-shattering, and the stage begins to flood with smoke. "Let me hear you make some noise for the one, the only, Doechii!"

As Doechii runs on stage, I scream, too distracted by the

presence of one of the hottest rappers in the game to press Kelvin any further about what he just said.

twenty-two

THE PASSENGER SEAT windowpane feels cool against my temple as Ama cruises towards Kokrobite, the beach town and home away from home for the Mensahs. Chelsea, Whitney and her friend Mo are fast asleep behind us, their usual chatter replaced with soft snores that drift toward us every so often. I shake my head as I glance at them in the rearview mirror, where they lie like fallen dominoes. Whitney is leaning on Chelsea, who is lying on Mo, who is pressed against the door. While I appreciate the silence, I'm most grateful to have a moment to speak to my cousin without unnecessary interference.

A blue Toyota RAV4 catches my eye in the rearview mirror, and I follow it as it picks up speed and slides into the opposing lane on our left. The driver, a young guy around our age, zooms to overtake us while a girl in the passenger seat is turned with her back to the door and her head bobbing in the wind. My nose crinkles as I turn to Ama, who remains focused on the uneven road ahead.

"What?" She chuckles, watching me from the corner of her eye. Her tone is mindful of the sleeping beauties behind us.

"Why aren't you doing that?"

"Doing what? Speeding?"

"Yeah, that is like the fourth car you've let overtake us. Come on, I wanna throw my head back in the wind, too," I joke, causing Ama to shake her head at me.

"Did you not hear your grandma before we left?" Before we left for Detty Rave, Grandma Lily rattled off all the ways we could get into a car accident if we weren't careful. Ama kept reassuring her that this wasn't her first time driving the one-hour journey, but Grandma Lily was insistent that Osei or Will should be the one to drive us. Since Will is coming late, and Osei's car is full with the others, Aunty Naa had to convince her to let us go, but Ama had to swear on a bible that she'd drive carefully.

I chuckle, remembering the theatrics. "You know I'm only kidding. If we got into a fatal car accident because of reckless driving, my dad would find a way to bring me back to life just to kill me again for being careless." I look at my phone, half expecting to see it ringing because I mentioned him. Between the festivities in Accra and his nonstop hours at the pharmacy, we haven't found the time to have our call, and I'm growing more anxious as we continue to play telephone tag.

"Everything okay?" Ama asks, noticing I've gone quiet.

"Just thinking about my dad," I admit.

"Don't worry; you two will get your chance to talk soon," she reassures me.

Ama and Uncle Emmanuel finally had a heart to heart in the days following Christmas. From what she told me, he's still a stereotypical Ghana dad, stubborn in his ways and void of emotion, but he acknowledged his neglect and said he would try to do better to mend his broken relationship with Aunty Ellen.

"I hope so," I mutter, biting my bottom lip. I felt level-headed when I first told Grandma Lily I'd talk to him, but as time passes, I fear I will only explode during our first interaction.

"Come on, let's talk about something less depressing," Ama says. "You and Kelvin seem to be progressing along nicely."

Involuntarily, a sigh escapes my lips. It's loud and heavy and shocks both myself and Ama. She whips her head at me, and I quickly cover my mouth. Where the heck did that come from?

"Um, is there something you want to tell me?" She turns her attention back to the road but glances at me from the corner of her eye.

I look up at the rearview mirror. The girls are still fast asleep, and Whitney has even started drooling, but the sight of dribble running down her chin does little to cheer me up.

"Have you ever," I start, my fingers itching as I fiddle with the hem of the biker shorts I changed into after Detty Rave. "I don't know, caught feelings for two people at once?" I whisper, fearful to hear the words at any louder volume. Ama is silent momentarily, presumably thinking of how best to respond to my question that has seemingly come out of nowhere.

"Well, no. I haven't," Ama finally replies. "Are you, um, do you have feelings for someone that's not Kelvin?" Ama asks gently, but a groggy voice filters up to us before I get a chance to respond.

"I mean, isn't it obvious that she likes Osei?'

I can't bring myself to turn around, but I already know it's coming from the one person who would join a conversation they're not part of.

"I was asking Robyn, Whitney," Ama says sternly, her eyes flicking to the rearview mirror and then back to the road. I can hear Whitney stirring around and consequently waking Mo and Chelsea in the process. Great, now everyone is up for this painfully embarrassing conversation. Of course, I don't mind Chelsea hearing it because I would have brought this to her eventually, but Mo? She seems nice enough, but I don't feel comfortable airing out my dirty laundry in front of her yet.

"Sorry," Whitney remarks, sounding the least bit apologetic. "You guys were talking so loudly and woke me up. Anyway, I have no idea why you would want Osei when Kelvin is trying to give you the world. Besides, anything is better than a local."

I wrinkle my nose, wondering when I asked for her approval, but I don't say so.

"What's wrong with someone who lives in Ghana?" Ama asks, subtly correcting Whitney's choice of words in a way that only Ama can. Now fully awake, Chelsea comes to her sister's defence.

"Dating a boy from Ghana is not bad per se, but look, dating is hard enough as it is. And even though we are all Ghanaian, we know how difficult it can be to date someone from back home. It's honestly a huge culture shock for most people."

"Especially for someone like you," Whitney adds sharply, and her words land like a hot slap across my cheek. I try to whip around to face her, but my seat belt tightens against my chest, limiting my mobility.

"What the heck is that supposed to mean?" I huff, unbuckling my seatbelt so I can glare at her. Chelsea quickly interjects. Her voice is abnormally high, and her arm flails out beside her as if to protect her sister from my wrath.

"I think what Whit means is since you're only half Ghanaian and didn't grow up in the community, there's just certain things that you're still coming to understand."

Okay, ouch. I stare at my best friend, my face scrunching

with hurt and betrayal. Please tell me how you really feel, Chelsea.

"Take it from us, Robyn," states Whitney, tilting her head like a preacher about to read a verse to a congregation. "We know a lot of girls who have tried it, and their relationships always end in tears because their mindsets were just too different. One girl from our church almost gave up her whole career and life because the guy she was seeing couldn't understand why she would rather work than be a stay-at-home mom."

Mo nods at Whitney's account before adding one of her own. "Another guy we met a few Decembers back fell madly in love with one babe and brought her back to the States. They married, had kids, and appeared to have a normal, happy life. The minute she secured citizenship, she took the kids and sponsored her secret boyfriend from Ghana." I watch as horror fills Chelsea's face as if she herself is the man Mo is talking about. "I'm telling you, that man was never the same. You see him now, and he's like a zombie. He lost everything!"

"I mean, that sounds awful, but I'm sure that's not everyone's experience," I counter as I glance over at Ama, hoping she'll back me on this. Besides, didn't Chelsea say something about Whitney having a horrible experience one December? Maybe she's just projecting her fears onto me.

"Sure, there are one or two good stories, but from what I can see, it's always easier to stick to what you know," Whitney concludes, crossing her arms. "Listen, all we're saying is falling in love with a boy back home during December in Ghana is a risky game only rookies dare to play. Don't be that rook, Robyn."

The sound of Apple's FaceTime ringtone floods the car, and Whitney pulls out her phone to answer it. Whoever's on the screen causes all three of them to squeal loudly.

"Oh my gosh! You didn't tell me you're in town," Whitney shouts at the person.

'Hiiii," Chelsea sings, leaning into the screen.

"When did you land?" Mo asks, clamouring over Chelsea to get a better view.

Distracted by the person on the phone, our conversation abruptly ends. I turn around, refasten my seatbelt, and sit back to reflect on everything they've said.

I have no experience with guys my age who were born and raised in Ghana. I've only recently met Africans my age who are from the continent, and even then, it's a Nigerian girl named Bisi. Bisi is an international student who's in the same program as me and we always find common ground with hair, music, and schoolwork. And while Kelvin may have been born in Ghana, he's so Canadian-ized that I've never thought twice about whether he's from here or there.

Osei's the only one who's lived in Ghana his whole life. I know at first he wasn't my favourite person, but I don't think it had anything to do with where he's from. But what if what Whitney's saying is true? Are our lives that different? Are we really worlds apart?

"Don't mind them," Ama says, interrupting my thoughts. She brings the car to a lull as a young woman holding hands with two toddlers crosses the road, and uses the opportunity to look at me directly.

"Whether he's from here or not, just be smart about it. Ultimately, you're still young, but if you feel like you have more feelings for Osei than you do for Kelvin, then you should be honest about it. To both of them."

When the woman crosses, she turns onto a dirt road and rolls down our windows. I know Ama's right, but how can I be honest when I don't fully understand what I'm being honest about? Do I like Osei more than I like Kelvin? Kelvin has always been straightforward about how he feels about me, while Osei, on the other hand, sends me mixed signals. First he flirts with me, then he says we're better off as friends. It's hard to know for sure where he truly stands.

Weighing my options I sigh deeply, and my lungs stock up on the salty air that welcomes us to the seaside town. We're moving slowly up a winding road, swerving around potholes every few feet and at the top of the hill lies a stretch of newly built beach houses. They're bright with fresh white paint and stretch three stories high, but 'house' is not the proper term for the mansion perched on a grassy mound facing the Atlantic Ocean. The modern structure boasts oversized windows and an unconventional slanted roof that opens up to reveal a vast balcony.

"Oh shit, Rob! I knew Kelvin had money, but you didn't tell us he was a proper d-bee," cries Whitney as she pokes her head between Ama and me, trying to get a better look at the enormous property.

"First of all, back up," I say, nudging her gently. "And secondly, a what?"

Ama chuckles as she pulls the car in front of the house.

"D-bee is short for *Dada ba*. A rich kid living off their daddy's money."

I don't respond because I don't have to. We both know that describes Kelvin to a tee.

Ama slows down in front of the oversized rectangular doorway before turning off the ignition. The sound of the gravel crunching under the weight of the tires must have somehow travelled throughout the house because the door swings open just as we get out of the car. A shirtless Kelvin is strolling towards us in white slides, with a much more clothed Jojo, David, Osei and Kuukua tailing him. Seeing them both right in front of me makes my entire body prickle like it's being poked with a thousand needles. How am I supposed to make it a whole weekend under the same roof as Osei and Kelvin while I try to sort out my stupid feelings?

"You guys made it! Welcome to my little slice of heaven," Kelvin says. His Ralph Lauren navy blue swim trunks hang dangerously low on his torso, showing off his tawny, razor-sharp v-line.

"Robyn," he says, opening my car door. My name rolls off his tongue smoothly like freshly whipped shea butter. "Look at how effortlessly beautiful you are."

It's a lie, but I grin anyway. After the festival, I'd thrown on one of my oversized T-shirts, biker shorts and Crocs. I'm hardly making a fashion statement right now. He steps toward me and takes my hand in his, and it takes everything in me not to untangle his fingers from mine. I hate that I don't feel comfortable holding hands with Kelvin in front of Osei, but I don't want to create a scene, either. Ignoring the discomfort settling beneath my skin, I turn to Osei, his sister and friends to make the necessary introductions.

"Hey, David. Hey Jojo! This is my cousin Ama," I say, resting my free hand on her arm. "My friend Chelsea in the blue and her sister Whitney in the orange. And the one in green is Mo, Whitney's friend," I say, pointing out the girls by their various athletic sets.

"Hi," they sing, their voices in perfect harmony.

"Kelvin, this place is stunning," coos Whitney, forcing her body between us so we have to release each other. I have to fight the urge to drag her out of the way by her Brazilian bundles.

"Do you mind showing us around?"

Whitney blinks her lash extensions at him so fast that I fear she might fly away. Actually, no, I'm not afraid of that. Her flying away right now would be lovely.

Much to his surprise, she doesn't wait for a response to link her arm with his and turn him toward the house. Mo also takes Jojo's arm, and Chelsea hands her travel bag to David, following Whitney's lead. Ama and Kuukua link arms while laughing behind them, while an exasperated Kelvin swivels his head back at me as they walk away. I can't help but giggle at how adorable he looks in distress. Don't worry, Kelvin, I'll come to your rescue soon.

"You two are cute," Osei's voice bursts through my inner dialogue, reminding me he's been standing there the entire time. An internal furnace flushes against my cheeks, realizing he just witnessed that interaction. The awkwardness in the air is as thick as the smoke I saw coming from burning garbage when we left the city this morning. Avoiding his remark, I focus on heading towards the trunk of Ama's car instead.

"Come on, let's just get these bags inside."

twenty-three

IF THE MARBLE island in the beach house's kitchen looks like it belongs in a Restoration Hardware catalogue then Osei, who stands next to it, looks like the model hired to help sell it.

He can't see me from where I stand, but I have an ample view of his side profile as he pops bright green grapes into his mouth. He's still in the sleeveless tank he was wearing earlier, and it's hard not to stare at the stretch marks that run across his upper arms and trail onto his slim, yet muscular chest. Observing him, I wonder what it would be like to press my lips against them. Does his skin feel as soft as it looks?

Shit, shit, shit. Robyn, you need to quit thirsting over this damn boy!

I take several deep breaths to clear my head, then beeline toward the fridge as if I didn't see him sitting there and wasn't fully fantasizing about him just moments before. I can feel his eyes boring into my back, and I try my best to ignore him. But when I pull open the fridge door, I instantly notice the top shelf is fully stocked with countless bottles of pear-flavoured Alvaro.

"No way," I shriek, pulling one out. "Kelvin didn't mention picking any up when he went on his food and drink run."

"That's because he didn't get any," Osei says nonchalantly from behind me. I slowly close the fridge and then turn to face him.

"Let me guess," I start, smiling against my better judgment. "All you?

"All me," he confirms, tossing another grape from the bowl before him into the air and catching it in his mouth. He angles his body to parallel mine, and a wide grin spreads across his face. The sight of it alone causes thousands of butterflies to ricochet around my heart and I know I can't deny it any further.

I *really* do like Osei Mensah.

This. Is. Bad. No, this is downright catastrophic. My mind whirls with all the horrible outcomes of being trapped in a house with the two boys I know I have feelings for.

How can I even begin to figure out who I like more when they're both right here, only further confusing me with their good looks and very different personalities? I need to shut this down, and I need to shut it down now.

"Well, I don't know what you're trying to prove, Mr. Mens—" I start, but the sound of Osei's laughter fills the kitchen, abruptly cutting me off.

My mouth snaps shut as the sound of his laughter satisfies my eardrums, scratching an itch I didn't even know I had.

"Geez, Robyn. Can you relax for once? I'm not trying to prove anything. It's a drink. If you like it, then enjoy it," he says as if it's the only obvious conclusion to draw.

I know he's talking about the Alvaro he bought me, but my mind can't help but apply the same principle to my current predicament. If I like something, I *should* enjoy it. I can deal with the consequences of overindulging after. With a smirk, I crack open the bottle and take a long, cold sip.

* * *

Once everyone is all settled in, I take Osei's advice and push my worries to the back corner of my mind. Instead, I focus on running around like a carefree child.

From the house to the beach to the backyard pool and back, we play volleyball and compete in swimming races. We fill our bellies at lunch with gourmet burgers and fresh-cut fries cooked on the spot—courtesy of the Williams' private chef—and soak in the sun until we can't take the heat anymore.

When it's just me and Kelvin, I'm in full-blown lover-girl mode, but whenever Osei catches me alone, we don't hold back, our banter becoming more addictive by the second. Half of me feels like I'm teetering on the edge of a steep cliff. But the other half, fueled by a combination of Pear Alvaro and Pineapple Smirnoff Ice, doesn't seem to care. It plans to enjoy every last drop until I can't stomach it anymore.

Now that it's New Year's Eve, we sit sprawled out in the Mensah's entertainment room, split into three teams to play an intense round of our version of Aux God. I sit between Osei and Ama on the brown leather couch and take in the faces around the room. Each one gives me more satisfaction than the last. It grows within me like a wildfire, and I relish in it. I know that the chance of this exact moment happening again is slim to none, so I want to be able to remember it forever. Picking up my Praktica from beside me, I snap the moment of the faces around the room. The laughing, the yelling and the playful gazes are happiness personified.

"*Chale*," Jojo cries. "How can you say Ghana's biggest

contribution to rap music is Stormzy when a whole Sarkodie *dey*?"

"Nah, bro, Sark? He fall off longest," yells Osei in defence and I have to stifle a laugh. Of course, the rapper Osei chooses is the one who's known for singing his melodic hooks and choruses. An R&B stan, through and through.

"Well, it doesn't matter what the two of you think," Whitney barks at Jojo and Osei from the leather recliner. "Pretty boy, and I get to decide who's right."

Kelvin rolls his eyes at his newly-minted nickname, from his seat at her feet, but I know he secretly loves it. That boy is pretty, and there is no denying it.

Chosen by a random generator website, Ama, Mo, Osei and I are on one team. While Kuukua, Jojo, David and Chelsea are on the other, a trio of Kelvin, Whitney and Will make up the remaining team. We wait as they huddle together, deliberating which Ghanaian artist has done more for rap music.

"Having fun?" Osei asks, turning to me.

"Sure thing," I say, trying not to think about the feelings I've been working so hard to keep at bay.

"Look at that! You do know R&B," grins Osei.

"Huh?"

"Oh, come on, you don't know 'Sure Thing' by Miguel?" He's groaning now, his face buried deep in his palms.

"She's just uncultured, Osei. Don't mind her," teases Ama.

"Oh, whatever." I cluck my tongue at my cousin. Obviously, Ama has known Osei longer than I have, so they've had plenty of time to bond, but it's still nice to witness their sibling-like dynamic with my own eyes.

"I always knew you were my fave cousin," laughs Osei, leaning over me to give her a high-five, and I playfully push them both off of me.

"Okay, okay, we've decided our winner," calls out Whitney, summoning the room's attention.

"Even though Stormzy has contributed a lot to rap music," starts Kelvin. "The question asked which 'Ghanaian' has had the biggest contribution to rap music, not which 'British-Ghanaian'." He concludes with a smug look, daring us to debate his ruling. I glance over at Will, and he shrugs, making it clear who decided the winning vote.

"Ah, are you serious?" Osei's voice is laced with an unreasonable amount of disgust.

Kelvin doesn't answer. Instead, they stare each other down and the daggers being shot across the room make the stakes of the game seem much higher than they're supposed to be.

"Okay, I'm officially over playing this game," Ama says, jumping up to break the tense moment of silence and blocking Osei from Kelvin's view. "Who's hungry?"

* * *

Kelvin chooses a nearby chop bar he says he and his parents used to frequent for dinner. The wooden sign on the entrance has 'The Lord is Merciful: Authentic Ghanaian Dishes' carved into it, and the smell of peppery, smoked meat wafts around us. It's vastly different from the restaurants I have been trying with Kelvin and the girls, but I don't think they seem to mind, as giddiness bounces around the group.

"*Afenhyia pa*," greets a scrawny dark-skinned man passing by the entrance.

"*Afe nkɔ b3to yɛn*," everyone but me replies. I still can't hack the holiday greeting response yet. There's no hostess at the front, so we move inside, searching for a space to accommodate us all. I trail behind the group, taking pictures on my Praktica as we find seats. Snapping a picture of the friendly face behind the bar and a young couple sharing a meal at the table near the side entrance, I don't realize I'm holding my breath until I hear the click of the shutter. Not knowing how the picture will come out makes a thrill run down my spine. The image can either develop like a work of art or an out-of-focus waste of film. I pray all the pictures come out as good as they look in my viewfinder, but there's no way to know until it's all said and done.

"I already know what I'm getting. Banku and tilapia," I hear Jojo shout, and I turn my head in his direction. Everyone is seated at a long, dark green, wooden table with a bench on one side and five chairs on the other. "Don't even look at my plate if you order anything else. I won't share o!" He yells as he slams the menu down on the table.

I begin to laugh at his dramatics but fasten my mouth shut when I realize the only remaining spot is between Osei and Kelvin. I throw a desperate glance in Ama's direction, but it's no use. She shoots me back a 'Sorry babes, you're on your own' look, before looking at her menu.

Okay, this is nothing you can't handle, Rob. Just three people enjoying some food. My feet feel as if they're moving in slow motion as I approach the table, and they both jump to stand, their hands landing next to each other on the back of my chair.

"It's cool, bro," quips Kelvin. "I got it."

Osei holds on to the chair for a second, hesitating as he glances down at Kelvin's hand and then back at me. Begrudgingly, he releases it and gingerly sits back down.

"Thanks," I whisper sheepishly to Kelvin once I'm seated, and he pushes me in.

"No worries, babe."

When I look up at the others, I notice all the girls are looking at everything but us, trying their hardest not to laugh.

I already know that when we get back to the beach house, they will go on non-stop about this.

"What's everybody eating?" I ask while placing my camera on the table. Maybe steering the conversation to everyone's favourite topic will lighten this mood that's descended over our group. "Well, everybody, minus Jojo, since he's already announced to the entire bar what he's having."

"Fufu," they all say, their voices synchronized perfectly.

"Oh." My gaze drops to the cement floor. I was eyeing something tried and true, like fried rice and chicken, but now I'm not so sure.

"Is it a bad time to admit I've never tried fufu?" My voice comes out barely discernible as I sink deeper into my chair. Once again, my lack of Ghanaian experiences has me in the hot seat of shame.

"What!" Eyes bulge out at me from every angle. Well, from everyone but Chelsea, Whitney, Will and Kelvin.

"Ei, so you're telling me you've never had fufu and light soup on a Sunday morning after church? You don't know what you're missing *o*," David cries, letting out an incredulous gasp.

Kuukua shakes her head at me as if she doesn't even know the person sitting across from her. "You must try it tonight," she insists.

"Guys, don't forget she was raised by her father who is not Ghanaian, so it really shouldn't be this shocking." Kelvin's voice is reassuring, and I shoot him an appreciative smile. "Order whatever you want, babe," he insists, nodding at me.

"I don't know, Robyn. I agree with Kuukua on this one," Osei says, sitting back defiantly. "If you've never had it before, why not try it?"

"It's really not that serious," counters Kelvin.

"So you don't think she should try something different for once?" Osei shoots back.

"I didn't say that. I just—"

I drop my menu on the table and put my hands up in defeat, agitation quickly rising within me. "Just drop it, okay! I'm gonna get the fufu," I say, my voice slightly rising as regret inches up my throat like bile. If this is what it feels like when two of the cutest boys on this side of the globe are vying for my attention, I'm not sure I want it anymore.

Once the waiter who welcomed us earlier returns to the table to take our orders, the others start talking amongst themselves while we wait for the food. Kelvin, Osei and I on the other hand, sit in unbearable silence. I can sense the two boys sulking beside me, and my earlier regret morphs into a growing annoyance. What is their actual problem? I know Osei said things haven't been the same ever since Kelvin moved to Toronto, but it's starting to feel like they're using me to take out their unresolved resentment on each other and I want no parts of it.

When the server returns to the table, he and another waiter are carrying big plastic bowls filled to the brim with water in one hand, and little bottles of soap in the other. They place them down in a row on the middle of the table, and I watch as the water in the one in front of me shifts as it settles from the motion.

"Here, let me show you how to use it," says Osei, dragging the bowl towards him. "Since we eat fufu with our hands, we use this water to rinse off before and after we eat."

"I'm pretty sure she doesn't need someone to explain how to wash her hands," Kelvin grunts, rolling his eyes as he pulls it back.

"You guys," I say anxiously, eyeing the water sloshing around in the bowl. It's awfully close to splashing out and landing all over my camera.

"Bro, just let it go," Kelvin insists, tugging it back towards him, his mouth forming into a hard line.

"Kelvin," I try to warn, but it's no use. Osei is already pulling it back with immense force in his direction.

"You first!"

It happens so quickly that we barely have enough time to jump out of the way when the bowl tips over and water floods the entire table.

"Osei!" I exclaim, jumping back and out of my chair.

"Woah! You both need to chill the fuck out!" Will demands, but even his stern voice is not enough to undo the damage. My camera was first in the line of contact, and it's now drenched in water.

Slowly turning to my left and right, I see both boys are overcome with remorse. Osei's eyes desperately plead his case, and Kelvin's head hangs low with shame, but neither acts move me. It feels as if flames have engulfed my entire being, and if I don't get out of here, I will burn this whole chop bar down.

Snatching my camera off the table, I push past their outstretched arms and take off at full speed without looking back.

twenty-four

THE HOUSE IS EERILY QUIET, but I don't mind the silence. After what I've just witnessed, solitude is what I need right now. Luckily for me, no one has chased me back, so I have a moment to myself to process everything that just occurred.

Kelvin and Osei better count their lucky stars that there seems to be no damage after drying my camera. Well, the truth is, there's no way to tell until I send the roll for development, but until then, I'm trying to remain optimistic.

I still have four images left to shoot for my photo essay, and now, more than anything, I want to use my mom's camera to take them. The only remaining shots to take are a picture of Ama and me, a self-portrait of myself and two more that require the man I'm still trying to get a hold of, my dad.

Settling into the leather lazy boy, I curl my feet underneath me and bring the camera close to my belly. It's a weak attempt to ease the discomfort stirring inside, but I desperately need to feel any kind of pressure against it to keep me calm.

The boys have left me both bothered and conflicted. They've each texted me some form of an apology, but I've left their messages on 'read'.

This evening has shaken me entirely, and it's starting to feel like all my butterflies have been set free. I feel tempted to cut them both off and force myself to forget any of this ever happened. Maybe Whitney was right. What happens in Ghana is just better off left here.

A deep sigh escapes my lips as I blink back tears. Despite everything I've discovered, there's only one voice I want to hear right now. Dad has always been the person I've run to in times of crisis, even when he can only help in ways I don't always understand. This time apart is the longest I can recall not really talking to each other and it's beginning to hit me that up until now, I haven't allowed myself to miss him.

I've been too caught up trying to unearth his secret to feel anything other than rage toward him. But at this moment, I know I need him. I pull out my phone and tap on the FaceTime app.

"Dad," I yell when he answers on the last ring. I'm in shock that I've caught him.

"That's my name," he says dryly. Usually, his snarky sense of humour has me rolling my eyes, but right now, it's what I need to hear. My breathing steadies at the sound of his familiar voice. It's been so long since I've heard anything remotely like it.

From what I can see, he's sitting in his usual spot on the living room couch, and I can hear the Toronto Raptors losing again in the background—no surprise there.

"How are you doing? How are things at the pharmacy?"

"Things are finally slowing down around here," he says, glued to the screen. "The interns all caught the flu back-to-back, so we were short-staffed for a minute there."

"I'm sorry to hear that. But hopefully, you can get some rest now that things have settled down."

"No time to rest when I have a daughter to send to pharmacy school," he declares, finally looking me in the eye for the first time since the call started. "Speaking of school, any update on your grades yet? Today is New Year's Eve. How hard can it be to upload some grades?"

From the way he looks at me so expectantly, awaiting one specific response, I know that it's time to come clean. I'm tired of all the secrecy and deceit. I just want a safe space to figure out who it is I want to be and the only way we can do that is by being honest with each other about everything.

"Dad, I know about Mom," I exhale. He doesn't reply but doesn't look back at the television either. Instead, he mutes it, everything around him going painfully still.

"I know she was a photographer, and this isn't news to you since she was studying photography when you met. I saw her dark room and her work. I even used her camera, and as much as I am annoyed that you kept this from me, I'm sure you had your reasons for not telling me, so I forgive you," I say, the words leaving my mouth in a frustrated stream.

"I'm not mad at you for keeping this from me. I mean, I was mad, but I'm not anymore, because to be honest with you, I've been keeping things from you too. Dad, eMarks hasn't been down. I've known what my grades were all semester, but I've just been too scared to tell you that I'm not doing as good as I was in high school. No matter how hard I study, how many all-nighters I pull, or how many office hours I attend, I just can't seem to keep up. The only thing I've been doing really well in is this photography course I've been taking, and my professor thinks I have a real shot at doing it professionally. But in order for me to do that, she thinks I need to apply to this one-year fellowship in London that can help launch my career."

There's no response to my confession and his eerie silence is almost enough to stop me from continuing.

"So, um I've been shooting out here for the application and

everyone–Ama, Chels, even Grandma Lily–thinks I have what it takes to get in!"

At this, he makes a slow grumble that sounds like a mangled laugh and there's a look on his face I can't quite decipher.

"Your grandma encouraged this?" He clarifies.

"Um, yeah," I say hesitantly. "Dad, I really am sorry for keeping this from you and for lying about my grades. I know that was wrong of me, I do, but Pharmacology is just not for me. I know how much it meant to you for me to follow in your footsteps, but I'm tired of running from what my heart desires."

My eyes flicker around his facial features for something to hang on to, any emotion to keep me going, but they remain unwavering. Instead, I dig deeper within myself, channeling my mom's passion to give me the extra push I need not to back down.

"I'm good at this, Dad. If I can go all in and dedicate the next chapter of my life to working on this, I could make a real living from it. And if you don't believe me, we can crunch the numbers, or I can show you what other professional photographers are making these days. Trust me, I wouldn't be suggesting this if it wasn't a viable option."

There's a long moment of silence as Dad absorbs my pleas. His face still lacks emotion, so I suck in my cheeks, hoping for the best as I wait for his response.

"Robyn, when your mom was alive," he starts, then stops. He breathes in a long air stream through his nostrils, and my bottom lip trembles. He's never even come close to saying those words before. I've begged my whole life to hear him acknowledge her, but I've never considered just how painful doing this is for him.

"When your mom was alive, she was the centre of my

universe. It was as if I didn't even realize I was living in darkness until I met her, and suddenly, everything was as bright as day. She was optimistic and wide-eyed and hated me right off the bat," he says, slightly chuckling.

"I represented everything she didn't believe in. Structure, realism and staying within the lines. She shocked me, if I'm being honest with you. People from Ghana and other parts of Africa are usually raised just like us West Indians. We follow the rules society has set for us by excelling academically in school. But your mom wasn't like that. From a young age, she had a father who put a high-voltage battery in her back that made sure her brightness never dulled, even long after he passed. I don't know if it was out of curiosity or envy, but I couldn't help but be drawn to her. Eventually, I won her over, and we rubbed off on each other. I helped her structure her dream so she could profit from it, and she helped me to be less rigid and enjoy life. Or at least I thought that's what was happening." He shakes his head with a faraway look in his eye.

"There was a period while she was pregnant with you that she didn't have much energy for anything, but after you were born, it was as if a flip was switched, and your mother turned back into the careless young adult I first met. Without warning, she quit her stable bank job before her mat leave ended and went into photography full time. She was back to being the woman who didn't care if there were consequences to her actions. The woman who would whisk you away to Ghana for an entire summer to chase a creative idea she had in a dream, not considering how I felt to be left behind, paying all the bills and maintaining our home. I know you don't remember much, but in the years leading up to her death, our marriage was falling apart, Robyn. She lived for herself and didn't care who got burned in the process. She didn't care about you and especially not about me," he spits out, each new revelation haunting me more than the last.

"The day she died was the same day I realized I had reached my breaking point. But there was no discussion of separation or divorce. I didn't have the time. In typical Nana fashion, she left us abruptly and unexpectedly. There was no sickness or warning beforehand. She was just here one day and gone the next."

Tears are forming in his eyes now, the whites behind his irises slowly turning bloodshot.

"That day, I left to pick you up from school, and your mom was sprawled out on the living room floor with her work printed out around her. She had been invited to show at a local gallery and had been painstakingly deciding which photos she would be submitting for the last several days. When we got back, we found her lying on top of her work, dead from a heart attack."

I'm speechless. I was there the day she died. Not a single word can form on my lips. The story I've waited so many years to hear has snatched my voice right out of my throat in one swift motion.

"I don't know what you know about her people and funerals, but Robyn, I swear to you, I wouldn't wish a Ghanaian funeral on my worst enemy. We had been so distant in those last few years I didn't know your mom had cancelled her life insurance and taken out several loans to launch her business. So, while I'm finding this all out, I have your grandma demanding I pay to fly your mom's body back to Ghana for the funeral. Going on and on about colours and traditions I couldn't care less about. I was a new widower, a single father, and expected to plan a funeral on an income being eaten away from the debt your mom left behind. At that point, I was too drained to put up a fight. Your mother may have been a light, but she shined so bright she burnt me out in the process," he sighs.

"She left us with absolutely nothing, Robyn. I brought you to Ghana for the funeral but washed my hands clean afterward. I didn't want you or me to be sucked in by her family ever again. I've worked hard to get us out of the hole your mother put us in, Robyn. And I'm sorry if I didn't do it the way you would have liked, but keeping this from you was the only way I knew not to hurt you. To me, you knowing nothing was far better than you knowing the truth. So, while I'm not happy with you for lying to me for several months, if you want to go ahead and follow in her footsteps, be my guest. I will even support you financially through your undergrad, but I promise you, Robyn, whatever you do after that—if it resembles your mother's path, I want nothing to do with it."

* * *

My dad's words ring in my ears long after we get off the phone. I've even moved her camera far away from me and onto the coffee table, unable to even look at it. How can something as small as this bring my family so much pain?

"Robyn, are you in here?" Osei calls out from the door of the entertainment room. I don't respond, but he comes in anyway. Thankfully, no one follows him.

"Everyone is out by the ocean," he says, as he sits down on the arm of the lazy chair I'm seated in. "Ama told us to give you some space, but I just wanted to check on you. Did you get my text?"

What text? Oh yeah, his apology. Right now, water damage to that cursed camera is the last thing on my mind, but I nod absentmindedly to acknowledge that I read it. Osei sighs with relief.

"Okay, good! I truly am sorry, Robyn."

I don't feel up to talking about what transpired tonight between the three of us, but I don't want to think about my mom either.

"Were you at Detty Rave?" I ask, blinking back tears. He eyes me oddly for abruptly changing the topic, but decides not to question it.

"Yeah, I was. A classmate of mine was covering the show, so he brought me backstage for most of the night," he says carefully as if he's deciding if this is what we should be discussing right now. He hesitates, then takes the plunge. "Rob, is everything okay?"

I nod quickly, brushing over his concern. "Backstage for what?" I ask, pushing him to distract me further. His eyes scan mine with contemplation and I force myself to look genuinely interested in wanting to hear about his backstage experience. It seems to do the trick because he begins to go off on a tangent about it, instead of continuing to question me.

"Oh, Robyn, I wish you could have seen it. It was incredible. My friend Paa was a backstage photographer, and he let me shoot with him."

When I hear this, I want to smack myself. Of course, Osei was backstage for something photography related. It's the last thing I want to talk about right now, but Osei has already started running his mouth at 1000 kilometres per minute, and there's no way to reel him in now.

"The rush I got from being back there, capturing artists in the moments before they hit the stage? Man, I can't stop thinking about it. It's made me realize that I can't let this dream go to waste. I want to go all in and bet on myself, so I've decided to apply for the fellowship."

My body tenses as he makes the announcement, and a weak "good for you," is all I can manage to blurt out. He continues to talk, but my brain is working too hard trying to reboot from the conversation with Dad to catch the details of what led him to this decision. I don't have the energy to feign any emotion. Not joy. Not shock. Not envy. I simply don't care. Not when I know for certain it won't be worth it in the long run.

It's all so clear to me now. The reckless decisions my mom made destroyed the people around her, and I refuse to let the same thing happen to me.

"I just want to thank you, Robyn. For pushing me to apply. You might have thought that it was me helping you, but truthfully, you're the one who was helping me."

The air seems to shift between us as Osei stares at me with an intense focus. I gulp, knowing full well that this conversation has nothing to do with cameras or photography.

"So in the spirit of trying new things and taking chances, I know I can't let you go back home thinking all I want is to be your friend," he says.

"You don't?" I whisper, my head spinning from the revelation.

He nods slowly. "I'm not going to lie to you, Robyn. It was pretty clear to me from the moment I first saw you."

"Osei, please don't. I-I-I can't right now," I stammer, squeezing my eyes shut. I can feel my body tensing for the impact of another confession. I don't know if I have it in me right now to hear any more.

"Please, Robyn. If you'll let me. I just need you to hear this."

My heart stumbles over its own rhythm at the sound of his soft plea. This vulnerable side of Osei, the one I only get to see at his most raw moments, might as well be my kryptonite. I slowly peel my eyes open and when our eyes meet, he exudes the warmth of a thousand sunbeams.

"I was immediately attracted to you, Robyn. I mean, who wouldn't be? But after working on your photo essay together and getting to know you better, I knew you were more special than I initially thought. Robyn, you deserve a connection that is well-rounded and wholeheartedly cared for. Something that goes beyond just chemistry and compatibility. That kind of connection doesn't happen overnight, and it definitely doesn't happen if I come off too strong, so I fell back. But I guess my ass fell back too far because before I knew it, you were in Kelvin's arms, and when I tried to pull you out, we all fell into this tangled web."

"Every time I tried to pull away, and trust me I tried, I found myself drawn to you even more," he admits softly. "It was almost as if whenever we interacted you were curling that cute little finger of yours, calling out to me to follow your lead. Daring me not to be attracted. As if that's even possible," he scoffs, his voice dropping an octave.

I swallow dryly, taken aback by the person he's describing. It doesn't sound like the person I've been my whole life. No, this depiction of me is damn right terrifying because it sounds so similar to the woman Dad described to me moments earlier.

The instant adoration. The magnetic pull. Do I have the ability to dull Osei's light in the same way my mom did with Dad?

I'm not sure, but I do know that I don't want to find out.

But before I can even find the words to express how I feel, Osei jumps up from the armrest almost as if a bright flash has gone off and snapped him back to his senses.

"Look, you are in no way obligated to respond," he says frantically, an embarrassed expression settling across his face. It is so unlike him; I wince at the sight of it. "I know this is a lot to take in, considering everything going on between you and Kelvin, but I just didn't want you to go back home without knowing how I truly felt."

Osei rubs the back of his neck as he backs up in the direction he came. "I'm going to give you some space now, but I'm here for you if you um, need me," he rambles, before turning on his heels and leaving me in a complete daze.

twenty-five

KELVIN FINDS me curled up in a fetal position, but before he can even reach me, the sounds of the others come trickling in behind him. My body freezes with panic—not wanting to be seen like this—and Kelvin immediately notices. He moves swiftly, helping me to my feet and leads me to a side door that takes us outside without anyone noticing.

Once outside, we wander down a stone-covered path that starts as steps near the property and transforms into flat ground. It leads us toward a secluded beach area where thick, tall palm trees border the path and sway gently in the coastal night breeze. Where the stone steps meet the sand, we kick off our shoes and approach the ocean. As my feet slide into the sand, he doesn't ask me any questions, and I don't offer any answers. His quiet demeanour reminds me of why I like him as much as I do. Even in silence, Kelvin feels comforting and familiar. Kelvin feels like home.

"This place is gorgeous," I croak as we slowly stroll on the beach, watching the waves cascade. They dance at the shore, pulling back like a bow in an arrow, then launching toward us again. At night in Accra, the clouds seem to stretch on and on, but here in Kokrobite, there appear to be fewer white puffs and more blue sky stretching over the horizon. It's all so idyllic.

"It is, isn't it," he whispers, and I feel a strong need to be closer to him than I already am. I lean into his firm body, and he wraps his arm around my shoulders. His body, pressed tightly against mine, feels solid and dependable. Someone you know you can count on. Someone who makes sound decisions based on logic and reasoning, not feelings that can change at the drop of a hat.

As I lean on Kelvin, the realization that he's the only support I need, makes me feel safe enough to bare my soul. He remains quiet as I unravel in front of him and open up about how my mom destroyed Dad and their union, not caring about how it would affect me in the long run. I cry out about the role my grandma played in my prolonged distance from my family, and detail how she treated Dad during one of the most challenging chapters of his life.

I tell him I've decided to not go through with the fellowship application and that I want to pursue my original plan to study pharmacology. As long as I'm my mother's daughter, there's no way that her inherent selfishness isn't ingrained in my DNA, so I need to do everything I can to ensure that it never surfaces, starting with not following in her footsteps.

He doesn't tear his gaze away from mine as I tell him about the feelings I caught for Osei. Not only does he deserve to know the truth, but I also want him to have it. A relationship will only work between us if he knows exactly what he's dealing with. All of me, without restraint. If he doesn't want to continue after that, so be it, but he can never say I didn't try.

"I just want to say thank you for being honest with me. I know opening up like that isn't easy, so I want you to know that I meant it when I said I'll always be your biggest fan,

Robyn. As long as you remain transparent with me, within reason, I'll try my best to understand you."

I wrap my fingers over his knuckles and squeeze them gently to acknowledge his words without interrupting him.

"I'm sure you can tell from how stupid I was acting earlier, but I knew I was losing a part of you to Osei. You've always been open with me, but sometimes it felt like you were giving me the a-side of Robyn, and he was getting both the a-side and the b-side."

"I truly am sorry, Kelvin. I hope you can understand that it wasn't intentional. The b-side was just the things that I thought only Osei could relate to. But I no longer care about photography or the fellowship. I know what I want now. It was foolish of me to reconsider anything just because I had a few bad grades. I'm going to buckle down next semester and get back on track."

"It wasn't foolish of you, Robyn," he says, stroking my cheek. "You're human. Sometimes, we accidentally take a longer route to a destination we already know, but that's okay. All that matters is you made it."

I try to muster up a genuine smile, but even I know it doesn't reach my eyes. I know I've made my decision, and I'm ready to stand by it, but the weight of all the emotions from the last day makes it hard to rejoice in it just yet.

"Thanks, Kelvin," I say weakly.

"And don't worry about your grades. Next semester you will have a personal tutor who will make it their mission to ensure you pass each class with flying colours."

"I will?" I ask, scrunching my nose in confusion. "Wait, who?"

"Me," he smirks. "I will give you my old assignments and study notes. Or we can go through each course reading line by line. Whatever you need, Robyn, I'm there for you. I'm just glad you didn't give up on the goal you've been working so hard toward. It will all pay off, okay? It always does," he says, reaching out to angle my chin toward his mouth.

I force my smile to stretch wide, wanting Kelvin to know how grateful I am, and he leans down, slowly planting kisses all over my face. He traces my jaw with his lips, spending an elongated moment at my neck, and I sigh as a ripple of pleasure leaves my body when he sucks on the skin, allowing myself to revel in the pleasure of his sweet touch. Kelvin seems to know my body better than I do.

We make out on the beach, the lower half of our bodies getting soaked by the ocean waves until we hear cheers and loud popping noises. Startled, we break apart to see firecrackers racing to the sky, bursting over the beach house community in an extravagant flourish. I turn back towards Kelvin with my most effortless grin of the night plastered across my lips. I know more than anything this is where I need to be. No one else matters.

He lowers his head, his breath warm and familiar, as his lips hover over mine,

"Happy New Year, Kelvin."

"Happy New Year, Robyn. I have a feeling this year will be your best year yet," he says, sealing his toast with a long, steady kiss.

twenty-six

BY THE TIME Kelvin and I trek back to the house, the others have fallen fast asleep in the entertainment room. The scene reminds me of the slumber party Chelsea threw for her sweet sixteen. The fond memory bubbles to the forefront of my mind and makes me smile when Kelvin and I peer into the unlit room. They've yanked out the couch cushions and brought down all the duvets and pillows from the five bedrooms to create a massive mattress in the middle of the ample space. Will and Ama are closest to the door and are spooning near a snoring Jojo. Whitney, Mo and Chelsea sprawl out, so their limbs lie on each other, and Kuukua and David are the furthest away, sleeping nose to nose. But when it clicks that Osei is not among them, my throat burns. Where is he? Did he ring in the New Year alone? I shake my head as the impending thoughts try to take over my current state of happiness. Snap out of it, Robyn! Osei's whereabouts is no longer your concern!

"Since Chelsea is down here, do you want to sleep with me tonight?" Kelvin asks, interrupting my momentary spiral. His voice is hushed as he draws the door closed, his free hand still in mine. Even with the door closed Jojo's snores are still audible in the hallway. "I'd hate to leave you alone after the night you've had."

He's right. I don't want to be alone right now. Even though it's late, and this day has been taxing, sleep has not come for me yet. I'm scared to be alone with my thoughts right now. What if they try to convince me I've made the wrong choice? Feeling Kelvin's firm body next to mine should be enough to keep my mind occupied through the night.

"I'd love that," I murmur, squeezing his palm with all the strength I can muster.

His room is the primary bedroom where his parents stay when they visit. After living among the hustle and bustle of Accra for seven years, they knew they wanted to be far away from the city when visiting Ghana. According to Kelvin, it's their little slice of heaven on earth.

The California King mattress sits in a mahogany wood, canopy bed covered in a thick duvet. Four pillows, two shams, and one throw blanket crowd the headboard. I let Kelvin shower first, needing a moment to collect myself so I don't pass out from the steam. So by the time I've showered, dried off, completed my night routine and thrown on the UofT T-shirt he left out for me, I find him bobbing in and out of sleep.

"Navy blue looks good on you," he sleepily murmurs as I crawl into the empty spot beside him on the bed. His T-shirt falls just under my bum, and it's not a regular stiff Gildan like the shirts we got in our Frosh Week welcome bag, but the good nylon stuff. Something Kelvin probably paid a lot of money for at our school's campus store.

He stretches his arm across the pillow, and I fill the bare space with my body. We're both radiating so much body heat that I can't help but wonder how long we'll be able to sleep in this position before we have to pull apart.

"Thank you," I whisper into his bare chest, but there's no response. He's already fallen fast asleep.

* * *

Several hours pass by and I'm still blinking in the darkness burdened by my non-stop thoughts. As Kelvin snores beside me, I toss and turn, trying to find an optimal position to block them out, but recollections of every moment that has led me to this point still sneak through. Even things I haven't thought about in years come flooding back. Like the conversations with the therapist my elementary school suggested I visit in the weeks after my mom's death. She told me memory loss after experiencing the death of a loved one was normal, and after a few weeks, my memories of my mom and I would come back, but they never did.

For so long, I felt as if something was wrong with me for being unable to recollect them. I can't help but wonder if that was my brain's way of protecting me from the crippling reality of who she was. Even at eight years old, my body didn't want me to continuously re-live the pain of being betrayed over and over again.

But here I am, ten years later, relieving it anyway, because I chose to go looking for it. I went and opened the Pandora's box housing all my mom's dirty little secrets, and now nothing will ever be the same because of it.

As sunlight begins to spill through the curtains, I'm still wide awake, but when I hear Kelvin rustling beside me, I force myself to shut my eyes. I don't want him to know that I haven't slept yet, and I know just one look at me will give it away. The last thing I need is for him to fret over me more than he already is.

I lie still as he climbs out of bed and enters the bathroom, listening to the sounds of his morning routine—the toilet flushing, the tap running, the whir of his electric toothbrush. It's not long before he re-enters the room, and I can feel him plant a kiss on my temple before leaving. With Kelvin gone, I attempt to reopen my eyelids, but they feel too heavy to lift. Giving in to the exhaustion, I finally allow my mind to decompress, but just as I feel myself about to drift off, two familiar voices burst through the bedroom door.

"Knock, knock," they say in cheerful tones.

I groan as they enter, then peel my eyes open to see Ama walking toward me with a plate full of breakfast food and Chelsea trailing behind with a glass of apple juice. They place them on the nightstand beside me and hover near the bedside.

"Kelvin told us you weren't feeling well," Chelsea says, leaning over to connect the back of her hand to my forehead. He's right. I'm not feeling well, but it's not the kind of sickness that can be confirmed by checking a temperature.

"Yeah, sorry for missing the countdown last night," I mumble, slightly turning away so that her hand slides off. I haven't been able to get what she said to me on the drive out here out of my head, but I can't bring myself to address it right now. Sorry, Chels, but you rank at the bottom of the list of worries taking up space in my mind right now.

"Oh, okay," Chelsea stutters. Even though I can't see her, I know what rejection looks like on her face. It automatically causes her bottom lip to stick out and her button nose to crinkle. Well, at least she knows how I felt in the car.

"We just wanted to let you know that everyone is finishing up with breakfast, and we'll be leaving soon." Ama relays the information calmly yet professionally, which I can only imagine is how she runs Surplus Ghana. "Will you be riding back with us or Kelvin?"

"You," I say quickly. There's no way I'm getting stuck

between Osei and Kelvin again. Not when Osei is still waiting for a response that I know I can never give him. That is a guaranteed disaster. My game plan is to get back to Grandma Lily's, avoid Osei by hiding out for the next two days, then rush to the airport and leave all of this behind me. If I don't respond to his texts or calls, eventually, he'll forget about me and move on, right? It's not foolproof, but it's the best I can come up with running on zero hours of sleep.

"Okay, sounds good. Get ready and meet us downstairs in the next thirty minutes."

When I hear the sound of the door softly closing, I force myself to sit up in bed. It's not that I don't want them to know what's happening with me, but I can't hash it all out again. Not now, anyway.

I find my bag and neatly packed clothes at the foot of the bed. It's in nowhere near the frantic state I had left it in. I pull out my black Lululemon tights and a faded black cropped tee with an image of a spitting Tupac. It feels like a fitting outfit, considering the series of unfortunate events. Once I've changed, freshened up and repacked, I peek out the bedroom door, checking the hallway for the one person I don't want to see.

Great, everyone is already gone. I need to dash down these stairs and get into Ama's car, and I'll be one step closer to being back home. As I turn my back to the hallway to pull the door shut behind me, a hand lands on my shoulder and from the weight of the palm alone, I already know who it is.

"Hey, Miss Carter," Osei sings cheerfully, as if nothing transpired between us the night before. I turn around slowly, trying to delay our confrontation for as long as possible. When we're finally face to face, I notice the door to the room Osei was staying in down the hall is no longer closed. Was he waiting this whole time for me to come out?

"Osei," I reply, fiddling with the straps of my bag. I'm not sure what else to say. Are we going to address what he confessed? Because I don't understand how he is acting as if everything is normal between us right now.

"Well, I just wanted to apologize again for last night," he says.

"You do?" I ask.

"Yeah of course. I hope everything is okay with your camera so you can finish your application. Wouldn't it be so amazing if we both got into the fellowship?" My heart plummets as Osei's eyes gloss over. Of course all he cares about is that stupid camera. When he begins to detail all the galleries he hopes to visit in London, a faint ringing starts to go off in my ear. As the sound gets louder, it transforms from a high pitch ringing to a clear taunting. *Do you want to be like your mom, Robyn?* It says. *Live a life so bright that it burns everyone around you, Osei included?*

"No,' I shout abruptly. It's the first thing I've said since Osei started rambling, and the volume catches him off guard.

"No?" He repeats back to me. The devastation on his face almost crushes me, but I know I can't stop here. I have to keep going.

"I said no, Osei. There's no *us*, and there's no London. I'm not applying anymore." I start for the stairs, trying to brush past him, but he grabs my arm, stopping me in my tracks

"Wait, what happened? Robyn, talk to me. What made you change your mind? Is it something Kelvin said? I always knew he didn't get it."

"No," I yell, jerking my arm away from his grasp. "None of this has anything to do with Kelvin. I just decided to stick with my original plan because this is what *I* want."

"This isn't like you," Osei says, his body trembling as he

shakes his head furiously. He's getting worked up now, and his forehead is glistening with sweat.

"Well, maybe you don't know me as well as you thought, Osei." It's a lie. He and I both know it, but it's what I need for him to hear right now.

"But I do know you, Robyn. I know what makes you tick and what makes you smile," he shouts, exasperated by my constant rebutting. "All the things you think no one else can see, I see them clear as day. I see every single inch of you, Robyn. The full damn picture!"

Time seems to still as the severity of his words hit me, because I know it's the truth. From the first day at the airport, he's seen right through me despite my best efforts. But whether he's telling the truth or not doesn't matter anymore. I need something, anything else, to be the reason as to why I'm pushing him away and not applying for the fellowship. Because I know if I tell Osei what I found out, he will not let this go without a fight. He won't let me sink my dream. He'll do everything in his power to keep it afloat, and I don't need that right now. I can't afford to keep venturing out into unknown waters. I can't afford to keep making the same mistakes my mom did.

My mind flashes to the conversation with the girls in the car, the things Whitney said about me being with Osei, and I know I can use it. It makes me physically ill just thinking about it, but maybe if I cut him where I know it will hurt, he will let me go. That way, we can both be free.

I take a deep breath, mentally load the ammo that I know will cause irreparable damage, and then set it off.

"No, Osei. You *think* you see me, but what you see is the version of me you think I should be. It's the same thing you've been doing with Kuukua and Kelvin, and now you're doing it to me." I shake my head with so much conviction that I almost believe it. "I don't want to end up with a guy like that, Osei."

Disbelief seems to shock him to his core, and he staggers slightly.

"A guy like what, Robyn?"

"Like you, you . . ." I stammer, ". . . you locals!" My sneering tone delivers the low blow like a spray from a machine gun. "You all have secret agendas. Trying to get with girls like me, only to want to change them to fit whatever mould suits you!"

My words couldn't be further from the truth. In fact, Osei has been nothing but understanding, emotionally intelligent and not afraid to drift from the status quo. But I need to walk away. I can't keep going down this path he so desperately wants me to walk on. In order for me to walk away, he needs to let me go.

"Wow. Is that how you truly feel about me, Robyn?" Osei is stricken with disbelief.

"I said what I said," I say, tilting my nose in the air, fighting to keep my tone unbothered.

At this point, Osei's shock seems to have settled in. He lets out a slow, manic chuckle, making drawn-out claps with the same hands he was trying to console me with not less than twenty-four hours ago.

"Well done, Robyn. You truly had me fooled. I didn't think it could be you, but I should have known better. This shit is typical for girls like you."

"Now, what is *that* supposed to mean?" I shout.

"You know the girls who come down here and turn their nose up while they go looking for guys like Kelvin. You heard his foreign accent, saw his flashy shit, and went running into his arms. He fits the bill on paper, so he's the one for you, right? That's something I expected from someone like Whitney, Robyn, but not you," he scoffs.

The look of discontent on his face makes my insides boil, but I try to force myself not to take it personally.

"But me, a guy from Ghana," he beats his chest with his palm. "The same Ghana that *you* claim to love. The country you would 'trade your life in Toronto for' isn't good enough for you? If that isn't some bullshit, I don't know what is!"

This one stings, making me respond honestly.

"That's not fair, and you know it!"

"Okay, so if that's not the issue, why did you choose him over me?" he asks, a fierceness flashing through his eyes. "Don't lie. I know you felt what I felt every moment we've spent together. The hours we've put into your photo essay? The late nights? The different conversations all over your grandma's property? You mean to tell me you haven't felt any of that? I may live halfway across the world, but I know what we have transcends distance, Robyn. I see you, and you see me."

I'm trying to hold back my tears, but there's no use. The emotion is charging throughout me, making me fully believe that the lie I've told Osei is why I'm ending this.

"Osei, please. You know it would have been too hard."

"So because it's hard, it's not worth fighting for? Just because something appears to be easier doesn't mean it's what's best for you. But whatever, Robyn, continue to lie to yourself if it makes you feel better. I'm sorry I'm not good enough for you beyond your little holiday, but I can't control where I was born or raised." He shakes his head, and I watch as anger subsides into something that looks like disappointment. "You know, now that I think of it. You're right, Robyn. You don't care about photography. No, you're just obsessed with optics. But real life isn't a picture. You don't always get to choose the outcome."

His words whip me, pulling off chunks of my skin as they

land. I know he's only responding based on what I've said, but hearing this still hurts. It leaves me raw and bleeding, but I can't back down now. I let my frustration flow full force ahead, like a runaway train with no one in the locomotive, and let it steer me to destruction.

"Just face it, Osei," I say, gesturing between us. "You and I? It was never going to happen. I have learned my lesson. What happens in Ghana should stay in Ghana. You are not worth the trouble."

I spit the last part out and watch the words burn as they land on Osei. Closing his eyes, he nods slowly as if finally accepting that after the words we've just exchanged, there is no way we can go back to the people we once knew.

"Message received, Robyn. Loud and clear. You go with Kelvin, and I'll ride with Ama. We wouldn't want you to have to be around people like me for any second longer, would we?"

With that, he sprints down the stairs and out the door without looking back, leaving the house as empty as I feel.

twenty-seven

I SPEND the next two days with my cheek pressed to the pillow in Grandma Lily's guest room. The overwhelming weight of disappointment makes my limbs feel heavy, pinning me down to one spot. I never would have thought that this trip would go up in flames like this. I don't want to discard all the memories I've made, but it's hard not to see them all as facades now that I know the truth. But I guess I got what I wanted. I came here to find out what tore my family apart and I got my answers and then some. I just never considered that the truth would be something I never wanted to know.

My phone buzzes from under my pillow and I have to force myself to scrounge up the will to pull it out from underneath my head.

> **KELVIN**
>
> Hey, babe. I just landed at Pearson. Waiting to get off the plane.
>
> How are you feeling? Are you packed for your flight?

JESSICA CARMICHAEL

> **ROBYN**
> Yup. Just ready to get out of here.

KELVIN
I know how you feel. By the end of the trip, I was missing my bed more than anything. Don't worry, you'll be leaving in no time.

'In no time' means tonight, but even that doesn't feel soon enough. My packed suitcases are waiting at my bedroom door and I'm counting down the minutes until I can get out of here. Once I'm back home, I have to focus all my energy on bringing up my grades and finishing my first year of university like I did in high school, with the highest GPA in my program. This vacation was a setback that had me taking a detour with too many unnecessary stops. Once I land in Toronto, all that changes. I'm getting my life back on track.

A light rapping on the door causes me to stir in the direction of the sound.

"Can I come in?" Grandma Lily asks softly from the other side. I want to say no, but I know better than to be disrespectful in her own home.

"It's not locked," I reply and the door groans open, mirroring my inner feelings as Grandma Lily shuffles inside. It's the first time we've been alone together since I got back from Kokrobite and the tension in the room can't be missed. I'm assuming she knows I've spoken to my dad from how distant I've been since coming back. If someone were watching us without context, they'd probably think we weren't related. As if we didn't just spend the last few weeks bonding and catching up on all the years we lost out on. If it wasn't so sad, it would be funny how quickly we fell back into our respective roles as relatives who barely speak.

I sit up in bed as she settles into the rattan armchair,

smoothing the wrinkles of her black dress with her tiny palms, and I realize this is the first time I've seen her in a colour that doesn't instantly brighten my mood.

"My dear, how are you feeling? Will you be okay to fly?" Her face is curious as she holds my gaze.

"I'll be fine to go home," I say, hiding behind a mask of impassivity.

Grandma Lily nods and a pregnant pause follows, both of us unsure what to say or do next. From the moment we first reconnected, Grandma Lily and I had an immediate bond, so I don't know how to navigate this new-found awkwardness.

"Well, I think I'll go look for Ama," I say, slowly peeling off the covers to reveal the airport outfit I put on first thing this morning. The flare of my black yoga pants hits the ground as I swing my feet to the floor. I'd rather sit at my gate for four extra hours than endure this discomfort.

"*Tena ase.*"

She says this calmly, but the familiar Twi phrase makes me freeze, momentarily calculating how much trouble I'll be in if I disobey our family's matriarch. It doesn't take much mental math to determine it won't be worth it, and as I sit back down, the bed seems to sink for an eternity under my weight.

"I love my daughter, but she wasn't perfect," Grandma Lily starts, not facing me. She's looking out the window, her gaze locked on the water tank that sits at the side of the house. "When Nana was doing something she loved, she was like a driver who never checked their blindspots—speeding at full force, not caring who she clips in the process. In her teenage years, I spent so much time chasing after her. Cleaning up the wreckage she left behind. But this wasn't the same deal for your grandfather. The way Nana talked about her passions would suck people in and cause them to make decisions they wouldn't otherwise choose. Your dad fell for *that* woman, and so did your grandfather," she says firmly, turning back to face me.

"I struggled to understand this when she was younger. When I wanted her to do education, your grandfather pushed her into the arts. They had that in common, the two of them. He knew what it was like to be unable to follow his dreams." She looks at me and smiles fondly. "He wanted to be a musician but was a terrible singer, so instead, he wrote music. But music wasn't something his parents wanted him to do, so when his good friend brought him the printing company idea, he jumped at the chance to make something of himself."

"He wasn't like the other businessmen in Ghana who wanted to be rich for status. He couldn't care less about any of that stuff. He wanted to be so successful that his kids could do whatever they pleased. After he died, I knew I had to let my feelings about her dreams go, or else I would lose Nana, too. She needed someone to step into those shoes, so I did that. I don't know if it made any difference to her, being that I had spent so many years opposed to her dreams, but in those final years, especially after you were born, I tapped into the support he was known to give her until the day she died."

Dad had scoffed when I said Grandma Lily supported me. Maybe Mom told him what it was like to grow up with Grandma Lily constantly discouraging her. It probably sounded ironic to hear me say that.

"I didn't always handle everything right, Robyn. When she died, the pressure I placed on your dad for the funeral and the burial was not fair, especially because he is not a Ghanaian, and our customs are not the same. But I only found out months after the funeral that your mother wasn't as successful as she claimed to be. While we thought she had finally launched her full-time photography career and was reaping the fruit of our labour, she was taking out loans she knew she couldn't repay. But it was too late, and the damage was done. When the funeral was over, and her body was buried, your father didn't want us to speak to him, or you, ever again."

A fragment of a memory filters through my brain as she says this. Dad is carrying me in his arms at a burial site as dirt is being thrown onto a glossy black casket. The air is muggy, and loud wailing is coming from all directions. Dad's face is stony, but not in the way you'd expect from the widower of the deceased. He almost seems to be burning with rage. I squeeze my eyes shut, trying to block out the image. I have tried so long to conjure up any memory of my mom, our time in Ghana, and her funeral, but I've never been able to. Now it's back, and all I get is a clear visual of how much pain and suffering my dad's been through at the hands of my mom and her family.

"If I could go back and change everything, I would, but I can't, Robyn. None of us can. The only assurance we can hold on to is that even in all her flaws, your mother left this earth being the person she wanted to be. I don't say this to tell you to follow in her footsteps, but so that you can understand that life doesn't have to be black and white. You don't have to live one way or the other. There are a lot of good things that come out of being well-balanced. I saw what I did wrong with your mother and vowed not to make the same mistakes with my grandchildren. I will always encourage you and Ama to follow your dreams. Even with other kids like Osei, I go out of my way to tell him to do the same thing,"

My body flinches at his name, still raw from the lashings from our last conversation. "But all I ask is that you do so wisely. It's okay to live in the grey, Robyn. Listen to your father, advocate for yourself and don't make your mother's selfish mistakes."

I mull over her words, still unsure what I should be feeling right now. So much information has been dumped on me these last few days, and I need time and space to think it through.

"Thank you, Grandma," I mumble. I don't know if I'm genuinely thankful for her words just yet, but I know it's what she wants to hear. And deep down, underneath all my rage, I still want to be able to give that to her.

"You are welcome, my child," she says, rising from her seat, looking satisfied with our conversation. "Ama tells me you have one more photo to do out here. One of the two of you?"

"Oh, well, I'm not applying to the fellowship anymore, so we don't have to do that."

"How about for memories, then? You and Ama deserve that much. Come on, don't be hasty," Grandma Lily retorts, sounding like herself again. She exits the room in her usual waltz, and I reluctantly rise from the bed, walking into the shea butter-scented haze she leaves behind.

twenty-eight

ALTHOUGH THE DRASTIC drop in temperature is vastly different from the city I've just spent the last four weeks in, landing on the frigid, slush-covered runway makes me feel an immense sense of relief. My life is finally back to normal.

After waiting an hour for my luggage, it finally whirls out of the carousel. Once I gather my bags and enter the arrivals area, I'm surprised to see Dad there waiting for me. Not idling in the pick-and-ride like I expected him to, but inside among all the other families carrying their rose bouquets and signs. The sight of him standing there, eagerly scanning the crowd of travellers, causes a jolt of childlike energy to course through me and makes me run into his arms. He stumbles back when I collide into him, but his grip is firm around me, and I hold on like I'm afraid he might dissolve in my hands.

On the drive back to my apartment, I listen as he rambles on and on about the pharmacy, but for the first time in my life, I don't mind it. It makes me realize how easily he can read me. The way he instantly knows I'm not in the mood to talk about what happened on my trip. I feel a pang of guilt when I remember how just four weeks ago our easy bond wasn't enough for me. Never again will I take that for granted.

The next morning, Bisi greets me as I enter the lecture hall on our first day back to school.

"Welcome back!"

"Thank you," I reply, my teeth chattering as I peel off my jacket and sit beside her. "How was your winter break, Bisi?"

Both of Bisi's parents are Nigerian diplomats who moved their family to Toronto when Bisi was in high school. When her parents and siblings moved to Berlin this past summer, she decided to stay and go to UofT instead of following them. When she first sat next to me in Introduction to Physics II last semester, I could have sworn she was a model who got lost on her way to the runway. Her legs stretch for miles, and her angular face is a makeup artist's dream canvas. This semester, our course schedule is practically identical, so we'll definitely be seeing a lot more of each other.

"A bummer since I didn't get to go back home like you, Miss Ghana! I was *tuned* in to your Instagram stories! Like, I could not tear my eyes away! I had no idea you got down like that! I never see you at any parties around here." She jokingly swats me on my arm, but I can't bring myself to laugh when I think back to my trip. She's right. I was quite literally having the time of my life up until the last few days.

"Yeah, I guess Ghana brought out some alternate version of me or something. But it's back to regular scheduled programming for me. I have a lot I need to focus on this semester," I whisper as our professor Dr. Garcia walks down the steps and to the front of the room. Dr. Garcia, a man whose age is only evident by the mound of salt and pepper curls on the top of his head, is one of the most tenured professors in the faculty.

Nervous whispers follow him as he descends the steps. It's widely known across the department and on every rate my prof site imaginable, that the man does not play around when it comes to Biology. As Dr. Garcia bends over to connect his laptop to the projector, Bisi leans toward me, blissfully unaware of the minute panic attack that just coursed through my body.

"Well, all I know is that Robyn 2.0 better have come back home with you," she says in a hushed whisper, before turning to pull out her MacBook. I have to fight the urge to scoff at the suggestion. Becoming Robyn 2.0 is the last thing I need this semester.

"Hello everyone and welcome to Molecular and Cell Biology," Dr. Garcia barks. His voice booms around the auditorium and silences us all. "In this course you learn the key principles and concepts in molecular and cell biology. Not only will there be lab work to go along with weekly lectures, but at the end of each class I will be assigning a short quiz to test your general knowledge. This course won't be easy so if you're in fear of failing, I suggest you leave now."

His eyes narrow as he looks around at the sea of first year science students and for a second, I swear his eyes lock with mine. I gulp nervously but don't dare to move a muscle. It's almost as if he can smell the fear emitting off of me or something. When no one leaves the room, Dr. Garcia nods approvingly at our frozen state.

"Lovely. Let us begin."

* * *

"I don't get it. What is going on between you two?" inquires Jalen as he shovels a handful of sweet potato fries into his mouth. He's sitting across from Devon and me in our usual booth at El Furniture. The food here is less than mediocre, but everything is under ten dollars which makes it practically

Michelin Star worthy to broke-ass university students like us. I grimace as pieces of the crispy fried vegetable land all over his shirt. He may be the one for Chelsea, but his table manners are not it for me.

"Nothing," I say, handing him a napkin, since the person who'd typically do it isn't here yet. As usual, Chelsea is running late from her placement at her aunt's hair salon across town. With both boys studying at Toronto Metropolitan University, all three of our campuses are located downtown, so we try to meet up at least once a week for lunch.

"It's definitely not 'nothing' because Chels won't stop talking about how something shifted between you two while you were in Ghana. She kept going on and on about it last night and made us wake up late for practice this morning," Devon insists, shaking his shoulder-length locs.

He and Jalen are both starters on the TMU men's soccer team and are quite literally consumed by it. "And I don't want to hear about it again tonight so you two need to make up quickly." As he says this, I notice the puffy bags under his eyes for the first time. Damn, Chelsea must have really worn him out.

With me spending the last two days in Accra hiding and Chelsea on last-minute market runs with her mom, we didn't get to see each other before leaving Ghana. And since she spent last night at the boys' place, today will be our first time seeing each other in person since the beach house incident.

"Yeah," Jalen chimes in. "She kept on mentioning an Osei and a Kevin."

My eyes roll as he mispronounces Osei's name as 'O-see'.

"It's pronounced, "Ow-say," I say, not bothering to hide my annoyance. But it's only after I say this that I realize he also said Kelvin's name wrong.

"Who's Osei?" Devon asks, before I can correct him. He

wiggles his eyebrows with a mischievous curiosity and I glare at him in return. He's really making me regret agreeing to remain friends after our failed dating attempt right now.

"Yeah, Robyn, who's Osei," mocks Jalen. From his teasing tone alone, I'm confident that my best friend, better known as the snake, has already filled him in with everything and anything he needs to know about the boy I've been trying to forget.

"Osei is no one," I state, my lips forming a tight line. I hate that I can feel my body start to go weak from just repeating his name, and if it weren't for the colour of my skin, my face would probably be as pale as the salt in the shaker in front of me.

"No one?" Chelsea asks, magically materializing at our table. She slides into the seat next to her boyfriend and shoves the oversized cosmetics bag she takes to her Co-Op placement in the space between them. "Since when was Osei no one, Robyn? If that's true, I clearly missed something." Her tone is laced with genuine confusion that would typically get me to spill my heart, my soul and a whole lot more, but today I'm not moved.

"Well, things change," I shrug, focusing on scraping out the remains of my spicy vodka rigatoni with my fork. With my lack of response, the boys lose interest in our conversation and start discussing Premier League soccer instead. Chelsea, on the other hand, leans toward me while brushing her latest hairstyle, a chestnut curtain bang wig, out of her eyes.

"Does this have something to do with what we were talking about in the car on the way to Kokrobite?" she asks in a hushed voice even though I know the boys aren't listening. "Whitney was just joking, Rob."

I look up from my empty plate to meet her eyes. "And you?" I ask, trying to appear casual as I lick the vodka sauce off my fork. "Were you joking when you said I wasn't a Ghanaian?"

"Oh, come on," Chelsea sighs, throwing her hands up in defence. She sits back in her seat. "That's what you're mad about? It wasn't like that, and you know it."

Chelsea has never given me a reason to think otherwise, but right now, it feels easier to be upset over this than to go into the details about my mom, Kelvin or Osei. Deep down, I know it's a copout but I couldn't care less.

"Yeah, well maybe I don't," I shrug, standing in front of my seat and tossing a twenty dollar bill on the table.

"Robyn, just talk to me," she pleads and when I look into her eyes, I almost break down in the middle of the restaurant.

"I know that's not the real reason you're this upset," she insists. "I saw Osei's face when he got into Ama's car, and he mentioned you weren't applying for the fellowship anymore. What happened at the beach house? What happened between you and Osei?"

Throwing my backpack over my shoulder, I shift my weight from one foot to the other as I pick up my jacket.

"Can we just talk about this later, Chels?" I sigh, while zipping myself into my coat. I know she won't drop it until we do, but this should be enough to get her off my back for now.

"Fine. Later," Chelsea agrees, with one last pointed look before turning to her boyfriend to steal fries off his plate.

Once I escape El Furniture, I decide to spend my time between classes hiding out in my favourite library on campus, but it's only when I get to the building that I realize I have to pass Dr. Beal's office and the media lab in order to get to it. I pick up my speed as I approach the lab. Hopefully, if I zoom past fast enough, Dr. Beal won't see me passing, through her office's big window that faces the hall.

My heart rate steadies as I'm able to sneak by without incident then instantly quickens when I see her wild curls bobbing behind a sea of students heading in my direction.

When she spots me, she stops in her tracks smiling wide. As usual, she's dressed more casually than my other professors, in her bright blue skinny jeans and faded black Rolling Stone T-shirt.

"Robyn Carter. Just the student I was looking for. I wanted to tell you how happy I am that you decided to apply for the fellowship. I have such a good feeling about this."

"Hi, Dr. Beal," I mumble, looking down at her scuffed Vans. I'm seriously regretting replying to her email right now. I don't think I will be able to handle hearing the disappointment in her voice when I tell her that I've changed my mind.

"I, um, decided not to go through with the application after all."

"You're joking, right?" She sounds so surprised that I'm scared to look up at the face that probably matches it.

"Um, no. I just decided it's best if I continue down the Pharmacology path. I've had this dream of becoming a Pharmacist for a long time now and I want to stick with it. I've put in too much work to deviate now," I confess, mustering up the courage to look Dr. Beal in the eye. Her neat eyebrows furrow as I say this, but that's the only thing that indicates she's disappointed in me.

"If that's what you want, then I support your decision," she says with so much kindness I might cry. "This is your life after all, and you have to do what's best for you. I will be rooting for you regardless. Have a great semester."

She smiles at me one last time, then calls after a student behind me. My feet feel pinned to the ground as she walks away. Wait, is that it? Isn't she supposed to push me for more information or ask me why? I don't have photography this semester, so it's not like she'll have any other opportunity to press me on this. Is she really giving up on me just like that?

Up until this point, I've felt so assured in my decision to

not go through with the fellowship, but the realization that Dr. Beal was the last line of defence and even she has given up, has shaken me in a way I wasn't expecting. My bottom lip trembles as it begins to hit me. It's official. The fellowship is now a thing of the past.

twenty-nine

I SPEND the first half of the week dodging Chelsea by camping out at the library until ungodly hours, but even I know it's getting ridiculous. While my anger directed at her has subsided, I've yet to figure out how to tell her about what happened at the beach house. Since becoming best friends, we haven't gone this long without being in constant communication before. Petty arguments here and there, sure. But nothing that's lasted longer than a few hours. It feels abnormal that we haven't spent any time together this week, especially since we live together, but now it's Thursday and Dad has summoned me home to strategize on how to improve my grades, so Chelsea will have to wait one more day.

The house is quiet as I enter through the garage. It's only half past three, so Dad is still at the pharmacy and won't be back until six at the latest. I kick off my shoes and head into the kitchen for a glass of water. He was so excited this morning when he called to confirm what time I'd be coming over. He kept going on and on about how he can't wait for us to be able to work together one day in the future. All I could do was nod as he spoke, the reality of the new semester not being any easier than the last, making it hard for me to focus on what he was saying.

While hiding out in the library, I've been trying to get ahead on my readings, but I still feel so far behind. Dad is convinced that spending at least one day a week with him to go over my schoolwork will be the thing the helps to get me back on track, but I'm already starting to have second thoughts about that. While I see where he's coming from, a part of me feels as if the additional pressure will just make things worse for me.

My phone vibrates from my jacket pocket and I pull it out to see Kelvin responding to my request to be picked up from the Ankrahs' tomorrow, instead of Dad's place. He wants to take me on our first official date in Toronto, but tomorrow is the only time Chelsea is free to talk, and luckily for me she also happens to be back home.

> **KELVIN**
> That's one more hour added to my 'Seeing Robyn Again' countdown but I think I can manage. 😉

Instinctively, my lips twist into a frown as I read his message. Kelvin's been texting me nothing but encouraging and sweet messages all week. Checking in on me and not shying away from telling me how badly he wants to see me again. If it wasn't for the fact that he's been so busy with classes and his part time job as a researcher for his Human Biology professor, he said he would have taken me out much sooner than this.

His constant support and consistency feel like something straight out of a rom-com. The actions of the leading man you're supposed to love. Something you rave about to your girlfriends, and they fall over themselves just listening to you go on and on about it. But for some reason, I haven't been able to fully bask in it.

I should be enjoying the fact that what we had wasn't just a holiday romance, and he likes me here just as much as he did in Accra, and maybe even more. Kelvin is everything I should want. If I decided to let him go, I'm sure at least ten other girls would be waiting to scoop him up. He aligns with my future and shows up for me in ways most girls my age can only dream of, yet I can't shake the lingering feeling that it's not enough.

It's like he's been miscast for the role he's playing or something. I don't know why I can't enjoy the boy that's right in front of me. Maybe I'm just being overly indulgent. Haven't I learned that you can't always have your cake and eat it, too?

I shut my eyes and shake my head quickly to divert my train of thought. Robyn, you're overthinking again. Kelvin is good to you. Kelvin cares about you. Kelvin *understands* you. That is all that matters.

I rinse out my water glass and grab my bag to head up to my room in the townhouse I grew up in. When I open my door, I'm greeted with the familiar bubblegum pink walls and white trimmings that line the floorboards. The backdrop of my childhood.

Dad always said there was no point in making any significant changes because young girls go through too many phases to keep up with, but as I stand in the doorway, I feel painfully aware of how little has evolved here over the years. When was the last time I even wore something pink? When I was twelve, maybe? I glance around the room feeling increasingly dissatisfied as I take it all in. None of this used to bother me before, so why do I care now?

Sighing, I walk over to my white L-shaped desk, toss my backpack on the bed and pull out my MacBook to get a head start on next week's readings. Once I'm seated, I open my laptop to see a notification indicating that Dr. Garcia has already uploaded the grade for our first quiz on eMarks.

I take a deep breath and click on the notification, gnawing at my bottom lip as the screen refreshes. The first quiz was pretty generic. It was just ten questions that went over the key points from the introductory lecture. Bisi even texted me after she did hers to tell me how easy it was, so I'm expecting nothing lower than 80%.

When the site finally loads, my eyes zero in on the first grade and my heart immediately sinks to the soles of my feet. 60%?! How is that even possible? I didn't feel unsure when I was taking the quiz. In fact, I was feeling quite confident from all the hours I spent going over and over the course material at the library. How is it possible that I can invest so much time and effort into this and still can't get this right?

I slam my laptop shut as I feel my palms start to itch. Without thinking, I rub them against my jean-covered thighs to draw as much friction as possible, but once again the grounding trick proves to be pointless. If it's the first week of the semester and I already feel as if I'm out of my depth, how am I supposed to survive eleven more weeks? I don't know how much more of this I can take.

A wave of sadness seems to descend upon my room and before I can even process what I'm doing, I slip out of my clothes, and trade them for the only items that remain in my childhood dresser. Once I'm in the pair of slightly tattered house shorts and my high school gym shirt, I climb into bed, curl up into a fetal position, and cry myself to sleep.

* * *

"Robyn?"

The sound of my name causes me to peel the comforter off my head. When I emerge from under the darkness, I find Dad sitting at the edge of my bed.

"What time is it?" I ask, wiping the grogginess from my eyes.

"It's half past eight. You looked so comfortable when I got home, so I didn't want to wake you, but when I realized you were still asleep, I came to check on you."

"Damn," I groan. "I wasn't planning on sleeping that long."

"That's alright. We can postpone our talk about school if you're too tired. It's just the first week anyway."

The way he shrugs after saying this looks so foreign to me that I ogle him wildly as if locs have just sprouted from his bald head. Dad has never skipped an opportunity to talk about my education. Once, when I was in elementary school, I caught a fever on the night of a parent-teacher interview and instead of skipping it, he lathered me in Vicks and made me wait in the car while he ran inside for the meeting.

"Who are you, and what have you done with my father?"

Dad chuckles and gives me an earnest smile.

"I'm just so proud of you for sticking to the plan. I know it's not always easy, but I think you'll soon see that you made the best choice," he concludes before briefly patting my leg and standing up. But his words don't stir up any sort of pride in me. Instead they make my throat burn with unshed tears. He has no idea how hard this has been for me, and even if he does, he will never truly understand.

Just as he's about to leave my room, our eyes connect in the mirror hanging above my dresser and I watch as the pride slowly falls from his face and shifts into fear. It's as if he's seeing something in me for the first time, but I'm not sure exactly what it is. I turn my attention to my reflection and realize what has him in so much shock. I look unrecognizable. A disheveled version of myself with sunken-in eyes and chapped lips from constantly being gnawed at.

"You look so much like her," he whispers, watching me in horror through the mirror. "That, that, look on your face. I'm just realizing that I've seen it on her before. Right after she got pregnant, she decided to put photography on hold to focus on raising you and I guess that with everything that was happening, I never really took in how hard it was on her. How the nine months leading up to your birth turned her into a shell of herself. It was only after she had you that her spark returned, and I was just so happy for your arrival that I completely disregarded how much it all affected her."

My mouth drops open as I watch the horror on his face in the mirror. Where is this coming from and why is he bringing it up now? Does he think I made the wrong choice? My anger flares up like a match has been swiped within me. He doesn't get to drop this on me now, not after everything I've already given up.

"Are you kidding me?"

The words come out sharply, popping the bubble we've kept around this topic since I got back, but I'm sick and tired of dancing around things. I'm tired of holding my tongue and being disappointed time after time because I have to navigate his feelings. Enough is enough.

"Are you seriously backtracking right now?" Rage rattles inside me as I watch him slowly turn around. His eyes are closed as he takes several long, deep, breaths.

"Robyn. I know you're upset, so I will let the fact that you are speaking way out of turn slide," he starts, opening his eyes to reveal they're cloudy with concern. "But you have to see where I'm coming from."

"That's just it, Dad! I'm tired of doing that," I cry. "All my life, I've tried to understand you, and it's exhausting. I'm tired of pushing past things and acting like things are okay. We've spent years tiptoeing around everything and anything that has to do with her, and now that you've finally revealed why, you're changing your tune. I tried to understand, Dad, I really did. I know you're coping with this in your own way, but what about me? Did you ever stop to think that maybe your coping mechanism would only make things harder for me?"

Hot tears are racing down my cheeks, and snot bubbles are dripping from my nose, but I don't care. Everything I've kept down has rushed to the surface, spilling out in a rush.

"Having Grandma Lily back in my life allowed me to open the door you never dared to. Suddenly, I was in a world where Mom's pictures were plastered everywhere, and her existence mattered. Then you shattered that for me by revealing the truth, and now you're trying to humanize her again? I'm not —" My voice cracks, and I pause, clearing my throat. "I'm not a baby anymore, Dad. Can't you see that I'm my own person? I know you want to protect me, but can't you see how this hurts me instead? I need the truth, Dad. I need the full picture to grieve my mom for the woman that she was. The good, the bad, the ugly. No more secrets, Dad. Let me draw my own conclusions," I croak, looking down at my hands.

My mattress depresses under his weight, and he pulls me into his body. Instantly, a loud cry releases from deep within me. Years of untouched emotion pours out and floods the room. He holds me as I wail, gently rocking me in his arms. It's the first time in a long time he's held me like this. When the tears dry up, and my sniffles are the only sound in the room, he gently curls his fingers under my chin to shift my head to look in his direction.

"Robyn, look at me."

Hesitantly, I drag my eyes to meet his gaze. I've never

freaked out on him like this before, so I don't know how he will react. With anger no longer clouding my judgment, I remember that I'm speaking to a middle-aged Caribbean man, and I clench my jaw preparing for the worst.

"First things first, no matter what happened between us, I will never run out of love for your mother."

He's staring at me so intensely that I want to shift my gaze again, but I fight the urge to break eye contact.

"Secondly, you're right. All I ever wanted to do was protect you. A part of me knew that going to Ghana would fully unlock the traits your mother passed down, and I was so scared of how they would show up in you. But I forgot that you're not just your mother's child, but mine, too. You're the perfect combination of the two of us, and I should have been able to trust that with guidance, you could follow your heart without losing yourself completely. You've proven time and time again how responsible you are as a child and a teenager. I had no real reason to believe that would change just because you decided to explore photography." He observes me earnestly before he continues to speak.

"But lastly and most importantly, I am sorry. I am sorry if it seemed like I was trying to rush you out of your grief. That was never my intention. It's hard to explain, and one day, if you have kids, you may understand, but raising a child is not easy. Raising a child alone is even harder. Every day, you make decisions that can alter your child's life and who they become. You try your best to choose the right option but don't always get it right. You hit the nail on the head, Rob. For me, it was easier not to dwell on the fact that not only had I lost the love of my life, but when I needed her the most, she left our family in ruins. I knew if I tapped into that pain, I would not have been able to be the father that you needed."

He hangs his head as he says this, his hands folded in his

lap. The man who has been a tower of strength my entire life has shrunken beside me. Reaching out to grab his hand, I give it a light squeeze, and he looks up at me with a faint smile and shiny eyes. Dad cups my cheek into his palm, a bittersweet expression on his face.

"I was forcing you to push past something you never even had the chance to process because you were in the dark for so long, and for that, I am deeply sorry," he says. "You're right. It is hard for me to accept that you aren't my little girl anymore, and I no longer have to protect you from pain. You are a budding, bright, beautiful girl becoming a young woman. You have your own feelings, dreams and way of processing things, and from here on out, I'm going to try my best to remember."

"Thanks, Dad," I sniff. "It means a lot to me to hear you say that."

"Robyn, your mom and I may have been two misguided souls trying our best to navigate parenting, but you must know we loved you more than anything in this world. She may not have always shown it in the best ways, but it was always you that she loved most. If this fellowship is what you want to do, then I want you to go for it."

"Let's say I don't get into the fellowship," I whisper. "And I want to switch to an arts program instead, will you still support me?"

"It's going to take me a minute to get adjusted to your new reality, but I'll try my best to support you. I love you and I want you to be happy, Robyn. I just don't want your head to be completely in the clouds."

"I can promise you that I don't want that either. I want to stay grounded, Dad," I insist. He's right; so much of me comes from him. My discipline, my drive, my ambition. He's instilled these traits in me, and they aren't going anywhere soon.

"Then I promise to hold you down, Rob. Not to keep you

from soaring, but so you know where home is if you ever feel like you've gone too far."

"You promise?"

"I promise," he swears, squeezing my hand tightly for good measure.

thirty

THE COOL JANUARY wind assaults my exposed face as I stand outside the Ankrahs' front door. I know Chelsea is expecting me any second now, but I'm still hesitant to go inside.

"You know you have to turn the handle for the door to open, right?" I whip around, and a smirking Jalen is at the bottom of the front steps. The hood of his light grey Moncler jacket is pulled tightly around his fair, freckled face. Jalen is part Jamaican and part Bajan, but most people assume he's half-white from his fair complexion.

"I know, I was just checking my phone," I lie. I don't know why I suddenly feel nervous around him. It's as if it's the first week of high school again, and I've learned that my new friend Chelsea comes packaged with a built-in boyfriend, her middle school sweetheart.

"Come on. Let's get out of this cold," Jalen shudders, moving past me and opening the front door. Chelsea almost always leaves it unlocked, even though Aunty Lydia has told her a million times not to. "I know your girl. She's been waiting for you."

Trailing behind Jalen, I take in the familiar home. I've spent so much time here after school these past four years, it may as well have been my own home. Walking past the sitting room, I smile when I catch the family pictures of the Ankrahs over the years, lining the floors. The first time I visited, Chelsea had asked me if I found it funny that Ghanaians had so many pictures in frames but never hung them.

At the time, I didn't know enough Ghanaians to know if that was true, so I just shrugged. Something she seemed to find even funnier. But she wasn't laughing at my expense. It's never like that with Chelsea. Chelsea never makes me feel like the odd one out. All she's ever wanted was to immerse me in the culture she grew up in. She makes her mom bring me to every hall party, encourages her Dad to quiz me on Twi words, reminds Will to bring me gifts from Ghana, and even makes Whitney send me the latest trending songs from her uni parties. Chelsea has never pitied me for what I don't know, all she wants is to help me where she can. It was unfair of me to think—even for a second—she would suddenly switch her tune.

"Chels! Where you at? Rob is here!"

Jalen's voice bellows as we enter the kitchen. As I wait awkwardly at the bottom of the steps, he disappears into the pantry. Jalen is the only person more comfortable at the Ankrahs' family home than I am. After several moments pass, I hear Chelsea's heavy footsteps padding down the stairs.

"Hi," she mumbles, as she gets to the bottom.

"Hi," I mutter back, fiddling with the zipper of my jacket.

"Oh, you two have got to be kidding me," Jalen sighs with a mouthful of Doritos.

"Shut up," Chelsea and I cry, flashing scowls in Jalen's direction as chip pieces fall from his mouth and litter the kitchen floor. Turning back to Chelsea, I'm not surprised to see that she has a slight smile, identical to mine, on her face. We've been in sync for four years. One minor setback doesn't change that.

"Come on," she sighs, nodding towards the stairs.

I follow Chelsea to her bedroom, drop my jacket on her chair and we both plop down on her bed. In high school, whether we were talking, crying or laughing until our stomachs hurt, you could almost always find us here lying side by side like this.

"Chelsea, I'm so sorry," I start, turning toward her side profile.

"No, I'm sorry," she replies, facing me. She props her head up with one hand, her elbows sinking into her sheet-covered mattress.

"For what? I know you weren't coming from a bad place. I was just all up in my feelings and took my frustrations out on you."

"No, Robyn. I should have been more understanding. I don't know why I get like that whenever Whitney's around, but it's not an excuse. I should have been backing you, not her. I should have been way more empathetic because it was clear that you were going through it."

From her earnest expression, I can tell she's missed me as much as I missed her. I sit up to fill her in on everything that has unfolded, from finding out about my mom, cutting off Osei, and deciding to go through with the fellowship application after all. By the time I'm done, she's upright, moving closer to hug me.

"Aww, Robyn. I hate that you had to go through all this alone. I am so sorry I wasn't there for you." Her words reverberate into my neck.

"It's not your fault," I say, into her embrace. "You didn't know because I didn't tell you."

"That still doesn't make it okay. As your best friend who

knows more than anyone about your complicated feelings regarding your identity and your mom, I should have never let anyone speak to you that way. Not even my older sister. And to make it up to you, I'm here to help you with whatever you need to complete this photo essay. I'm scheduled to work this weekend, but I will call in sick so that I'm all yours."

"You'd do that for me?" I ask, genuinely surprised. I know how much Chelsea loves her part-time her job at Sephora. She always brags about the fact that she gets to stop older Black women from using the wrong shade of foundation. She calls it her contribution to the beauty industry.

"What else are best friends for? I'll even make Jalen and Devon help too. It's Friday, and the application is due on Sunday at noon, right?

I nod.

"Then you need all hands on deck," she exclaims, jumping up from her bed to find her phone. She waves it at me when she locates it sitting on the counter in her ensuite bathroom. "If I don't catch them before they start playing FIFA, we'll never get a hold of them."

She strolls back into her bedroom, tapping her phone quickly, and my phone vibrates when I receive the message she's sent to our group chat. As she nears the bed, she freezes as if a sudden realization just hit her.

"Wait! What happens if both you *and* Osei get in? Are you ready for that? Even if you don't, he's your grandma's neighbour and, strangely enough, one of her good friends. If you go back to Ghana, you can't exactly avoid bumping into him."

Everything Chelsea is saying right now are scenarios I've already considered. They've been running through my mind ever since my conversation with Dad, and each time, I draw the same conclusion. There is absolutely nothing that I can say or do for Osei that will make things right between us. Looking down at my hands, I shake my head in shame.

"I don't know, Chels. I spent all night and the entire morning stringing together countless apologies, but they all feel insignificant compared to what I said." I inhale sharply as the words I used to hurt him prickle my memory. If just the thought of them still causes me pain, I can't even fathom how he must feel.

"I think the real reason you're struggling with this is because, deep down, you know it's not just an apology you want to say," Chelsea says, sitting next to me with a serious expression. "The same way you decided to go through with the application after you found out about your mom, don't you think you owe it to yourself to take that leap with Osei too? You need to tell him how you feel without restraint, Robyn. Those cards you like to keep so close to your chest? Lay them all on the table. Go all in."

"But what about Kelvin?" I whisper, searching her eyes. I hope to hear a response that will leave him unscathed by my decisions.

Chelsea sighs, and I know she feels my sentiments. "Look, don't get me wrong. I think Kelvin is a great guy, but that doesn't mean he's what's *best* for you. Even if you feel like you're choosing the right person, if you don't choose yourself first, it will never work, Robyn."

I've hated how weird things have felt since getting back to Toronto, but I think I was just too scared to admit that I was only choosing Kelvin because he fit into the life that I thought I had to live. And even if Osei wants nothing to do with me, it would be better to be alone than to give Kelvin only a fraction of what he deserves. Not when he's set his heart on giving me the world and then some. Being together would only leave us both unhappy. If my parents have taught me anything, it's that discontent breeds resentment, and I don't want that for either of us—Chelsea's right. I need to tell Osei how I feel, but I need to end things with Kelvin before I do.

* * *

"And this is the building where I live," Kelvin states, slowing down his silver Tesla in front of an outdated brick building. After our date, Kelvin wanted to go on a late night drive around the city. At first I was hesitant to go out with him at all. I just wanted to end things over the phone, but Chelsea and Jalen insisted that it needed to be in person and I knew deep down they were right.

After everything Kelvin has done for me, it's the least I could do. What I failed to remember is that he would spare no expense on our first date. So unfortunately for me, I had to endure the lengthy, albeit delicious three-course meal at Akira Back, a high-end restaurant I've only ever seen on Instagram stories, because there was no way I was going to break up with him in front of all those people.

"Oh," I say, straining my neck to glance at the high-rise. It looks like it was built before our parents were even born.

"The brick is, um, a nice shade of red."

"You don't have to lie. Everyone knows that UofT housing sucks," he laughs, reaching over to turn down the old Kendrick Lamar song he has on. "After my second year, my parents are letting me move into a condo by the waterfront, but they wanted me to experience campus life first."

"I can't lie to you. I was struggling to find something nice to say. Seeing this just makes me feel relieved that my dad agreed to let me stay with Chelsea off campus this year," I say, turning toward him with a sheepish grin on my face. It's my first genuine reaction since he picked me up from Chelsea's house, and from the shock sparking in his amber eyes, I know it's caught him off guard.

"Wow, I was starting to think I'd never see that smile again," he chuckles, but it's not one of his usual laughs. It's quieter and lacks its familiar warmth. Even though I've felt on edge all night, I've tried my best to maintain normalcy between us; clearly my attempts were futile.

Taking a deep breath, I prepare myself for what I must do. I try to locate the girl I became in Ghana, Robyn 2.0, as Bisi put it —the girl who went after everything she wanted and wasn't afraid to choose herself. Once I feel that familiar courage swelling inside me, I turn to face him.

"Look, Kelvin, I have to be honest with you," I start, but his hand lands on my knee, cutting me off abruptly. I glance down at his hand then back up at his face. He's smiling softly at me and a week ago I probably would have melted at the sight of it, but tonight it has the complete opposite effect. I squirm in my seat as an icy chill runs down my spine.

"I knew this was coming," he admits, and a mixture of relief, confusion, and sadness ripples through me. "My ego couldn't let me see it before, but I felt the shift when you returned from Ghana. And now that I'm seeing you in person again I can't lie to myself about it anymore. You did your best to play it off tonight, but I know your heart's not in this, Robyn," he stops to clear his throat, but when he speaks again, he sounds even more strained. "You have to do what's best for you. Even if that includes not being with me."

"I am so, so, sorry, Kelvin," I say, the words coming out in a sputter. I can feel my tears threatening to fall, but I don't let them. It would be selfish of me to cry when I'm the one who's inflicting the pain. "I never meant to hurt you." My excuse sounds pathetic in my ears.

"I wish I could say that makes it hurt less, but it doesn't," he admits, his eyes focused on the Friday night traffic spilling into the street before us. Like all the other buildings on UofT's campus, his residence is smack in the middle of the big city. The outdated architecture and cohesive signage are the only indicators separating it from the rest of the downtown core.

"But don't worry about it. I'll be okay, Robyn. We both will," he shrugs, glancing at me with a strained smile. It looks like he's trying to lift the disappointment from curving his lips downward. "At least we gave this an honest shot, right?"

I sniff. "You think so?"

"Well, it was the best we could do, while one of us was, no *is*, in love with someone else." The word slams into my chest, and I choke out several coughs, making Kelvin laugh loudly.

"Oh, come on, did you think I'd be letting go of us this easily if it was for anything less than true love," he asks, raising a playful brow at me.

I bury my face in between my hands to hide my embarrassment. Have I really been that obvious?

In the darkness of my palms, memories of Osei come surging back, hitting me strongly, one after the other, powered by a force that can only be described as an intense feeling of deep affection.

Oh shit, I'm in love with Osei Mensah.

Peeling my hands off my face, I turn to face Kelvin.

"It's about time you finally figured it out." he says with a sad smile, as the realization dawns on me. With one last squeeze of my knee, he puts his car into drive and begins the journey to take me home.

thirty-one

THE FIRST OF my remaining three images is easy to shoot. A cropped image of my parent's wedding rings, hers lying on top of his, in the palm of dad's hand. The brown lines etched into his skin are a textured backdrop for the silver bands I didn't even know he'd kept for all these years. It's a closeup that requires no specific location, so I took it as soon as I got home.

But I need more than one hand to bring my next vision to life. After Chelsea promises to buy the boys cookies from the cafeteria every day for the next week, Jalen and Devon meet us on Saturday morning at University College Library. Since we aren't technically allowed to take pictures inside, the boys act as lookouts while Chelsea, Dad and I rush to a back corner of the library that no one has occupied yet. I can tell Dad is slightly uncomfortable with breaking the rules, but he now understands how much this means to me and pushes through for my sake.

University College Library is where my parents first met. Dad had been studying for an upcoming quiz at a two-person desk when my mom sat beside him. According to him, he didn't notice her until she started talking loudly to herself about a book she was looking at. Just as he was about to tell her to keep it down, he glanced at her side profile and was so mesmerized he forgot his plan to tell her to shut up.

It's important to me to include a photo that symbolizes the inception of their love, even if they fell out of it by the time she passed. With only one shot of film remaining and time not on our side, I work quickly to position Dad, getting him to hunch over the desk as if he were studying. Then I walk backwards until I'm between two bookshelves, far enough to frame the desk between them and rotate the Praktica horizontally before shooting. I want to capture him with his back to the camera and an empty chair slightly pulled out from the table next to him to symbolize her no longer being here.

Once I'm done, Jalen and Devon take the completed roll of film to a local photo lab that promises next-day development while Dad takes Chelsea and me back to the house for my final shot, the self-portrait. As Dad tacks a white bed sheet to our living room wall, Chelsea and I use her makeup lighting and a kitchen stool to create a makeshift studio. I set the DSLR camera I signed out from Dr. Beal on a tripod and turn on the self-timer. With my mom's camera around my neck, I wait for the indication that the shutter is about to go off and try my best to emulate her aura. Our resemblance is uncanny thanks to Chelsea's finishing touches—thin brows, powdery foundation, and a thick rim of brown lip liner tracing my lips.

Now, I glance up at the black-rimmed clock that hangs over my desk just as the minute hand races to join the hour hand at twelve. I'm running out of time to submit my application, but the words I thought best summarized the story I wanted to tell no longer resonate. Instead, Osei's voice is all I can hear. There are only five minutes left to submit my fellowship application, but the sound of his voice is stopping me from sending it as is. It's unmistakably clear as if he's in my bedroom with me teasing me with his gap-toothed smile.

"*I think we can still go deeper.*"

When I arrived in Ghana, I only wanted to learn more about who my mom was. I never expected the truth to uncover not only my family's deepest secrets but parts of myself as well. This is no longer a photo essay that tells the story of a woman who was as loving as she was creative and complex. It's much deeper than that. It's an exploration of grief, not just for myself—but for her family and dad too.

I stare at the Dropbox folder containing my completed photo essay and my index finger jabs fervently on the delete button, erasing the words 'The Life and Death of Nana Antwi' from my screen.

There isn't enough time to mull over the new title, but I've learned to trust myself enough to know that I don't need to. With the new title saved, I add the completed Dropbox link to the body of my email, attach the completed application and click send.

thirty-two

I FALL BACK in to my desk chair in relief as I come down from the euphoric high of cutting it so close to the deadline. I actually did it. No, *we* did it. I let out a hysterical laugh. Despite all the distance I've put between us, Osei still found a way to be a part of this moment. My laughs grow louder as I think of how ecstatic he would be if he were here right now. None of this is possible without Osei.

    I bite down on my lip, contemplating all the different directions I can approach this conversation, but nothing seems right. Osei has always been able to decipher my thoughts without words, but that was when I was right in front of him, and he could see me and feel my energy. Being halfway across the world, I don't have that luxury anymore. I chew on the corner of my cheek as I wonder if I should write my feelings out instead. People like that, right? Isn't the whole love letter thing a sign of true romance? Or even if I don't send it, maybe just seeing my thoughts written out will make it easier to navigate them over the phone.

    Springing up in my seat, I pull my MacBook toward me,

swiping my cursor quickly across each icon at the bottom of my screen in search of my notes app. But instead of opening the white and yellow notepad I aim for; my finger slips and accidentally clicks on the icon next to it.

When the Apple Music window takes over my screen, I first notice the song paused at the top of the screen. 'Find Someone Like You', by Snoh Aalegra. It's one of the songs Osei added to my library on our first day of shooting. I stare at it momentarily, debating whether I should listen to it or just exit the screen, but something tells me to press play.

Snoh, backed by a choir, breaks out into song where she left off, and I scroll through the playlist. Most of the artists he's added are familiar to me because they're mainstream, but there are a few I've never heard before. As I reach the end of the playlist, I feel myself losing interest, but just as I'm about to switch to my notes app, I see the cover art of the last song and a sharp breath leaves my lips.

It's a song plucked directly from the *Beyond the Lights* soundtrack. His favourite, no, *our* favourite movie. I press play and inch toward the edge of my seat as 'Extraordinary Love (Fall Version)' by Stacy Barthe begins to play. As she sings about two ordinary people falling in love, her voice seems to get stronger and stronger, repeating the same lines repeatedly and permeating her point with steady runs and riffs.

A million emotions rush through my body as I realize that Stacy has managed to put all my feelings into words. But it's not just the words. It's the harmonies mixed with melodies and the sound of cymbals crashing against steady drumbeats. Like a powerful image, it captures something far more significant than words alone can convey.

The song is still playing as I click on the 'share' option, select Osei's contact and begin to type.

ROBYN

> I finally understand why you love R&B as much as you do. Sometimes words alone just isn't enough.

My finger hovers over the 'send' as my eyes scrutinize my message for typos. This text is nothing close to the apology he deserves, but something is telling me it's the right place to start. Just moments after it is delivered, his read receipt appears under the image of the song's cover art, and I gasp. It's as if he's been lurking in my message thread, waiting for me to reach out. I inch closer, waiting for his message to come through, but it never does. Instead, an incoming audio call pops up on the right corner of my screen.

Not wanting to take the call from my laptop, I jump out of my seat and begin frisking my bed, searching frantically for my phone. Once every last pillow is off my bed, I spot my black phone case lying face down in the middle of the light pink bedsheet.

"Hello," I gasp into the phone, trying to catch my breath.

"What does Robyn Carter know about Stacy Barthe?" His question rumbles in my ear, and I close my eyes, soaking in the sound of his sweet voice.

"You didn't know I listen to R&B now," I say, then hold my breath. I know he started the call on a humorous note, but do I have the right to keep it going? To banter with him when all I should be doing is pleading for his forgiveness? I want so badly to switch the call to FaceTime so I can gauge his expression. If I could see him, I'd have a better idea of how he feels right now. If he still cares for me like he said he does, but even I know that would be asking for too much. I barely deserve a response, let alone a video call.

"Oh yeah? What changed?" I wince from the way he spits out the words so bluntly.

"My feelings for you."

The words rush out as if I'm using a calling card and we're running out of time, but the deflated sigh that fills the line makes me want to recoil and take it all back.

"Robyn, please. Let's not do this. You've already made it perfectly clear how you feel about me."

"Osei, please. Just give me five minutes to explain. If you never want to speak to me again after that, fine," I plead, pacing across the length of my bedroom. Even through the phone, the tension between us feels as thick as the smog in the Accra air.

"Fine. Five minutes."

"From the first day we met, Osei, you saw right through me, and I hated it. I had worked so hard to become this person I thought I was supposed to be, and after being around you for five minutes, it was as if I was opaque to you. Then, on top of that, you were unapologetic about the one thing I was told I could never love. So yes, my feelings toward you were complicated from day one. Something switched in me when I found out that my mom was a photographer. I no longer cared if you could see me because I wanted you to. But that night at the beach house, right before you told me how you felt, I had just learned that my mom was responsible for destroying my family. Before she died, she was willing to do anything, even if it meant putting her family through hell and back, to chase her dreams. That terrified me, Osei. How could I follow in her footsteps without ending up at the same destination."

"But why didn't you just tell me this?" Osei asks quietly.

"At that point, my feelings for you were so strong that I knew that if I gave you the chance, you would have been able to change my mind. So I panicked and decided right then that I would play it safe. But to do that, I needed you to let me go. And I know it was hurtful and wrong, and so, so stupid, but at the time, pushing you away felt like the only way you would let me go."

"I won't lie to you," he starts. "These last few weeks have been hell. I couldn't understand how someone I had developed such strong feelings for could switch up on me like that. I've spent several nights replaying that argument. Trying to understand where things went wrong, until I had to force myself to accept that I didn't know you as well as I thought I did. So now that I've started to move on, you're telling me it was all a lie? I'm struggling to wrap my head around this. Truth or not, your words cut deep, Robyn. And to be quite honest with you, I feel as if I'm still bleeding from them."

I drop my head in shame even though he can't see me.

"Osei, no amount of apologies can make up for the awful things I said, but I want you to know how deeply sorry I am for deliberately hurting you and lying about my feelings for you. But I need you to know that even as I was saying those awful things, I didn't think they were true," my chin is wobbling as I speak, and I quickly try to pull it together. "You are nothing like that, Osei. You are the best thing that has ever happened to me." I confess, baring my soul to a boy thousands of miles away.

The line goes silent, and it feels as if he's waiting for me to say something more, but what more can I say? As every second passes without him responding, it doesn't escape me that this is the first time he's been speechless around me. My pulse hammers as I pace around my room waiting for him to say something, anything, at all.

Desperate to fill the silence, I decide to speak up.

"Sorry! That was a lot to dump on you, and I understand if we can't move past this." I say, trying not projectile vomit from the rejection.

"Robyn," he sighs. "I've already forgiven you. His voice is

full of sincerity and the words cause me to freeze in the middle of my room.

"Wait, what? When?" I ask in utter shock.

"If I'm being honest, I forgave you the moment you sent me the song."

We're both quiet for a beat and then, in unison, we burst into unrestrained laughter. The sound transfers me to every heated disagreement that pulled us apart and every vulnerable conversation that drew us back. It's clear to me now that it should have always been Osei. Yeah, Kelvin was everything a girl could want, but he just wasn't *him*. We breathe in sync as our laughter dies down and we sound so alike that it's hard to differentiate his breathing from mine.

"Thank you for apologizing and telling me the truth about your feelings," he continues. "It makes me feel better knowing I wasn't completely alone in this. What we had, though brief, was real, and I'll forever be grateful for that. But—"

"You need more time to heal," I say, finishing for him. As much as the finality in his tone hurts, I can't say it completely surprises me. It's exactly what I would have done if I was in his position. Holding back my sniffles, I use my shirt sleeve to wipe the tears that have started to streak down my cheeks. I don't want him to hear how much this is breaking me.

"Don't worry about it, Osei." I'm trying to keep it light, but I'm pretty sure he can hear how much effort it's taking. "Besides, there's the whole long-distance thing, right?"

At this, I can hear his smile through the phone. We both know long-distance wouldn't have been an issue. Even halfway across the world, I can feel the magnetism that drew us together in the first place. Osei was right. What we have transcends distance, and we would have crossed the ocean by foot to make this work.

"Take care of yourself, Miss Carter."

"You too, Mr. Mensah."

thirty-three

SEVEN MONTHS LATER

IT'S BEEN three months since I received the first email informing me I've been accepted into the fellowship. It came shortly before the end of the second semester, when I was in the middle of trying to switch to UofT's Visual Studies program. With the admission to the fellowship not guaranteed, I needed to have a backup plan in place. Pivoting from a science degree to the arts wasn't an easy feat, but Dr. Beal made an appeal on my behalf to the faculty, that allows my acceptance if I complete all required first-year prerequisites. This means that it will take an additional year to graduate, something I wasn't too thrilled about, but I knew would be worth it if I meant I got the chance to do what I loved.

Luckily for me, the news about the fellowship came just in time, saving me from having to head down the academic route at this point in time. While Dad is still pushing for me to get my degree, we've agreed to see where the fellowship takes me before committing to paying several thousands of dollars for a piece of paper I may not need.

Now, as I stand in arrivals at Heathrow Airport, the email that has just appeared in my inbox reveals the nine others joining me in London for the following year.

TO: Robyn Carter
FROM: The Emerging Black Artists' Fellowship
SUBJECT: Meet Our Emerging Black Artists' 2025 Fellows
DATE: AUGUST 18, 2025

In just two short weeks, ten young creatives will join us in London to begin the one-year journey that will change their lives forever. Since 2019, over 10,000 young artists have applied for the Emerging Black Artists' Fellowship. A program launched by The London School of Film, Media, and Design to fund, foster, and elevate young Black artists from around the global community. This year, we received over 1,000 applications. Our selection committee, composed of five critically acclaimed artists, have chosen the ten fellows they believe demonstrated a high level of creativity and skill in each respective art form. From writing to music, from visual art to photography, get to know our 2025 fellows below.

My full name is written in a large, bold, serif font, followed by a picture of me and the small biography that I sent in. Right after that, they inserted three images from my photo essay. The shot of Grandma Lily, the one of dad in the library and my self-portrait. I stare in awe at the three images as if I didn't take them myself. I still can't believe they picked me. Everything about this still feels so surreal.

The seven-hour overnight flight from Toronto to London was complete with the wails of cranky babies and complaints of whiny adults. I let out a small giggle, watching people grumpily shove past each other as the baggage carousel spurs to life. It feels like I'm the only one genuinely excited to be here.

"Excuse me," says an airport attendant, pushing an elderly woman in a wheelchair in front of me. As I step back to let them through, my phone vibrates with a FaceTime call.

"Robyn, can you hear me?" Dad says once the call connects. His forehead takes up the entire frame.

"Yes, I can hear you." I laugh, surveying the terminal for somewhere less crowded to talk.

"Were you able to switch to the e-Sim I got you without any issues then?" He asks as he adjusts the camera to show more than a quarter of his face.

"Yeah, it was pretty straightforward, so I did it before we even took off," I say, finding a row of empty seats next to an out-of-service conveyor belt.

"And the flight? Was the food okay? Is it cold in London? Have you spoken to your cousin yet?"

After years of not mentioning them, it still surprises me when I hear Dad refer to my mom's family so casually. While Ama and I texted daily in the weeks after my trip, it took some time for me to feel comfortable speaking to Grandma Lily again. Even when I wanted to, I knew I needed space to process everything I had just discovered. It wasn't until she reached out to Dad in February to apologize, that I could move past things. Seeing both of their deliberate efforts to make amends was the bridge I needed to get over the remaining pain. After that, Grandma Lily and I have never missed a Sunday check-in, and if I'm at Dad's, he always happens to be lingering around nearby. Their initial brisk greetings have developed into small talk and the occasional shared memory of something from my mom's past. Things aren't perfect, but I know he's trying, and for that, I'm grateful.

"The flight was fine. There was barely any turbulence, and the food was actually pretty good. I haven't been outside yet, but it was drizzling when we landed. I'm waiting for my suitcases now, but Ama should be outside by the time I'm done here."

When I told Ama I was moving to London in September, she invited me to come out two weeks early to stay with her while she was visiting her mom and brother for the summer.

"Okay, that's great. I'm sorry I wasn't able to get out of this medical conference to bring you there myself," Dad says, his face consumed with regret. "But I promise, I'll be on the first flight out the week of Thanksgiving. By then, you'll be settled into your place, and you can show me around your new city."

"Don't worry about not being here. You've done more than enough for me. None of this would be possible without you," I say, genuinely meaning it.

In the last eight months, the dynamic of our relationship has shifted drastically. I've always known dad would do anything to provide for me, but now his provision goes beyond my education and financial needs. Without the overbearing weight of my mom's secret holding him down, he moves around me as if he's ten pounds lighter. He's scaled back on being so rigid and has allowed himself to relax with the acceptance that he's doing his best to raise me.

Before I left for London, he even shared some of the wild things Mom used to do to spark inspiration, like placing rolls of film under her pillow because she swore it helped her conceptualize in her sleep, and we laughed until our stomachs ached. I didn't understand it before, but I get how someone as eclectic as Mom could fall for a guy as dogmatic as Marvin Carter. All he wants is the best for the people that he loves. And if anyone knows how easy it is to fall for someone like that, it would be me.

"This is all you, baby girl. Stay focused on the dream, and I'll be here whenever you need me."

When the call ends, I look toward the carousel and see that my suitcases have begun their journey around the conveyor belt. The crowd has lessened, but I still recognize quite a few faces from the flight hovering nearby. I grab a trolley and make my way toward the carousel. When I see my suitcases approaching again, I ask the guy standing next to me to help me grab them.

"Damn, are you moving here or something?" he asks jokingly. He pauses to wipe the sweat forming above his eyebrows, then heaves my last suitcase onto the trolley.

"I am," I reply, my entire body brimming with pride.

thirty-four

"WELCOME TO LONDON, MY LOVE," Ama sings once she answers my call.

"Thank you! I'm so gassed to be here. I just got my luggage, where do you want me to meet you?"

"You've walked over to the short-stay car park, yeah?"

"Yup. I just got here," I reply, watching people load suitcases into cars around me. Others wait patiently for their travellers to come out, but none look like Ama. "Did you park toward the back? I can meet you half way if you want me to."

"No. No. You stay right where you are and don't move," Ama says, before ending the call abruptly.

Usually, I'd be annoyed by her ending a call so suddenly like that, but today, I'm far too excited to think about it too deeply. When I pull my phone away from my ear, the screen flashes to life, and I notice that the email I was reading before Dad called is still open. As I wait for Ama to find me, I continue to scroll where I left off. My excitement grows as I learn more about the talented artists I get to meet in just two short weeks, but when I get to the seventh fellow, everything around me seems to come to a standstill.

THE FULL PICTURE

I know it's him by name, age, and location, but I still find myself swiping frantically to his picture just to be sure. In one of our first weekly check-ins in February, Grandma Lily briefly mentioned that he completed the application. But she never brought it up after that, so I assumed he didn't get in. Kelvin also didn't mention it the few times I've seen him on campus. At first it was awkward navigating the new distance we put between us, but after some time passed, he told me that he's been in touch with Osei who called to apologize for how he treated him in December. Other than that, I haven't heard from or about Osei since the last time we spoke.

As his familiar face gazes at me expectantly from my phone screen, I feel a warm sensation stir in my belly. His lop-sided grin makes me feel as if he's been waiting for me to find him and I finally did.

If Osei is in the fellowship, that means he will be in London in just two weeks. As in the exact city I'm standing in right now! My heart races as I speed past his biography, searching for the sample from the photo essay he submitted. When I finally land on the selected photos, my hand flies to my mouth as I whisper the title to myself.

"*Inner Child* by Osei Mensah"

The images feature two boys dressed in identical outfits, and from their resemblance, it's clear that the younger of the two represents the older boy's inner child. The first image is shot from above while the boys lie beside each other with their backs pressed into a grass field. Their heads meet in the middle of the frame like a yin and yang symbol. The younger boy is upside down, his face twisted in agony, while the older boy is the right side up, void of emotion. The following picture is similar, but instead of lying on the grass, they're standing outside the Mensah family home, facing the camera. The small boy's pain is less evident on his face, but traces of it remain in his eyes. The older boy is seated next to him, wearing the same stoic expression from the first image. In the last picture, they're standing on stairs in what looks like a lecture hall. This time, the older boy has his back to the camera, but at his side, the little boy is clinging to him. No longer in pain, he stares at the camera with a vacant expression.

Each photo draws me in as if Osei has embedded pieces himself in every last pixel—the little boy who just wanted to be heard. The twin who is trying to escape from beneath his other half's shadow. And the teenager who is tired of having to fight for his dreams. It all feels as clear to me as if he's here talking me through it himself. Through his work, I understand exactly where he's coming from, and it suddenly dawns on me the one thing he wanted to hear me say the last time we spoke. Frantically, I swipe to his contact information on my phone.

I told him I'd give him space, but I need him to know I get it now. I know what else he wanted me to say the last time we spoke. He wants to hear that I notice how his eyes light up when discussing photography, how they glisten while his pupils grow three sizes. And that an R&B song, no matter how depressing the lyrics may be, can be the one thing that can put a smile on his face. He wants someone who recognizes that he's devoted to Grandma Lily because she's the only adult who lets him be himself. Even with no guarantee that he still feels the same way, I need to tell him that I see him exactly how he sees me.

I'm in the middle of debating whether I should call or text him when someone yells my name, causing my head to snap up. As my eyes register the person approaching me, they widen in shock.

"I told you next time I'd be on time," Osei shouts as he strolls toward me.

I'm struggling to string together a sentence as he stops in

front of me. My brain is damn near malfunctioning trying to make sense of what is happening right now.

"Hello, Miss Carter," he grins. He wraps his arms around me, and I fall into him, nestling my face into his white T-shirt. As I breathe in the familiar fresh linen scent, it takes everything in me to stop my legs from giving out.

I'm still in shock, as he releases me from his grip and steps back but I take a second to drink him in. Besides his black coils being a few inches taller, everything about him is the same. The same even and dark complexion. The same lean but built frame and the same gorgeous full lips.

"What are you doing here?" It's the first thing I can think of when I finally get my cognitive skills back.

"I'm here for the same reason you are," Osei says with a laugh.

"But the fellowship doesn't start for another two weeks," I exclaim as he takes the trolley from my hands and pushes it toward a parked car.

"Well, my parents weren't exactly thrilled that I wanted to switch career paths and leave Ghana, but after a lot of back and forth, Grandma Lily managed to convince them under two conditions," he says, pausing to open the trunk. When it flies open, he starts to load my suitcases. "The first being that after the fellowship, I have to finish my degree, and the second condition was that I have to stay with Ama's family while I'm out here."

"So, did you know I'd be coming this whole time?" I ask, trying to process that Ama and Grandma Lily have pulled this off behind my back. As per fellowship policy, we couldn't share our acceptances online until they made the official announcement in the email we got less than twenty minutes ago.

"Nope, I found out today when Ama rushed into the room I'm sharing with Sammy, threw her keys at me and told me to come get you." He laughs, pressing the button on the car's remote to close the trunk automatically. "But I'm so proud of you, Robyn! What did you end up naming your photo essay?"

"You didn't see the email that went out today?"

He shakes his head as he leans back on the now-closed trunk. The sleeves of his plain white T-shirt are snug against his toned biceps and I bite down on my bottom lip as the tiny mountains lodged in his arm, shift ever so slightly as he moves.

"I was too busy ensuring I wouldn't be late to get you, to check my email. I didn't want to endure your wrath and fury for a second time in a row," he laughs.

I lean forward to try and playfully swat him, but he dodges me before I can even get close. I want to ask him how he knows I changed the name, but I already know the answer. Like always, Osei knew that the moment he told me I could go deeper, I would.

"*The Art of Loss*," I say, and our gazes lock with intense focus.

His brown eyes soften with adoration, and the approval causes every nerve ending in my body to feel like it's been set on fire.

"Now *that* is perfect."

"No, what's perfect is *your* submission," I gush. "How on earth did you come up with something that profound in such a short amount of time?

He rubs the back of his neck, a sheepish grin forming on his lips.

"I just followed the same advice I gave you."

"You've always been quite good at giving advice."

"Is that so?"

I nod, feeling myself getting worked up. "I just hate myself for taking so long to realize it."

"It's okay, Robyn," he starts, but I shake my head.

"No, Osei, it's not okay. I should have listened to you from the first day we met. Nobody gets me the way you do," My voice cracks as tears well up in my eyes. "Not my dad, not my grandma, not even Chelsea understands me like you."

Osei steps forward, and I hold my breath, not wanting even the slightest breeze to interrupt this moment. He leans toward me; our foreheads are so close they almost touch. Authenticity radiates off him, comforting my entire being, and I try to keep my tears from falling.

"Hey, hey. It's okay. Don't cry," he whispers, chuckling softly. Using his thumb, he wipes away a tear that has managed to escape. Without breaking eye contact, he strokes the side of my face, tracing along my right cheekbone. I shudder from his gentle touch, and it causes one of my curls to fall onto my face.

"By the way, I love this new colour on you," he says, admiring the loose strand coiled around his finger. "Your beauty truly knows no end."

I reach up to graze my ginger hair.

"I felt like doing something other than black for once. No more playing it safe," I say, matching his piercing gaze. "Osei, I really don't want to lose you again. I'm ready to give this a shot if you are. And no, it's not just because we're going to be in the same city."

I'm full-on rambling at this point, and it feels like snot might be running down my nose, but I truly don't care. I'm laying it all on the line, and there's no turning back this time.

"I mean, sure, being in the same city helps, but it's more than that. Osei, I *see* you and I love you for who you are. And who you are is better than everything I ever thought I wanted."

A soft smile graces his lips as Osei slowly unravels my hair from the tip of his finger, returning to tracing my features. As his thumb inches along my jawline, he leans in closer and by the time it glides gently across my bottom lip, our faces are just inches apart.

"I love you too," he whispers before moving in to close the gap between us.

As we kiss for the first time, I realize how pointless fighting my attraction to him was. I've spent years trying to fill the void my mom's death carved within me and despite my resistance, Osei seamlessly fits in. From the moment we met, we were destined to be together.

"Wow," he breathes, when we finally pull apart. His gaze is heavy, and his lashes flutter. "You have no idea how long I've wanted to do that."

"Osei," I say, as a wave of emotions flood my senses and the weight of how much he means to me fully sinks in.

"Yes, Robyn."

"Whether you're here in London or back in Accra. Heck, you could be in Timbuktu for all I care. I just want you to know that *you* are someone worth holding on to."

Osei leans back onto the trunk of Ama's car, stretching his arms to show off the length of his wingspan. The little gap in his front teeth looks wider than ever as his smile spreads from inch to inch of his handsome face.

"Come on and hold me already, then."

acknowledgments

First and foremost, I want to thank God. Not only for my life, but for the ability to see the world the way I do.

I want to thank my immediate family and my extended family. Thank you for humouring me and for your never wavering faith.

The Edmonton Arts Council and the City of Edmonton, the work you do to support independent artists like me is life-changing.

To everyone who contributed in making this book a reality; Wilhelmina Assam, Fatima Baig, Jenny Hoops, Ana Hoffman, Losa Eguavoen, Mimi Ezinne, Ruona Janere, & Nero Yalaju. Thank you!

My original Ghana in December crew! Thank you for the trip that changed my life.

To my cheerleaders. I am so grateful to have you. Deborah Acheampong, Leah Ennis, Anna-Maria Poku, Mowa Badmos, Camille Mawugbe, Jasmine Bell, Olatomiwa Sobande, Benedicta Mawuena Dzandu, Aseye Tsatsu, Léonicka Valcius, Christine Cowan, Elsa Kebede, Busayo Matuluko and many more!

Mr. Sebastian, if I can impact youth in the way that you do, I'll know that I've done something worthwhile.

For the girls who get *it*. Don't let your dream die in the hands of someone else.

And lastly, to my personal person. You are the softest and safest love I've ever known. Akpe na wo.